MW01153777

# PINNED

*An*
SSU Boys
Novel

#1

## MARIS BLACK

*Maris Black*
*Thanks for being*
*friendly.*

This book is a work of fiction. Names, characters, places and incidents are the product of the author's imagination or are used fictitiously. Any resemblance to actual events, locales, or persons, living or dead, is coincidental.

Copyright 2014 by Maris Black. All rights reserved, including the right to reproduce, distribute or transmit in any form or by any means. For information regarding subsidiary rights, please contact the Author:

Maris Black
maris@marisblack.com

First edition January, 2014

This novel is dedicated to my grandparents.
G, R, & M.
I know you would totally not approve of my racy content,
But you are proud I'm writing, and that's enough.
Thanks for the support — and the raisin'.
I love you all there is!

Thanks to Richard for everything you do, Mike for the help &
support, Chris for cheering me on, and Spence for the button!

And a special thanks to Gabriel,
For being so incredibly Gabriel.

# 1

*(JEREMY)*

*I'M FREE falling.*

And yeah, I'll cop to being a little bit scared. But I think it's okay for a guy to be scared every now and then, especially on his first day of college. And it's not just fear and nervousness. I'm almost high from excitement— blown away by what I consider to be the official beginning of my new life.

It's intimidating because there's just so much freedom, which is exactly what I want. It just takes some getting used to, that's all. Coming straight out of a small town high school where every last thing is decided for you, college is a bit of a culture shock. I can wander around campus all day, skip classes, do whatever the hell I want. No one is going to come along and usher me to detention or make me suffer through yet another embarrassing parent-teacher conference.

So far, I've got a really good feeling about this place.

"Hey man, nice shirt!" a guy calls to me from several yards away. I have to laugh when I get a good look at him, because we're wearing the exact same Pixies tour shirt.

"Back at ya," I say, making a cheesy finger gesture like I'm shooting a pistol. He smiles.

It's a relief to see that a lot of the students are wearing ripped jeans and ratty t-shirts like me. I was worried that everyone would have wardrobes full of expensive clothes and that I'd look like the same old loser I always have. Truth is, I've only got two pairs of jeans and six shirts, and one of those shirts is about two threads away from the garbage can. In other words, I'm poor. In high school it was well known that I— or more accurately, my father— had no money, but here in the relative anonymity of college, I just might be able to blend in with people who have more than I do.

That would really piss my dad off.

"Don't you go getting all uppity at college," he'd slurred when he hugged me goodbye two days earlier. "Remember, you ain't no better than anybody else around here."

What he really meant was, *You ain't no better than me.*

"Okay, Dad," I'd replied with a sigh.

What I really meant was, *Fuck you, you drunk bastard. I'm outta here, and you can rot in hell for all I care.*

It felt so damn good when my butt hit the duct-taped driver's seat of my Corolla, knowing I was about to be driving myself to freedom. It didn't matter that freedom was less than two hours away, or that I'd have to retain a B average to keep from losing my financial aid and ending up right back in Center Hill Trailer Park — or as I like to call it, Center of Hell Trailer Park. It didn't even matter that I didn't know a single damn person at Southeastern State University, or that I'd have a boat-load of student loans to pay off after college. Or that I'd have to start from scratch to qualify as a walk-on for the wrestling team.

As sketchy as my future seemed, fear of the unknown could never diminish the beauty of my parent's doublewide trailer retreating in the rear view mirror. Nothing has ever felt that good. When I could no longer see my dad swaying drunkenly on the front deck, I let out the breath I was holding. My muscles slackened, and I allowed a smile to steal across my face.

*Freedom. What an awesome word.*

Today that freedom is mine, and I intend to take full advantage of it.

Southeastern State University is more beautiful in person than in any of the photos I've looked at online. The distinguished buildings look like they've stood for at least a hundred years, their slightly crumbled bricks a faded red color. Everything is well kept and neatly landscaped.

I enter a square courtyard in the center of the campus where a fountain gurgles, flanked by purple-hued Japanese maples and low yellow shrubs. Must be fifty students hanging around the courtyard this morning, most of them busy chatting with other students or standing with their necks canted at that obnoxiously familiar forty-five degree angle characteristic of cell phone addicts. My own pay-as-you-go cell phone is useless until my dad makes a payment. Mom says I should have more minutes today, but sometimes it takes weeks.

And I can't trust her word, anyway. It's getting harder and harder to tell when she's fucked up and when she's not. Either way, my phone is in my pocket just in case.

I stop close to the fountain, a fine mist of overspray sending goosebumps racing up my arms as I pull my campus pamphlet from my pocket and flip to the map of the square. I know that my first class is at ten o'clock in the Wilson Building, but the problem is that the layout around the square is perfectly symmetrical. The buildings are like mirror images on each side, and since the map for it is on its own page, I can't figure out how the image reads in relation to where I'm standing. Of the two identical red brick buildings standing on each of the four sides of the courtyard, not a one of them appears to have a name on it. Tragic oversight, if you ask me. If only there was some landmark to distinguish one side of the courtyard from the other.

When I realize I'm going to have to ask someone for help, I scan the square. Most people are too busy doing their own thing to be bothered, and some of them look downright unfriendly.

My only good choices are a chubby guy with glasses who is busy searching for something in his backpack, or a pretty girl who is leaned back on the side of the fountain staring at the sky. She looks like spring with her light blonde hair and floral print dress, an unconscious half smile on her face. Before I can rethink it, I'm standing in front of her with one hand in my pocket, the other clutching the map.

"Excuse me."

She stops admiring the sky long enough to acknowledge me, and her smile widens. "What's up?"

"Um, are you familiar with the campus?"

"Sure," she says. "I'm a sophomore, so I pretty much know everything about this school. What'cha need?"

I hold the map out to her. "I can't tell which end of this map is up. My first class is in the Wilson Building—"

"Oh yeah, there it is right over there." She points to one of the quadruplet buildings and then to its representation on the map. "You can tell which way the map goes by the side of the buildings the walkways are on, see?"

I face palm and squeeze out an embarrassed laugh. "Crap, I should have noticed that. Guess my brain isn't awake yet."

"It's okay." Her voice is babyish, stuck in her throat like she's just huffed helium. "I think you're adorable, like a little lost puppy. What's your name?"

*Little lost puppy?*

I hate it when people talk to me like that. So fucking condescending. For a moment I consider biting her on the leg. It would serve her right for calling me a puppy, especially if she got rabies. Instead, I answer politely. "Jeremy Miller. I'm a freshman."

"Hi, Jeremy." She flashes a practiced pageant smile and flips her hair. "I'm Stephie. Nice to meet you."

"And here I thought it was going to be hard to meet people at college, but I think I just figured out the secret. I'll just wander around asking for directions."

Stephie laughs and runs a hand though her hair. "That's a classic pick-up ploy, freshman. You catch on fast. You shouldn't have any problem at all finding a girlfriend around here. Unless you already have one..." She looks at me from beneath her lashes. "Do you already have one?"

"Um, no…" I shift from one foot to the other, not quite sure how to answer that question. Should I elaborate? Tell her I don't have a girlfriend because I'm not looking for one? Tell her I like cock? That would be rude, but I'm tempted to do it just to see her reaction— and to get her back for calling me a little lost puppy.

"Well, there's a party tonight, if you're interested—" She looks over my shoulder, her smile faltering. Her posture snaps straighter, and she fidgets with the lacy hem of her dress.

"Who the fuck is this, Steph?" a deep voice asks from behind me.

*Shit. I don't have to be a rocket scientist to guess where this is going.*

He continues, his voice getting louder. "I can't leave you alone for ten minutes without some guy with a death wish trying to chat you up. Yesterday it was that frat boy at orientation, today it's a little faggot with a purse."

Someone less familiar with the dynamics of the bullying game might have spun around in shock, or even offered up some stuttered explanation, but not me. I simply take a calming breath and look straight ahead, waiting for whatever unpleasantness is coming my way, hoping this is not going to blow up like things have a tendency to do around me.

I try to ignore the too-familiar creeping burn across my shoulder blades that lets me know I'm about a breath away from losing my shit. I concentrate on slowing my heart rate, which has ramped up noticeably, rattling my ribcage and making breathing more difficult than it was only seconds before.

6

*Pleeeease... I don't want to get mad. Not on my first day. This is supposed to be a happy day.*

"What has gotten into you lately, Caleb?" Stephie has found her voice, but it's lost some of its affectation, like the helium has worn off. She doesn't look directly at Caleb, who is at the moment breathing down the back of my neck. Instead she stares at her skirt, running neatly manicured fingers back and forth across the lace. I recognize the look of intimidation well. She's afraid to speak, because she might say something to set her boyfriend off. "First of all, that's a messenger bag, not a purse. And Jeremy was just asking for directions to Wilson. That's all."

"Yeah?" Caleb asks. "Well, open your eyes. It's right over there, dude."

"So I've been told," I mumble under my breath. "Thanks, Stephie. I appreciate your help."

I turn to leave, walking to the left of where I can very distinctly feel Caleb's presence, but he purposely sidesteps in front of me. When I come up against his broad chest, it's like hitting a flesh-wrapped brick wall.

*Damn, he's big.*

"You a freshman?" Caleb's voice is threatening, even if his words aren't. He obviously doesn't have much of a soft spot for freshmen.

*Ignore the burn, Jeremy. Don't think about gouging this asshole's eyes out and force-feeding them to him with chopsticks.*

I ball my fists at my side, channeling every bit of control I have into keeping my voice steady, forcing a smile onto my face. · "Yeah. I just got here two days ago, so I'm not really familiar with the campus yet."

*I choose to remain calm. I choose to remain calm.* The simple mantra my high school counselor taught me loops over and over in my head. I usually have pretty good success with it, which is surprising because the truth is... I'd rather fight.

"Look," I continue, with an outward air of calm that surprises even me. "I was just trying to get to class, and I lost my way. Your girlfriend looked friendly—"

"Oh, I'll bet she did." Caleb is glaring down his nose at me. He's a good six inches taller, with dark wiry hair, dark eyes, and a wide, snubbed face. Built like that barrel-chested bulldog on Looney Tunes, or maybe a heavyweight wrestler.

*Shit. If this guy's a wrestler, we're in for some rough days ahead.*

"What I meant was—"

"I don't care what you meant." He interrupts in a loud voice, stepping toward me so that my knees bump against the edge of the fountain, almost toppling me in. "You have no business even looking at my girl, much less talking—"

This time Caleb is the one who gets interrupted, but not by me. "Lay off the macho bullshit, Caleb," says a guy who has come up behind him unnoticed. "People speak to other people. It's part of being human."

Caleb responds to the voice and instantly backs up, allowing me room to get clear of the fountain. Then he snaps his head around to look at the newcomer.

He's slightly shorter than Caleb and less bulky, but just as insanely fit. His medium brown hair is buzzed close to his head, and the lack of hair serves to accentuate a pair of golden brown eyes that

I'm already getting lost in. *Wow.* Everything about him is tailored to my tastes. Like if I went to the Hot Guy Store, he's exactly what I would order: amazing muscles, full lips, five-o'clock shadow, and an adorable chin cleft that begs to be kissed.

*Or licked.*

As soon as I lay eyes on him, the shoulder burn recedes, but my heart rate doesn't slow a bit. In fact, it's about to hammer out of my chest, but this time in a good way.

"Mind your own business, Beck. This freshman was trying to hit on my girl. You know I don't play that shit."

"I — I wasn't—" All I can do is stammer, which is unlike me. I'm just suddenly desperate to clarify the facts, but only for Beck's benefit. I don't really give a damn what Caleb thinks, with his pug nose and overinflated muscles. He and I can go round right here in the courtyard if that's what it takes to settle this thing. But I do care what Beck thinks. For the first time in my life, it seems like an absolute disaster that someone might think I'm interested in a girl. I've spent every day since puberty *allowing* people to think I'm straight, so this is new territory for me. "Um, I wasn't..."

*Totally incapable of forming a sentence. Way to make an impression, Jeremy.*

"Was he flirting with you, Stephie?" Beck asks.

"No." She shakes her head, yellow blonde curls bouncing around her shoulders. She stretches her blue eyes wide and slackens her jaw, becoming the picture of innocence.

Beck looks directly at me, and my face heats. "What's your name, kid?"

*Kid??*

9

"Jeremy," I practically whisper.

"Alright, Caleb," he says. "It's been officially confirmed by both of them. Jeremy was not flirting with Stephie, so there's no problem, right?" His expression turns playful, and he pats Caleb on the back of the shoulder. "What's the matter, big guy? You haven't gotten enough fighting in over the summer? Looks like you need to get on the mat and blow off some steam before you hurt somebody."

*Great. Caleb is definitely a wrestler. Instant rivalry, and I haven't even made it to my first class.*

"We'll see," Caleb says. He spares another glare in my direction before sitting down beside Stephie and jamming his tongue down her throat in what I can only assume is a show of ownership. *Like I care.* Stephie is ignoring me now, letting her boyfriend maul her, which is the smart thing to do.

With the confrontation officially over, I know I should just walk away, but I'm rooted to the ground. Or more accurately stuck like a magnet to the guy with the golden eyes. Either way, I just stand there like an idiot, staring at Beck while he stares back at me. I want to look away, but I can't.

"I was just asking Stephie directions to Wilson," I offer lamely, showing him my map as if it's some sort of proof of innocence.

Beck raises his eyebrows, and one corner of his mouth flips up in a sexy smirk that triggers an all too familiar pulling sensation in my groin. Now I'm imagining him on his knees, looking up at me with naked lust in his eyes, waiting for me to slide my cock between those pillowy lips. *Mmmm.* If I don't stop picturing it, I'm going to have a full-on erection to hide.

"Wilson?" he asks. "Lucky for you, that's where I'm headed. Follow me, and I'll be your official tour guide."

I hang back for a moment, still staring, warring with my imagination and the metamorphosis that's threatening to happen inside my jeans. Then the thought of the word *metamorphosis* cracks me up, reminding me of the Hulk and his tattered purple pants.

*Don't make me angry. You wouldn't like me when I'm angry.*

Before I realize what I'm doing, I laugh out loud. It's a short laugh, barely audible, but it's enough to get Beck's attention.

He turns and stares at me with a bewildered half smile. "What's so funny?"

"I was just thinking about a Hulk comic… and how it reminded me of this morning."

*Hey, it's not a lie. He doesn't have to know I'm imagining busting out of my pants at the mere sight of him.*

He chuckles. "Yeah, I know Caleb is huge, and he can be intimidating. I don't know what's gotten into him lately. He's not usually quite so aggressive. But I won't let him mess with you, okay?"

"What are you, his warden?"

"Something like that." Beck laughs, his eyes crinkling at the corners. "I'm his roommate. We share a four bedroom apartment with two other people."

"Oh, that's just great. Are they gonna try to beat me up, too?"

"Don't worry about it." He wraps his arm around my shoulders and squeezes in that buddy-buddy way jocks tend to do. "I won't let anybody beat you up. Besides, one of them is a girl, and she can't fight worth a shit."

We continue on toward the Wilson building, Beck walking at

a relaxed pace while I lag several steps behind enjoying the view. He's dressed casually in a blue Polo shirt and soft jeans that have memorized his shape. They ride loose and low on his hips, the hang of them all too suggestive of the muscled thighs and glutes beneath. All I can think of is snatching them down, or what might happen if they accidentally fell down.

*Okay, now I'm just torturing myself.*

"What class are you in?" Beck asks, turning to look directly at me. I jerk my head up and hope like hell he hasn't caught me checking him out, and that I don't look as guilty as I feel.

"Huh? Um..." *Shit, where are my words?* "Microeconomics, room twelve."

"Ah, business major. Or have you decided yet?"

"Oh yes, business. And I've been decided since eleventh grade."

"A guy who knows what he wants. I'm impressed." He grins and pushes open the door to the Wilson building, holding it for me as I walk through. It's still fifteen minutes before classes start, so there are students everywhere in the hall, leaning against walls, sitting on the floor, thumbs tapping on their cell phone screens. Everyone is so sedate. I wonder if there's any way I look calm on the outside, because my heart is knocking around in my chest like crazy.

"What grade are you in?" I ask Beck, feeling stupid as soon as the words are out of my mouth. "I mean, what do they call grades in college?"

"I'm technically a junior, but I'm in a six-year fast track Sports Medicine program, so it's kind of weird. I'm going to go out on a limb and guess that you're a freshman." His tone is unmistakably teasing, and he nudges me with his elbow.

"Is it that obvious?" I can feel my face turning red, but there's nothing I can do about it. Apparently, I'm destined to look like a dork in front of this guy. "I'm from a small town," I say, as if that explains anything.

He leads me through the crowd, and I begin to feel as though there's an invisible string stretching from him to me, connecting us, pulling me along. It feels almost like we're *together*. It's thrilling to imagine what it might be like if we really were together, me and this big, hot alpha. It's a harmless little fantasy, right?

Most of the people in the hallway step aside when they see him, even if they're not in our way, and I wonder if it's because he looks intimidating or if he's really popular. I almost hope he's not because, in my experience, popular guys are nothing but trouble. Especially popular football jocks.

"Here we are. Room twelve." Beck comes to a halt outside my classroom and leans against the wall in a spot away from everyone else, crossing his muscular arms across his chest and narrowing his eyes at me. "So tell me the truth. Who spoke first, you or Stephie?"

"I did. Hey, I owe you one. Another minute, and Caleb and I would have been swinging. The last thing I need is a fight on my first day of college. Thanks for convincing him we weren't flirting."

Beck laughs and quirks an eyebrow. "Oh, she was definitely flirting with you. I can guarantee you that. What I'm trying to figure out is if you were flirting back."

My face heats as I shake my head furiously. "No, no, I just wanted directions. It never crossed my mind to flirt with her. I swear it."

He moves slowly toward me, sliding his shoulder along the wall, coming so close I have to tilt my head back to look him in the eyes— those gorgeous eyes with little flecks of gold.

"Calm down, Jeremy." His voice is low, hypnotic. "I'm not going to tell Caleb or anything. I was just curious if you like her, that's all."

"Why?"

"No reason." He shrugs and turns his head to glance absently down the hall behind him, instantly breaking my trance.

"*You* don't like her, do you?"

"Hell, no." He grimaces like I've just suggested he might have the hots for a cockroach. "Look, she's a sweet girl, but she's also a shit disturber, if you know what I mean. She sees a hot guy, she flirts, as you witnessed for yourself this morning. I hear Caleb bitching about it all the time. And with his size and temper, somebody's gonna get hurt one day. The dude can whip some serious ass."

"Hot?" Out of all of the words he said, that's the only one that registers in my brain.

"Yeah, man. I'm warning you for your own good. If she starts trying to talk to you, run the other way. She's trouble, and now you're on her radar."

"Nah, she's probably already forgotten about me." I dispel the idea with a wave of my hand in what is probably the most unconvincing display of false humility ever. In reality, my brain is spinning with excitement at the thought that he's just *almost* called me hot.

"A pretty boy like you? Shit. You've probably already gotten the attention of half the girls in this school."

"Yeah?" I can't stop an idiotic smile from taking over my face. "Just the girls, huh? No guys?"

*Crap. Why did I say that?*

"Uh…" Beck chuckles and glances away, running a hand down the back of his neck. "Yeah, some of them, too."

He takes an unconscious step back, leaving dead space between us for a moment, and our eyes are like opposite poles of a magnet— unable to meet. I curse my own big mouth, and that reckless little devil inside that makes me say ridiculous things without thinking.

Rocking back on my heels, I shove my hands deep into my pockets. "Well, thanks for the advice about staying away from Stephie and her rabid hulk of a boyfriend. I do appreciate your concern, but I promise there's nothing to worry about. She's not my type, okay? Like not even in the same fucking ballpark."

*If you know what I mean... Jeez, why can't I stop with the innuendo?*

"Good boy." Beck smiles, rubbing my head playfully and ruining the perfectly disheveled hair I spent so long fixing— or rather messing up— this morning. "I don't want to have to scrape your ass off the pavement if Caleb gets a hold of you. I can only keep the monster at bay for just so long if you're poking him with a stick."

"Hey, I may not be as big as you guys, but I can take care of myself a lot better than you think."

"Whatever you say, pretty boy." He winks, releasing an army of butterflies in my stomach.

I'm starstruck. He's the Beatles, and I'm a girl in the crowd. Is it even possible to be totally smitten so quickly, to have a borderline nauseating physical reaction to someone I've just met? It's all very confusing, but I do know one thing for sure. If he's straight, he'd better stop with the fucking winking and standing so close and calling me pretty boy. Because it feels an awful lot like flirting, and if he keeps it up, he's gonna get a mouthful of Jeremy whether he wants it or not. That's all I'm saying.

He clasps his hands behind him and takes a few steps backward, smiling at me, before he turns to go to class. As I watch him walk away, I realize that he passed his own class when we entered the building just so he could escort me all the way to my door.

*Does that mean something?*

"See ya." I wave to his retreating back, watching the way his jeans slide over that hot ass and those thick thighs, knowing I won't be able to think of anything else until I see him again. His body is so what I like. Maybe he's a wrestler, too, like Caleb. *Like me.* The thought makes my heart skitter.

*No. My luck, he's probably a freaking football player.*

As I enter my classroom, which is almost completely full now, I'm wondering why a guy like him is so eager to talk to me anyway. Why he bothered to walk me to my class. He couldn't possibly want to be my friend, right? In high school, I didn't have a whole lot of really close guy friends. Girl friends, acquaintances and people who wanted something from me? I had enough of those. But as far as true friends go— the kind you have sleepovers with every weekend and go stag with to the homecoming dance— Eric was the only one. Most people weren't too keen on being seen with the poor kid who always seemed just a little bit *different*.

Eric and I were on the wrestling team together, which he

16

dropped out of when it got too competitive, and the chess team, which I dropped out of when it got too boring. Though we both grew up in the small town of Blackwood, he always had a lot more love for the place than I did. I couldn't wait to get out. I tried to talk him into coming to Southeastern State with me, but he chose a nearby tech school so he could stay close to home. Guess I don't blame him. He's got a pretty cool family, which is why I always stayed at his house as much as possible on the weekends.

Lately, I've been nursing the fear that it would be just as hard to make friends at college as it was in high school and that I'd miss Eric. But if my first day is any indication of things to come, I won't have any problem acquiring a new set of friends.

*Really sexy friends with golden eyes.*

I know it's too much to hope that Beck is gay. And even if he is, that he would be interested in me. Still, those damn butterflies start flitting in my gut again every time I think that maybe, just maybe, he could be.

# 2

WHEN I get out of class, Beck is leaning casually against the block wall outside his classroom, jaw muscles clenching ambitiously as he chews a piece of gum. I nod casually, as if we've never met. As if I haven't just been thinking about him all the way through class.

He falls into step with me as I pass, and we walk together toward the exit.

"Were you..." I jerk my thumb over my shoulder and glance back at his classroom door. "Did you wait for me?"

He shrugs. "Part of the official tour package. How was your first college class ever? Was it everything you hoped it would be?"

"And then some," I reply. "I never knew the fine art of pricing consumer goods could be so damn interesting. I think I'll bring a pillow tomorrow."

"Get used to it. College core classes for the most part are really dry. Except maybe for Psychology, Anthropology,

Physiology… That kind of thing."

"Oh, so you're an *ology* lover. Interesting."

"Shhh." Beck leans in close to my ear, bringing with him the scent of spearmint gum. "Don't tell anybody. I'd hate to ruin my dumb jock reputation."

I automatically check out his body when he mentions the jock thing, as if I haven't already half-memorized it. He catches my eyes raking him, and his mouth turns up in a knowing half smile.

"Uh, what sport do you play?" I ask, trying to keep the tremor out of my voice.

"I *play* wrestling."

"No joke?" I stop dead in my tracks and grin. "I'm on the wrestling team, too. Or at least I hope to make the cut."

"Are you sure you got signed up? I'm Team Captain this year, and I've already studied the roster. I didn't see anyone named Jeremy."

"Well, it probably says William J. Miller."

"Yeah, yeah, I do know that name. Freshman walk-on from Blackwood, Georgia…, 157-pounder, right?"

"Damn, Beck. You weren't kidding when you said you studied that roster."

"I take my position very seriously, William."

"Ew!" I grimace and shake my head. "Don't call me that. It's my dad's name. I'm gonna legally change it one day."

Beck holds up his hands. "Sorry, man. Didn't mean to offend you."

"It's okay. Nobody really wants to be called by their dad's name, right? It's just creepy." I try to play it off before he gets an idea

19

of just how much it really does bother me. I'm trying to make a good impression, after all. No need to advertise that I have the world's biggest asshole for a father.

"If you think it's strange going by your middle name, try going by your last name like me. Hell, it's not even the full name. Only a piece of it."

"So what is your full name?" When he refuses to answer, I push him gently, making him stagger to the side in an awkward little tap dance. "Now that you've teased me, you've got to tell. It's a rule."

"Okay." He smacks his gum a few times as a huge grin spreads across his face. "Calvin Barnwell Beckett, III."

"Ooh, sounds fancy. Is your dad rich or something?"

"Pretentious is more like it. My family used to have a crapload of money, before they lost most of it in the twenties stock market crash. Now all we've got is freaking debt, but old attitudes die hard, you know? By golly the Becketts have to keep up appearances." He laughs and starts walking again, and I have to stretch my legs to catch up. "What's your next class, Junior?"

"Junior?" I frown.

"Well, you're smaller than me." He spins around in front of me, making me almost crash into him. We're standing so close I can smell the spearmint again. "What are you, five-eight, a hundred fifty-five pounds?"

I nod, staring awkwardly at his throat, wishing he'd get even closer, wondering what it would feel like to rest my cheek against his chest and wind my arms around his waist.

"See? I've got four inches and thirty pounds on you... *Junior*. But there's nothing wrong with that, you know? Nothing at all." His broad smile and smooth voice make what he's said seem less like a diss and more like a compliment. "So where are you headed?"

"I'm on my way to the cafeteria for lunch."

"Oh, not the cafeteria." He makes a face that has me already regretting the purchase of a meal card. "How about if I treat you to the best sub sandwich in town, at Hotrod's? It's right around the corner."

"It's your lunch break, too?"

He crosses his arms over his chest and arches a brow. "Only if you want it to be."

"Yeah, sure." I have to clear my throat to get the squeak out. "Sounds great."

*Okay, either he likes me, or he's yanking my chain. Maybe he's feeling me out, like I'm doing to him.*

It's awkward being gay sometimes, I'm not gonna lie. When you've got a crush on someone, and you don't know if they even have the potential to like you back, how do you go about letting them know you like them? It's sort of a double-edged sword, if you think about it. On one edge— the safe edge— you may never know if the other person is attracted to you. On the dangerous edge, well… Straight guys tend to be very protective of their *straightness*. Some more than others.

As for me, I've always stayed on the safe edge for the most part. I'm hoping college will change that, because I don't want to live in the shadows anymore, acting like something's wrong with the way I feel— with what I want. As I follow Beck to the parking lot, it's starting to feel like maybe that kind of life is possible. Unless I'm reading too much into his attention, which is even more possible.

21

*What if this is just him making friends?*

"Here we are." Beck pulls a set of keys from his jeans pocket and uses the remote to unlock the doors of a jacked-up black pickup truck with knobby mud tires. I cough to disguise a laugh, and Beck stares at me. "What is it?"

"Sorry, just not what I pictured you driving."

"Oh, really? And what exactly did you imagine I would drive?" He opens the passenger door and steps out of the way for me to hoist myself up with the assistance of a sidestep.

Once I'm settled in the seat, I wrinkle my nose in thought. "I don't know. I guess an Audi or Lexus."

He laughs and nods. "Okay. Alright. So that's how you see me? Like some preppy boy?" He regards me for a moment, chewing his gum harder, as if it helps him think. "I guess I'll have to prove you wrong, then. Show you how good of a bad boy I can be."

*Oh shit. Definitely flirting. Right??*

As he closes the door and rounds the truck to take the driver's seat, my brain starts twisting around all of the possible ways he might prove to me that he's a bad boy. I so hope that what he has in mind is as dirty as the stuff I'm imagining. I'm gonna be pissed off if he's talking about taking me deer hunting at five a.m., or mud bogging in some soupy Georgia clay pit.

The ride to Hotrod's is short, and once we get there, we're barely able to squeeze into a space in the minuscule parking lot. Beck mindfully pulls closer to the car on his left so as not to block anyone's driver side door, and we both scoot across to exit through the passenger door.

Like the parking lot, the restaurant is small, and there's almost no atmosphere to speak of. Decorations are limited to a couple of posters of performance cars, a black-and-white checkerboard floor, and a colorful potato chip rack. Like most sub shops, the employees are putting the sandwiches together in plain view behind the counter. Personally, I'd rather not watch people make my food— slapping meat onto the bread with precariously gloved hands, slathering room-temperature mayo with questionable utensils. I'd prefer a little mystery, thank you very much. Just walk out of a back room with my food wrapped neatly in the basket and let me imagine that it just magically appeared there all clean and perfectly put together. Blissful ignorance has its appeal.

I'm probably more sensitive to stuff like that because I feel like I know a lot about how nasty people can be, having lived with William and Gina Miller for the last eighteen years. Take it from me, growing up in a shabby trailer with an alcoholic father and a schizophrenic meth head mother will definitely color the way you look at the world. Add to that having no money and being unpopular in school, and you've got a bucketful of reasons why I'd do just about anything to have a different kind of life in college.

I've resigned myself to spending money I can't afford on the meal in order to spend time with Beck, but when I try to give him my share, he waves it away without speaking. Hopefully he doesn't notice the relief washing over my face.

Once we've gotten our food— spicy Italian subs and potato chips— we sit across from each other in a semi-circle corner booth with red vinyl seats and a gray Formica table top.

"Mmmm, you're right about these sandwiches," I mumble around a mouthful of food. "Best ever." Truth is, between my nerves and lack of money, I've put very little in my stomach since I left home, but he doesn't need to know that.

"Enjoy the deliciousness while you can. When the season starts, we'll be on a crazy strict diet, you know?"

"Hey, I always try to eat right. Even over the summer I watched my carbs. I work out a lot, too."

"Oh yeah?" A mischievous grin spreads across his face, and he drops his gaze to my abdominal area, which is hidden from view beneath the table. "Show me what you've got under there."

I have to swallow twice before I can even speak.

"Uh… Under what?"

"Under your shirt. What else?"

"You mean here? In this restaurant?" There are two couples dining near us, a man at a table in the middle of the room, and of course the guy behind the cash register. I wouldn't normally balk at showing someone my abs in public. It's harmless comparing, right? Something people do when they work hard to have a nice body. The problem is that with Beck it doesn't feel like comparing muscles. With him, it feels distinctly sexual.

He shrugs. "It's okay, Junior. Don't worry about it if you're too scared."

"Hell, no, I'm not scared." I scoot to my right around the booth toward Beck, my jeans squeaking loudly against the vinyl seat, until he can see all the way down to my lap. After a quick glance around the room to make sure no one's looking, I pull my t-shirt up to reveal what I think is a damn nice set of abs.

24

Beck stares for a few seconds and licks his lips. "Is that an Adonis Belt I see peeking over the top of your jeans?"

I grin and push my waistband lower, giving him a better view of the two ridges of abdominal muscle that slant down toward my pelvis.

"Pretty impressive," he says nonchalantly, before taking another bite of his sandwich. "When the season starts, I'll help you work on your problem areas."

"Problem areas, my ass." I meet his gaze with steely determination. "If you think yours is so much better, then show me."

He watches me in silence for a moment while he chews and swallows his food, and just when I'm beginning to feel like we're in the midst of the most awkward staring contest ever, he looks away. "Nope."

"Hey, that is totally not fair. Don't be such a dick." Before I can stop myself, I've hit him in the chest with the back of my fist.

*Oh, shit.*

He narrows his eyes at me for a split second, and I wonder if I've ruined everything. He's probably about to knock me out and leave me drooling on the floor of Hotrod's.

Instead, he smiles, and there's something dark in his eyes I can't quite put a name to. Whatever it is, it makes my stomach flip over and lie quivering inside my body.

He returns his sandwich to its paper-lined basket and brushes the crumbs from his hands. "You really want to see what I've got under here?" He bites his bottom lip and slowly lifts the tail of his shirt with his thumb and forefinger, just enough for me to see a tiny strip of tanned skin and a fine trail of blondish hair that disappears

25

into his jeans. I nod mindlessly, eyes riveted to that one delicious little bit of skin he's allowed me to see, mouth hanging open like it's popped a hinge. As if in slow motion, he hooks the thumb of the other hand into his waistband and pulls down ever so slightly, revealing another half inch of happy trail, but nothing more. Unconsciously, I lean forward, following his movement, anticipating what he's about to show me. But he doesn't show me anymore. Instead, he slips his thumb out of his pants, drops the shirt, and leaves me hanging.

*Fuck.*

I raise my guilty gaze to meet his, registering the smug look on his face. Too late, I realize that he's much better than I am at this game, and I've just tipped my hand.

I sit back, swallowing hard, not knowing what to say. I feel like I've just been baited and tested, and I don't know whether I've passed or failed. One thing's for sure. If I had any reservations about letting him know I like him, they're out the window now. Hey, as long as he feels the same, I'm fine with it. Only I still don't know that for sure.

"My roommates and I are having a party at our apartment tonight," he says casually. "You can meet some of the team. Wanna come?"

"Sure. Yeah. Sounds like fun." I hope I sound nonchalant instead of like the ball of excitement I really am. He's already seen me panting like a puppy over a sliver of his abs. I don't want to make a total ass of myself by freaking out over a party invitation that probably means nothing.

"Eight o'clock at Players Club, Apartment 215. Second floor.

Do you have a way to get there?"

"Yeah. I've got a car."

"Cool." He touches his cell phone screen a few times hands it to me. "Type your number in here. If you don't mind, that is."

*Mind??* I'm so ecstatic, my heart is thumping. While I'm putting in the numbers, praying my dad has paid the phone bill by now, the electronic door bell dings to signal new customers have just come into the restaurant. Whoever it is has stolen Beck's attention, and I have to tap him on the shoulder to get him to take his phone back.

He watches two men approach the counter and place their orders. One is rugged and middle-aged with a clean-shaved ruddy complexion and a salt-and-pepper buzz cut. The other is significantly shorter, younger and blonder. Both are wearing Polos and shorts.

"Are you about ready to go?" Beck asks, eyeing my half-eaten sandwich. "You can wrap that up and take it with you."

"Uh, okay." Now I'm dying to know who these guys are that have Beck rushing to get out of here.

I'm totally prepared to sneak past them on Beck's command, but he surprises me by walking directly up to them and clapping the taller one on the shoulder. "Coach," he says warmly. "Haven't seen you in here before."

The coach turns and smiles, showing rosy cheeks and a chipped front tooth. "Beck, I thought that looked like your truck in the parking lot, so I took a chance. Now I can introduce you to the new assistant coach. James Bradley, this is Beck."

The coach might as well be introducing the president, as reverently as he says Beck's name.

27

"Wow, we finally meet." The assistant coach shakes his hand, flashing a fantastic smile that transforms his face from cute to Hollywood handsome. "I've heard a lot of good things about you."

"Yeah, I should warn you, the coach has a tendency to overrate me," Beck says, blushing slightly beneath his tan.

Coach Roberts laughs. "False modesty is for beauty queens, Beck. This is wrestling. I expect you to take a compliment with the same confidence you have when you compete. Besides, everyone knows you're a favorite for the National Championship this year. You're going to put this school on the map."

"Yes, sir," Beck replies without pause. He turns his attention back to the assistant coach. "Thank you for the compliment."

"Who's your friend?" Coach Roberts jerks his salt-and-pepper head in my direction.

"This is one of your new guys, Coach. Jeremy Miller, aka William J. Miller from Blackwood, Georgia."

"Ah…" Coach Roberts finally looks directly at me, assessing me with narrowed eyes. "Looks healthy enough. You ready to work hard this year, Jeremy?"

"Yes, sir, Coach. Ready to go."

He laughs. "Very good. You know, you're a lucky boy if Beck has taken a shine to you. He's one of the best people you'll ever meet, and a hell of a wrestler." He focuses once more on Beck. "Have you seen Jeremy's moves yet?"

Beck shakes his head. "Not yet, but I plan to tonight. Some of the guys are coming to my apartment for a party, and I'm sure we'll get around to putting him through his paces."

"Well, don't let anyone hurt him. I know how you guys get

when you've been drinking. He's still got to qualify, and I'd hate for him to miss it because Truck broke his collar bone."

Beck puts his hands on the coach's shoulders and looks him squarely in the eyes. "Trust me, Coach. Truck's not getting anywhere near this one. I take full responsibility for him."

"Good. And you take care of yourself, too. You're not invincible, even though you think you are."

Beck chuckles and waves over his shoulder as he pushes me toward the door. "I'll be fine, Dad. Don't worry about me."

When we've both gotten back into the truck and are on our way back to the school, I give in to the temptation to watch Beck while he drives, mesmerized by the movement of his strong forearms and hands as he maneuvers the steering wheel. He's so handsome in silhouette, staring ahead as if hypnotized by the road, the muscle in his jaw clenching repeatedly even though his gum is long gone. I'd give anything to know what he's thinking.

"Why did you call Coach Roberts *dad*?" I ask.

"Because he acts like he thinks he's my father." He smiles without taking his eyes off the road. "I don't mind, though. I've been wrestling for him the last two years, and we've gotten pretty close. He's real supportive, you know? Made me Team Captain this year, gets me involved in a lot of community projects, helps me beef up my resume. My parents are supportive, too, but not so much in the wrestling. They're just not really into the sports thing, so it's nice to have someone pulling for me."

"So are you going to be a doctor in Sports Medicine, or a trainer or something?"

"Doctor," he says. "I thought I wanted to work in pro sports someday, but the more I learn about it the less glamorous it seems. I'll probably end up going into private practice somewhere."

We ride the rest of the short distance to school in silence, and after promising Beck several times that I'll come to his party, I head off to hunt my next class. This time he doesn't offer to help me find my way, so I guess the tour is officially over. He still seems lost in thought, which is fine.

I need to think about things, too.


My other two classes, English 101 and Sociology, go by in a blur. All I can think about is Beck and his party, and the possibility of finally having a real boyfriend, and that maybe life won't be so utterly horrible here at college.

By the time I return to my dorm room, my entire body is humming with excitement, and I can't wait for eight o'clock.

*I should probably be fashionably late. Not seem too eager.*

My roommate Seth is already in the room, lying on his bed and playing a noisy app on his phone. He's a sophomore, and slightly geeky, but he's really nice. And cute, if you like the bookish type. After his phone emits a couple of obnoxious buzzes that sound like he's losing, he sets it on his bedside table and looks at me. "How was your day, roomie?"

"Freaking awesome." I sigh, falling back onto my mattress, which is harder than I remember and practically knocks the wind out of me.

"Oh. My. God." Seth sits up and pushes his long auburn bangs out of his eyes. "You met a girl, didn't you? That's all a sigh like that can mean. So who is she? I want details. If there's a romance going on, I need to know about it."

"Jesus, Seth, take a chill pill. I'm just excited because I had a good first day. And because I got invited to a party."

"Oh yeah? Where?"

"Players Club." I pick at my rumpled plaid comforter and concentrate on making my voice sound casual. "This guy named Beck's apartment."

Seth squeals and rushes me, landing on his knees beside my bed, his hands in praying position at his chest. "Jeremy... Dear, sweet Jeremy. If you have any love or compassion for your new roommate, I beg of you... Take me with you. I'll be your designated driver. Your butler. Anything."

I laugh as I take in the sight of him groveling at my bedside. He does pitiful so well.

"I don't know if it will be your style of party. It's just going to be a bunch of wrestlers, from what I can tell."

Seth leans back and stops praying, fixing me with a very serious stare. "Honey, do you really have no idea that I'm gay? Taking me to a party full of hot, muscular jocks is like taking a frat boy to Hooters. They've never invited me to one of their parties, but if I show up with you, it's legit, right?"

I can't even answer, because I'm in shock. How could I have missed such a crucial fact as my roommate being gay? Hell, he's not even trying to hide it.

*Must be nice.*

For a moment, I contemplate telling him exactly how much we have in common, but the timing just doesn't feel right.

31

Uncertainty over the whole Beck thing has me confused, and so in the end I decide to keep quiet. Just for now. Besides, Seth has already admitted he likes wrestlers. What if he starts crushing on me or something? As cute as he is, I'm just not interested in him that way.

Besides, I've already got my heart set on someone else.

# 3

*(BECK)*

"Damn kid," I mumble under my breath, shuffling out of my bedroom in nothing but a pair of purple boxer briefs, my skin and hair still damp from showering.

"What is it, Beck?" Truck is watching one of his old MacGyver reruns on TV. He bought the DVD box set over the summer, much to the chagrin of everyone who lives or hangs out here. Sometimes I think if I hear that damn theme song one more time, I'm going to snap his DVD's in half. While he's not looking, of course. I'll tell him Caleb did it.

"Nothing." I make my way carefully through the living room, stepping over the random shit that's strewn all over the floor. "Are these your gym shorts, Truck? What the hell are they doing in the living room? And these energy drink cans... What kind of pigs am I

33

living with?"

Truck pauses his show and stares at me, pushing an unruly strand of dirty blonde hair behind his ear. "Why so grumpy, man?"

"Could we clean up this place a little? We're having a party in an hour. Where are Gretchen and Caleb?"

"Out getting the keg." He softens his unnaturally deep voice like he does when he's trying to be charming. "Calm down. You're too uptight. I know when something's bothering you. Is the Pope coming to the party or something?"

"I said it's nothing. Jeez."

It's not nothing, though, and Truck knows it. At six foot two and two hundred forty pounds, Truck may look like a caricature of a dumb jock, but he's pretty damn perceptive— a fact that surprises everyone when they first get to know him. I feel like a total fraud denying my agitation, knowing that he can see straight through me with those warm brown eyes of his.

The problem, which I absolutely cannot share with Truck, is that I've invited Jeremy to my apartment, and I know it's a really freaking bad idea. Like the worst one I've had in... well, ever. I'm already going to have to see him at wrestling practice several times a week, in the locker rooms, in the showers.

*Good lord. I may just have to stop taking showers.*

Now I've invited him to my home to hang out with me in front of all of my friends. I'm about ninety-nine percent sure he's attracted to me, and if he is, there's no way in hell I'm going to be able to resist at least trying him out. I'm already aching to run my hands all over the ripped belly he showed me so proudly in the sandwich shop today. What worries me most is that I was about a breath away from crawling across the seat and kissing that defiant expression right off his face. Right there in public.

*Yep, he's definitely going to be a problem.*

I've always been very careful about dating, because it's a huge risk for me. My entire future depends on my being careful, because I'm on a wrestling scholarship, and I'd like to keep it that way. I live like a freaking monk. I don't drink much, I don't do hard drugs, and I absolutely do not fuck guys.

Well, not very often, anyway. I do visit the local gay watering hole every now and then to hook up with someone discreetly. But only because there's an unspoken code there; you don't out another dude. For instance, you would not approach someone on campus as he stood chatting with his friends and say, *Hey man, I saw you at the gay bar the other night.* We all know this— or at least I damn well hope we do. We hang out, we have fun, and we keep our fucking mouths shut.

The bar hookup thing is a calculated risk, and it's the only one I've taken until now. I always figured I'd hold my breath through these awkward college years, develop a really strong right arm, and then meet the man of my dreams after graduation. Live happily ever after in some city far away from here.

*But now I'm fucking up.*

The first clue was when I almost kissed Jeremy in the sandwich shop, the second was inviting him to the party, and the third was when I jerked off in the shower less than an hour ago. It wasn't the fact that I did it that bothered me, but rather what I was thinking. In my mind I actually referred to it as *taking the edge off before Jeremy gets here.* So now in less than twelve hours, he's got a jerk-off session named after him, like he's something special. To top it off, instead of my usual cast of hot, faceless guys gang fucking each other in the sauna, there was cute little Jeremy on his knees under the table at Hotrod's, sucking me off until I came all down the front of his shirt. I felt so pathetic, I almost stopped in the middle... Almost, but not quite. As I squeezed out the last of my load and watched it swirling down the drain, I had the crazy thought that my future was going down right along with it.

*Can I please have one single thought that doesn't revolve around this guy? This is how obsession starts.*

Thankfully, Truck helps me pick up the living room with no argument, and we get the place looking presentable just as Caleb and Gretchen return with the keg. Now we're all here— the Four Musketeers, as Truck likes to call us. Caleb just moved in this year.

Our old roommate Jack got married over the summer and followed his wife to Florida, taking most of the decorations with him, so now the common area of our four bedroom apartment is pretty much an empty shell with a distressed leather sectional and an entertainment center. Gretchen and I have been planning to go shopping for some pictures and knick-knacks, but so far it hasn't happened.

The place is comfortable and roomy, but I'm already feeling like Caleb takes up too much space. He's always insinuating himself into every situation, foisting his opinions on everyone else, using my expensive protein powder without asking. That kind of thing. He never seemed that obnoxious before this summer, otherwise I never would have agreed to let him move in. Thank goodness Gretchen and I share a bath between our bedrooms, while Caleb and Truck share one between their rooms on the opposite side of the apartment. If I had to share a bathroom with Caleb, we'd come to blows within a week.

At least he's pretty useful when it comes to manual labor. Tonight, he sets up the keg in a tub of ice on the kitchen floor while the rest of us get the cups and snacks ready for the party. Gretchen lays out several bags of chips, some dip, a platter of raw veggies, and some bottled water for the non-drinkers and to combat alcohol dehydration. I toss some protein bars onto the counter for the wrestlers, who always need to be striving for muscle mass retention, and then we're set.

When two girls in heavy makeup, low rise jeans and halter tops wander in, it officially signals the arrival of guests. For the next thirty minutes, people trickle in. Most of them are girls wearing similar low rise jeans and halter tops, which apparently is the official party uniform at Southeastern State this season. By eight-thirty all but two of the wrestlers we invited are here, Gretchen's favorite dance mix is pumping from the stereo speakers, and about twenty chatty girls are giggling and preening around the sectional sofa— but still no Jeremy. I know he hasn't slipped in without my noticing, because I've kept a close eye on the foyer.

*What if he doesn't even show up?*

Though it should be a relief, the thought fills me with a sense of dread, and I realize he's the only thing I'm looking forward to. Everything else is just beer and boredom. It makes me wonder... If I'd never met Jeremy today, would I be having fun right now?

*Probably, yes.*

"What's up with you, Beck?" Gretchen approaches, fresh-

37

faced and makeup free as usual, and hands me one of the two opaque plastic cups of beer she's carrying.

Killing half of it in one go, enjoying the foamy smoothness that is so unique to keg beer, almost makes me feel better. It's not a particularly good taste, but after three years of drinking it, the familiarity is soothing. I breathe out a long sigh and lick the foam mustache from my top lip.

"Nothing, Gretch. Just feeling a little bored, or tired. Maybe both." I reach out and yank her long brown ponytail like I always do, and she snatches it away, narrowing her hazel eyes at me.

Gretchen is the only one of my friends who knows I'm gay, and she worries about me a lot. She's also a Psych major, so she's constantly trying to shrink my head.

"I'm serious, Beckett. Maybe you should go *out* for a while? The club is probably crawling, first day of school and all. I can run interference. But you might want to put your shoes on first."

I look down at my bare feet, wiggling my toes into the carpet. "Too lazy." I laugh and down the rest of my beer in three solid gulps. "Tell me, do I have *I need to get laid* tattooed on my forehead or something?"

"Yes," she says. "In bold letters. And if you don't want the wrong people reading it, you'd better go take care of the problem."

"What about you?" I counter. "Don't you need to get laid sometimes, too? Haven't noticed you burning up the sheets with anybody lately."

"It's different for me, hon. I'm a female. We do have needs, but for the most part they're not as immediate as yours. We can get by on flirtation for a long time. The attention is what's most important for us, not the sex."

"How insightful, Dr. Freud. Does that mean someone's been flirting with you?"

"Maybe... Okay, yes. But I'm not ready to share yet."

"Ooh..." I raise a brow. "Now you've got me intrigued. I feel a Brat Pack movie marathon coming on, and a confession."

"You think you can use my weakness for cheesy romantic movies against me? I'm not that easy."

Movement at the foyer catches my attention, and my bones seem to liquefy when I see that Jeremy has finally arrived. I don't know how it's possible, but he looks even better tonight than he did when we met. His short, dark hair curls slightly above his ears, framing that angelic face. Pale skin, ruddy cheeks, strong jaw, muscular neck. A vintage red-white-and-blue Sex Pistols t-shirt hugs his body like a second skin, accentuating every contour of his chest and abs, the sleeves stretched tightly around his biceps. As if that wasn't enough, he's got a strand of black rawhide tied around his throat.

If he chose this outfit just to make my dick hard, he's damn well succeeded in his goal.

I'm not the only one who has noticed his entrance. Whether from curiosity or interest, nearly every eye in the room is trained on him and the auburn-haired guy standing behind him.

*Oh God, that's Seth. If Jeremy brought a date to my party, I'm kicking someone's ass.*

"Dang," Gretchen says, gawking at the door. "Who invited the eye candy? Is he a wrestler? Ooh, the artsy one's not bad, either."

Jeremy scans the room self-consciously, but I don't make a

move to get his attention. I'm frozen in place, stunned, feeling the complication factor of my life inching slowly up the scale with every second that passes. When he finally spots me, his shoulders relax visibly, and a tiny smile lights his face.

Gretchen doesn't miss it, either. She looks from me to him and back again. "Oh, hell no, Beck." She pinches me on the arm, but I don't even flinch. "Beck, this is not a good idea, hon. Oh my God, that is one hot little piece of disaster right there. Walk away while you still can, Beck. Oh, shit. It's already too late, isn't it? No wonder you've been so distracted. Are you sleeping with him?"

Gretchen keeps talking, but I tune her alarmed yammering completely out as I watch Jeremy make his way through the crowd.

"Hi," he says when he's finally standing in front of me. He smiles in that shy way that melts me, stuffing his hands into his jeans pockets and glancing at the floor.

"Jeremy." The air is so thick between us, I can barely speak. If there ever was a guy I felt like I had to fuck, this is him. And if I'm not badly mistaken, he wants me, too.

"Hi, I'm Gretchen." She shoves a hand between us, practically forcing Jeremy to shake it, and dispelling the fog of lust that's got me half blind. "I'm one of Beck's roommates, and apparently the only person who lives here who's got any sense." She shoots me a pointed look.

"Oh, nice to meet you." Jeremy shakes her hand. "This is my roommate, Seth."

"I'm the designated driver," Seth says, taking his turn shaking Gretchen's hand. He glances nervously at me, as if he's not sure how I'm going to react to his being here, so I narrow my eyes at him in warning.

"Well, designated driver…" Gretchen hooks her arm through Seth's, indiscreetly pulling him toward the kitchen. "How about you and I go get a beer? We've got a keg, and it looks like it's going to be an interesting night."

"Uh, sure." Seth allows her to lead him to the keg, looking back over his shoulder once before leaving me and Jeremy staring awkwardly at one another.

"Hope you don't mind me bringing my roommate," Jeremy says.

"Nah, I don't mind Seth being here, but he'd better keep that fucking lip of his buttoned."

"Oh-kaay…" Jeremy's eyebrows come together in confusion. "Do I sense some animosity?"

I laugh. "No, no. Don't worry about it. Seth and I are friends. Sort of. He can just be a pain in the ass sometimes."

"I guess I don't know him that well yet." He watches through the kitchen doorway as Seth and Gretchen help themselves to keg beer.

"You wanna go to my room?" I blurt, mortified by my own lack of finesse.

"Yeah." He answers without any hesitation.

We could stay out here and do the party thing, but the truth is I'm afraid to be around anyone else right now. I don't think I can hide my desire. I'm worried that if anyone out there bothered to look at me and Jeremy for more than a few seconds, they would know what was going on. It only took Gretchen about a half a second. Somehow, I'm going to have to figure out how to control my reactions to seeing him. It's just plain, old-fashioned lust, so I'm hoping like hell if I can just get it out of my system one good time, I'll be over it.

That's the plan, anyway.

(JEREMY)

Before we can make it to Beck's bedroom, Caleb and some huge guy with dark blonde hair come swimming through the sea of people toward us. When Caleb spots me, he doesn't even try to hide his disgust, and neither do I.

"Jesus, Beck," he whines. "Did you adopt this guy or something? Why does he keep showing up today?"

"Better get used to seeing him," Beck says. "He's on the wrestling team, so he's going to be around a lot."

"That don't mean shit," Caleb groans. "Look around. He's the only geeky freshman wrestler I see in our house. The rest of them are off doing geeky freshman things like they're supposed to. So why does he rate an invitation?"

I can't hold my tongue with him talking about me like this, and right in front of my face. "What's the matter, Caleb? Still jealous—"

Beck reaches back to silence me, only his fingers accidentally graze the front of my jeans. It shuts me up, alright. I take a step back, my face getting hot, but no one else seems to have noticed.

"Caleb, either be nice, or go to your room," Beck says with an edge of menace that cracks his boy scout image just enough to turn me on.

"Go to my room? Are you kidding me? Who do you think you are, my dad?" He's about half way to bowing up at one or both of us. I'll bet the two of us could really do some damage fighting alongside each other. I'm getting amped just thinking about it.

Beck doesn't sound like he's ready to fight, though. He seems more like the peacekeeper type. "No, I'm not your dad. I pay rent here, and I'm not going to let you treat my guest like that."

Truck chimes in loudly. "That's right, Caleb. What the hell's your problem? You can't treat our guests like that."

Caleb throws his hands up in the air and grunts. "Whatever. I'm gettin' some beer."

"Fucker," Truck growls after Caleb is gone. Then he turns his attention fully on Beck. "Um... I hate to drag you away from your friend, Beck. It's just that my cousin Anna is down from UGA, and you said you'd meet her. Remember?"

"Oh, yeah." Beck turns toward me with an apologetic look. "Well, Jeremy can come along."

"No, no." I shake my head, embarrassed that I seem to have become the third wheel. "Don't worry about me. I'll just sit on the couch with all the single girls and listen to music."

Truck laughs. "See? He'll be fine for a few minutes, Beck." He mouths the words *Thank You* to me over his shoulder as he pulls Beck across the room toward a bunch of people crowded around the bar at the edge of the kitchen. I can't help but wonder why getting Beck over there is important enough for Truck to thank me.

As soon as Beck joins the group, a guy I've never seen before stands and offers his seat to him. He refuses several times before finally accepting it. I feel awkward watching him like some creepy stalker, but I'm far too curious to look away. A beautiful girl with shoulder-length blonde hair approaches, and Truck introduces her to Beck. I can't hear what they're saying from this distance, and I'm definitely no lip reader, but her ear-to-ear smile says she's as smitten with him as I am.

A wave of hot jealousy washes over me. I have no right to feel this way, of course. I've got no claim on Beck, and I still don't even know if he's gay. With my luck, he's probably straight and about to hook up with Truck's cousin. If he's not gay, there's no way he'd turn her down. Not with that smile and those pale blue eyes.

*Damn. Couldn't my competition have been a little less attractive?*

Without looking away from Anna or missing a beat in the conversation, Beck slips his cell phone out of his pocket, tapping around on the glass for a moment. Getting her number like he did mine in the restaurant today. He's probably got a phone full of numbers.

*Damn.*

I lean back against the fat sofa cushion and breathe out a long sigh. Maybe I should go get a beer after all. The line to the keg is short, and Seth is in there chatting away with Gretchen. Unfortunately Caleb is in there as well, hulking over everyone and bitching about some erroneous call in a football game last season. Stephie's tiny body is shoved up under his armpit, and she looks like she'd rather be hang gliding over power lines than listening to his big mouth. I certainly don't blame her.

A vibration in my back pocket makes me jump, and I dig my cell phone out. There's a text message waiting for me from a number

I don't recognize.

*"Sorry I left you alone,"* it says.

My eyes automatically find Beck, who is swinging his legs from the barstool and looking all innocent. He winks slyly and wiggles his phone at me. I try not to give in to a smile, but it's impossible to keep it off my face. *Yesss!* Maybe the night won't be so bad after all.

*"It's okay,"* I text back. *"What r u doing?"*

He types another text without looking at me. *"Feeling like I'm in high school again."*

I shoot him a confused look, but he's watching Anna rather than me, listening while she talks to Truck.

*"What do u mean?"*

He looks down at my text and smirks as he types his response. *"Trying to work up my courage to make a move."*

My heart drops into my toes. I knew it was too good to be true. Instead of being Beck's date, I'm his fucking wing man. *"Go for it,"* I text reluctantly. *"Guaranteed slam dunk."*

*"Really?"*

*"Jeez, just man up. You're like the hottest guy in school. Who would say no?"*

He stares at me for a moment with a funny look on his face, like he can't believe I've just gotten so rude with him. Honestly, I shocked myself telling him to man up, but I'm exasperated with the whole thing.

As soon as I pick my heart up off the floor and shove it back into my chest, I'm grabbing Seth and getting out of here. Let Beck have his classy blonde babe, and I'll go rub down this all-day boner with some internet porn.

*Or not.*

Crap, I'm not used to having a roommate. Would it be poor etiquette to jerk off to porn with Seth in the next bed? Maybe if I invited him to join me—

*What the fuck am I thinking?*

Another text comes in from Beck. *"Damn. You don't pull any punches. I like that. I'm usually very confident, but I'm a little out of my element here. So go easy on me, okay? Not perfect. lol"*

I sigh as I'm typing. *"Dude, she's gushing already. Just do it. And don't worry about entertaining me. Gotta go. Thanks for the invite. Talk tomorrow?"*

Beck's eyes stretch wide when he reads my text, and he starts typing fast. After he hits send, he watches me intently, and I hold his gaze until my phone vibrates and I have to look away to read it.

*"WTF? She's not the one I want."*

I sit and stare at the text for a full minute, not knowing how to respond. I can barely hear the music over the sound of my own heart.

When I don't answer, he sends another text. *"Do you know who I want?"*

*"I know who I hope it is."* It takes every bit of courage I can muster to hit the send button on that one.

I watch Beck carefully as he reads the text, his expression telling me all I need to know.

His head is bowed toward the phone in his lap, but he cuts his eyes up at me, his lips curling into a naughty half-smile. That look alone makes my dick twitch to life, and I purposely let him see me

46

adjusting it in my pants.

Another text buzzes in. *"Wow, that was hot. Touch it again for me."*

Okay, he's gone and done it now. I'm fully hard, sitting on a sofa in the middle of a bunch of college girls who could look around at any minute and see my very obvious boner.

But who cares? I'll do whatever he wants. It's his house. Hell, I'll do a strip tease in the middle of the room if he tells me to.

For now, I simply pretend to stretch, reaching one hand over my head and straight back. I cup my balls with the other one and drag it slowly up over my dick before hooking my fingers casually under my t-shirt and pulling it up to expose my belly, as if by accident.

When my x-rated stretch is over, I glance back at Beck, whose lust-darkened eyes are locked on me. Then he glances at the girl next to me and nearly falls off of his stool laughing. She's gawking at me with her mouth hanging open. Apparently, I've been putting on a show for more than one person.

"Uh, hey," she says quietly, with an embarrassed giggle. "Sorry, I was... I didn't mean to look." She unconsciously casts her eyes toward my crotch.

"It's okay." I pat her on the leg with the same hand I've just used to grope myself, and her face goes crimson.

Suddenly feeling a little claustrophobic, I excuse myself and walk toward the front door, moving away from Beck, the crowd and the beer. As soon as I'm tucked away in the small foyer where I can't see anyone and they can't see me, I break into a silly little dance, gyrating my hips and doing a train whistle pump with my arm.

*He likes me!*

My cell phone buzzes again, abruptly ending my dance.

*"Where did you go? More touching please."* He tacks a frowny face onto the end of it, which ironically brings a smile to my face.

It's time to find out just how much more he wants, so I tap out what is either the bravest or the dumbest text I've ever written. *"Why don't you come touch it yourself?"*

After I hit send, it doesn't take long to convince myself I've taken it too far. It's not like I can take a text back. I keep half-expecting him to reply with, *What the fuck are you talking about, dude?* or something equally humiliating, in which case I'll slip quietly out the front door and go drown myself in the university pond.

As the seconds tick by, it becomes evident that either he's texting a novel, or he's not going to answer at all. Three times I turn toward the door to leave, but each time I change my mind. Just when I'm about to go for the fourth cycle, Beck moves into the doorway, his large frame blotting out the light from the living room.

I always thought people were exaggerating when they talked about their knees getting weak, but now I know exactly what they mean. At the sight of Beck, mine go so weak they nearly dump me into the foyer floor.

*He came for me.*

He doesn't say anything, doesn't come any closer, but his eyes communicate an incredible need that matches my own. There are people standing within a few feet of us, but we're in our own little world here inside the tiny entryway.

Beck looks up and down my body, clenches his fists, bites his lip, closes his eyes, sighs... His body language tells every detail of his inner struggle so vividly, it's like reading a book. He wants me badly, but he doesn't know if he should take me.

*I'm going to have to take charge, or this ain't happening.*

"Where's your bedroom, Beck?" My voice doesn't waver, and neither does my gaze. I don't know why, but the more terrified I am, the better I am at faking confidence. It's always been that way.

"Over...um...." He steps back and glances at the carpet, breaking our eye lock.

"Which one?"

He points haphazardly across the apartment. "The door closest to the kitchen on the right side."

"I'll be waiting in there for you. But hurry, okay?" As I squeeze past him to get out of the foyer, I let my fingers trail across the obvious bulge in the front of his pants, thrilling to the sound of his sharp intake of breath.

*Oh yeah. He wants me.*

This time the victory dance only happens inside my head.

# 4

*(BECK)*

ONCE I've finally gotten up the courage to join Jeremy in my room, I close the door and dive straight onto the bed, rolling onto my back and covering my face with one of my five over-stuffed down pillows. "Jesus Christ…" I growl into the pillow.

*I can't even think straight. I just wish these feelings would go away. This is a mistake.*

"What's wrong? Are you having second thoughts?" Jeremy asks in a worried voice. "Maybe I should just leave?"

"Fuck. Sorry I'm not being a very good host," I mumble through the pillow. "I'm just in a funky mood, that's all."

"It's not a bad mood, is it?"

I peek out from beneath the pillow at Jeremy, who is now standing near the door with his hands in his pockets. How can I want

50

him to go, yet at the same time want so badly for him to stay?

"Not a bad mood, no. Just... weird. It's hard to explain. Have you ever been so confused it's like you're stoned or something? Like you feel really good, but really messed up at the same time? Like you're dying for something, but you're not sure if it's really something you should have? God, I'm babbling aren't I?"

"Yeeaah," Jeremy draws the word out, sounding distracted, as if he hasn't listened to a thing I've said. "Is this door locked?"

Slowly, I remove the pillow from my head and stare at him, my heart jumping up into my throat. "Yes."

"That's good." He crosses his arms, grabs the hem of his t-shirt and peels it over his head, tossing it onto the chair in the corner.

His body is so fucking hot, it takes my breath away. The guy's not built so much as compact and sculpted. And that neck, smooth and slightly thicker than you'd expect for his body size. I've never been a neck man— *is there such a thing?*— but there's something about his that really does it for me.

At the sight of his naked torso, every bit of moisture has left my mouth, and I swallow around a dry lump. "Uh, Jeremy, I think maybe you got the wrong idea—" What the hell am I saying? I'm backpedaling now, pretending to be straight out of sheer panic, even when we both know I've just been sending him naughty texts. I can't finish my sentence, though. Not with him looking at me with those hungry eyes, and stalking me with that body.

The Jeremy I met at school today was a shy kid, but the one coming toward me now is unabashed, determined, almost predatory. My heart rate doubles when he hoists a knee onto the bottom of the bed and crawls toward me.

"Really, Beck? Have I got the wrong idea? Because I could've sworn you just asked me to touch myself for you in the middle of your living room. What kind of idea should I have gotten from that?"

I don't answer. He's right, of course. I want him so badly I can't think straight, but I'm also freaked out about it.

"What are you doing?" I whisper as he leans over me, bringing his face close to mine until I can feel his breath on my cheek.

"I'm doing what you won't." He covers my lips with his, planting several firm kisses before teasing my mouth open with his tongue. I have no choice but to let him in. I try like hell to hold back my reaction, but when the dam breaks, all that's left is my naked hunger for him and a blind willingness to satisfy it. "If you tell me you don't want me, I'll stop," he says softly before kissing me again.

I close my eyes and wrap my hands around the back of his neck, pulling him close and deepening the kiss. Maneuvering his body until he straddles my thighs, he pins me beneath him. His hands slip under my shirt, bunching it up as high as it will go, exploring my sides and belly with his fingers. I suck in a sharp breath when he bends to rain kisses onto my quivering abs, licking into my belly button and tickling my happy trail with his lips. Then he moves on to my nipples, sucking and biting at first one and then the other, back and forth in a tantalizing pattern that has me panting and groaning before I even realize I've made a sound.

"Your body," he says. "It's amazing. I should punish you for teasing me in the restaurant today."

I can't help but laugh at the memory. "You were so funny trying to look down my pants. I thought you were gonna climb in."

"Yeah, laugh it up while you can. I promise I'll get you back." He grabs my wrists and shackles them above my head with his hands, leaning up to run the tip of his tongue down the sensitive underside of my arm, making me shiver uncontrollably. Alarm bells are clanging in my head, and it occurs to me that I'm being dominated by this little freshman pup. He's taking me over, and I'm actually letting him.

*How did this happen?*

"Mmmm... you taste even better than I imagined," he says, moving down to kiss my lips, my neck, and the hollow of my throat. He releases my wrists, but I can't bring myself to move them. It's as if he's tied them with an imaginary string.

My eyelids flutter from the strange sensation. "You imagined how I would taste?"

"All. Day. Long." He punctuates each word with a kiss trailing down my sternum, the last one ending just above my belly button. "Especially here." He reaches down to rub my dick through my pants, and I moan and arch into his touch, begging for more.

That's all the invitation he needs, because he immediately unzips and unbuttons my jeans, working them down my legs along with my boxer briefs and tossing them onto the floor. He stands for a moment, long enough to undo his own jeans and fold them down his hips, releasing his cock and making mine impossibly harder. I've never in all of my life seen anything sexier than those jeans folded that way, exposing the top half of his ass, his trim hips, and the jet black bed of curls at the base of his shaft.

"So hot," I whisper.

He nudges up between my legs, drops onto his belly, and

props himself up with his forearms on either side of my hips. When he takes my cock into his mouth, I have to grit my teeth to keep from crying out.

"Oh, Jesus Christ," I babble in a jumbled rush, pressing my lips together, willing myself to hold off. It's been a while since I've had any real human contact, and his mouth is like hot, wet velvet sliding over me. I bite back the little noises that threaten to escape my throat as he works me over with his tongue, lips, and throat for several excruciating minutes. He lavishes attention on the head, alternately licking, sucking, and tapping it against his tongue in a hypnotic tactile symphony, while his hand strokes my straining shaft.

I don't know if it's experience, natural talent, or desire that makes him so good, or maybe it's my own overwhelming need. I'm in no condition right now to judge. Whatever it is, the entire world has just flipped upside-down with me in it. I don't know how to lose control. Never had any experience with it. Yet that's exactly what's happening now, whether I want it to or not.

"Be easy, Jeremy... Easy. I don't want to come yet."

The cocky bastard smirks without taking his mouth off of me, and instead of easing up, he doubles his efforts. My cock disappears deep into his mouth over and over as I watch, and he levels his blue eyes on me, pinning me with his fearless gaze just as surely as he's pinned me with his body.

His hips move in time with his mouth, with those jeans folded halfway down his ass, giving me the most delicious view of the top swell of his muscled cheeks and the tantalizing seam running down the middle. He moves just like he's fucking someone, and the sight makes me want to come so badly I have to alternate between panting and biting down hard on my lip just to draw it out another precious few seconds.

Suddenly it dawns on me that the reason he's moving like that is because he's humping the bed between my legs, getting himself off with the friction while he's sucking my dick. It's enough to snap my last tenuous thread of control.

"Fuck... Jeremy..."

My orgasm boils up inside of me, and I hold my breath, as if that can help stave off the inevitable. I know he can feel it, because at that moment he molds every inch of his mouth around me, lodging the head of my dick tightly into the notch at the back of his throat and finishing me off with concentrated little sucking motions. He groans loudly around my cock and grinds his hips several hard times into my mattress as I shoot everything I've got down his throat.

*Shit, did I just make a noise?*

In my mind, I think I've cried out, but I can't be sure. None of this feels quite real. As the world swims slowly back into focus, I see Jeremy still hovering between my legs. Gorgeous, masculine, ethereal.

*Yep, that's as real as it gets.*

He licks his lips nervously, his face coloring. "Sorry I made a mess on your sheets."

And just like that, the shy boy is back. He looks so innocent as he rests his cheek on my hip and looks sweetly up at me through lowered lashes. Like a little angel who should definitely not know how to do the dirty things he's just done to me. Or to my bed.

The two of us spend endless silent moments just blinking and grinning stupidly at each other before Jeremy stands and tucks himself back into his jeans. I stare up at the ceiling wondering what the fuck I've just done, or rather what I've let him do.

*He just dominated the hell out of me.*

The knowledge settles like an anvil in my belly, my stomach muscles clenching and releasing, quivering almost to the point of making me sick. Not so much because I lost control, but because it felt so damn good.

"Beck, I gotta know something..." Jeremy searches my face with his clear blue eyes. "Do you bring all the new wrestlers back here to your room and take advantage of them like this? Because I'm thinking I might file a sexual harassment suit."

I grab a pillow and heave it at him, but he ducks easily out of the way, laughing so loudly I have to shush him. He claps a hand over his own mouth until the laughter passes.

"I'm guessing you're not out, then?" he whispers. There's no judgment in his expression, only curiosity.

I shake my head. "Gretchen knows."

"She's the only one?"

"Sadly, yes."

He presses his lips together, turns an imaginary key at the corner of his mouth and kisses it, then pretends to slip it into his pocket.

I can't help but smile at the gesture. "Well, aren't you sweet."

He laughs and moves to retrieve his shirt. Reluctantly, I drag my sated ass out of bed and get dressed, too. There's a party going on outside my bedroom door, and as much as I'd like to skip it, I know it's not a good idea to stay holed up in here all night with Jeremy. People will begin to wonder, if they haven't already.

The scene outside my bedroom is different now— sharper, more vivid, grainier even. It's like walking into the sun after being indoors for too long. I make a beeline for the keg, needing to get a bit of a buzz between me and everything that's happened tonight.

*I just let a guy suck my dick in my bedroom. In my fucking apartment. With my friends on the other side of the door.*

"Beck, there you are." Truck claps me firmly on the shoulder, making me jump like a scared kitten as I bend to retrieve the keg nozzle. After I fill my cup to overflowing and down every bit of it in record time, I finally acknowledge him.

"Yeah. Sorry, man… thirsty. How's it going?" I'm breathless like I've just jogged around the block, but it's from nerves rather than exertion.

"Great. As always, we're putting on a badass party. The alcohol is flowing, and the girls are getting drunker by the minute." He does a ridiculous air-humping move with his hips that I don't think he'd dare try if he was sober. He's slurring his words, too. Hopefully he and everyone else here are drunk enough not to have noticed my disappearance.

Jeremy is still in my room, waiting a few minutes before coming out so that we're not seen exiting together. I fill another cup of beer, hoping to have a buzz going by the time he gets out here. At least enough to take the edge off.

There's that phrase again. *Take the edge off.* I've used it twice today in relation to Jeremy, which begs the question: *What edge?* If he's making me so damn edgy, I shouldn't be doing this, right?

"Hey, I want to thank you for the thing with Anna. It's not every day we get to go stay in a luxury chalet in the mountains. You won't believe this place. I haven't been there in years, but it's freaking amazing. Eight bedrooms, indoor-outdoor heated pool, huge hot tub, and nothing to do but hike, fish, and fuck. I'm thinking about inviting Gretchen. What do you think?"

I cough beer through my nose. "Um, Gretchen? I don't know. Does she even know you like her?"

Truck toes the carpet, blushing. "I've been trying to give her hints, but I don't know. I was hoping you could kind of feel her out for me."

"Sure, I'll do that. But I don't think I'll be going on the trip with you guys."

"Oh, Beck, why not? It's going to be so awesome. Listen, you don't have to get with Anna or anything. The deal was that if I introduced you two, she'd let us stay at the chalet one weekend. I'm not pimping you out, dude."

"You sure?" I ask, still skeptical.

"Yeah, man. It'll be fun. You can invite Jeremy."

"Really? You sure she won't get pissed if I bring a—" My mouth opens, but no words come out. I look like a fish choking on air. For one surreal moment, I've almost forgotten Truck has no idea I'm gay, and I've nearly said something that can't be unsaid.

*Date.*

Truck saves me by supplying a more appropriate word. "Friend?"

"Yeah, *friend.* You sure she won't get pissed if I bring a friend?"

"Why would she? I told you she only wanted to meet you. Our families are big into wrestling, dude. She's got three brothers and a father who wrestle, and me and my brothers. She follows the sport, so she knows who you are and respects you. I mean, yeah, she thinks you're dreamy and shit. But she already knows she's not your type." He winks and takes a big swig of beer, scanning the room with his eyes.

I give him a wary look. "How did she know that?"

"Because I told her. Duh." Truck rolls his eyes. "But she wanted to meet you anyway, so I said fine. Between you and me, I think she would have let us use the chalet anyway, but I didn't want to take any chances. I really want to take Gretchen. You think she'd be impressed?"

"Sure, I guess." I've almost worked up the courage to ask Truck exactly what he thinks my type is, when Seth suddenly pops up in front of me like a drunken Jack-in-the-box.

"Where's my roommate, Beck?" He shifts from foot-to-foot, flipping his hair out of his eyes in classic Seth fashion.

"Um, I don't know. Where's mine?"

He shrugs. "She went off with Caleb's girlfriend after we drank a couple of beers. You jocks better not be fucking with my roommate. He's new in town, and a little naïve, but that's no excuse to take advantage."

"What the hell are you talking about, Seth?"

He pokes a finger in my face, and the fact that he's Jeremy's friend is the only thing that keeps me from throwing him out on his ass. "I know what you jocks do to innocent freshmen. I've heard stories."

59

I bend close to speak softly into his ear. "You've been watching too much gay frat porn, Seth."

He gives me a nasty look, and I find myself on the verge of a laugh, wondering what he'd say if he knew what his innocent little freshman had just done to *me*.

"Hey," Truck says, crowding Seth with his enormous body. "Keep your finger out of his face. You'd better show some respect."

Some of the other wrestlers have begun to move in, sensing trouble. The high-level community functioning of a team never ceases to amaze me. After years of spending so much time together, training together, you sort of end up sharing a consciousness to some extent, especially when one member of the team is threatened.

Not that Seth is any physical threat, but my guys are not about to let someone verbally assault me in my own home. Besides that, most of them enjoy a good confrontation every now and then.

"What's going on, Beck?" Vlad comes to stand next to me, showing solidarity and adding to the increasing air of aggression in the room.

Like a dark cloud and a rumble of thunder on the horizon, all signs point to this situation turning ugly fast. If I don't calm Seth down quickly, he's either going to get his dumb ass kicked, or get mine in some serious hot water. Unfortunately, when he gets on something, he's like a trained pit bull; he'll shake it till it's dead. That combined with his legendary lack of discretion is a recipe for disaster.

"Nothing's going on," I say casually. "Just a misunderstanding. I believe he thought we were hazing his roommate, but he's mistaken."

"Oh yeah? If I'm mistaken, then where is he?"

*Jesus, can't this guy take a fucking hint?*

"I'm right here, Seth," says a voice from behind me. "What's up? I was just in the restroom." Jeremy has finally emerged from my room, looking put together and innocent. And hot. God, I'd already forgotten how good he looks.

Seth's shoulders relax, and he lets out a long, ragged breath. "Thank heavens. I thought these jocks had taken you away to do horrible things to you. I pictured you passed out on the floor somewhere with alcohol poisoning, or being hosed down with a group of naked freshmen and forced to do the elephant walk."

"Elephant walk? Really?" Jeremy smirks at his friend. "Seth, I'm perfectly capable of taking care of myself. You do realize that I'm one of these jocks, right?"

Seth blinks vacantly for a moment, then he lets out an embarrassed laugh. "Oh, yeah. I forgot all you sporty types share a common bond and all that shit. But you're still a freshman, and frats and sports teams are both known to haze their freshman members. I've seen it... online." He clears his throat, casting an embarrassed glance in my direction.

Vlad turns to stare at Jeremy, his eyes glazed red. "Dude, you're on the team?"

"Yeah," he replies smoothly. "If I qualify, that is. And I *will* qualify." He lifts up onto his toes and grins.

"Oh, that sounds like a challenge to me," Vlad says, getting that gleam in his eye that says we're going to have a fight.

"Yeah," Truck agrees, grinning. "Definitely a challenge."

"Whoa..." I step between Jeremy and the other two. "I don't think I'm in the mood to watch wrestling tonight, especially not in

61

the apartment."

"Since when?" Caleb steps forward, eyeing Jeremy. "Someone always ends up wrestling at our parties, for the last beer if nothing else. That's why we all chipped in for that expensive-ass practice mat. What's the matter? You afraid we're going to hurt your new little pet?"

All eyes swing to me, and I realize this conversation is officially going down a path I do not want to reach the end of. Just when I'm about ready to flip Caleb on his head, Jeremy steps up, putting his hand on my chest. The warmth of his fingers through my shirt sends my heart into overdrive, reminding me of his hands all over me, exploring me.

"I don't mind, Beck. I'd love to take on any of these guys. One at a time, that is."

"Jeremy, these guys are way out of your weight class. Let me find Greg—"

"I don't mind," he insists. "Getting beaten doesn't bother me. But I can take care of myself better than you think."

I rub my hand back and forth across my buzzed scalp, feeling the short hairs prick my palm. "You keep saying that, Jeremy, but—"

"Then let me prove it."

*Fuck. He's trying to impress me.*

"Yeah, Daddy, let him prove it," Caleb drawls in a smart-ass falsetto that has me imagining sticking my whole arm down his throat and ripping his fucking guts out.

I struggle within myself to remain cool. As obnoxious as Caleb is, he's my roommate, and I have to live with him whether I like it or not. Also, for obvious reasons, I have to be careful how I handle the Jeremy situation. One false move on my part and everyone will know my secret. Most importantly, though, I need to discourage this rivalry between the two of them. I don't understand it, but I know it could get dangerous if it goes too far. Especially with a hot head like Caleb and a guy who seems to want to prove himself as badly as Jeremy does.

"Alright," I say calmly. "But Jeremy only wrestles Truck and Vlad. Caleb, I think you have a conflict of interest going, since you and Jeremy had that little altercation on campus this morning."

Caleb opens his mouth to protest, but I shoot him a withering look that succeeds in keeping him quiet.

I don't like these impromptu party wrestling matches very much. There are no rules, no referees. Occasionally they can get rough, especially when there's alcohol involved, and I don't want to see Jeremy get hurt. But in this case, with everyone begging me, there's no way I can say no without giving myself away. If I refuse to let Jeremy fight, people will start looking at me funny— and with good reason. I can't have that.

I sigh and throw my hands up. "Okay. Move the furniture and roll out the mat. As always, no lifts, no points— pin only."

Vlad jumps up to high-five Truck, and they're both grinning from ear to ear, while Caleb rousts one of our guests off of a barstool and sits down to sulk. We definitely need to get the season started so these guys can work off some of their backed-up testosterone. They're way too emotional over getting the chance to whip up on the new kid.

Jeremy squeezes my shoulder. "Thanks, man. I appreciate it. We'll try not to tear up your living room too much." He faces the other two, his eyes alight with a dangerous brand of mischief. "Now how do we decide who gets first shot at taking me down?" He struts in a circle, smiling and opening his arms wide as if inviting them into a warm embrace.

Like flipping a switch, he's become one of them. Masculine, aloof, driven. Ready to take on whatever comes at him, consequences be damned. I want the shy boy back. Or the sexy guy who was just in my bedroom, whoever the hell *he* was. Not a shallow carbon copy of every other gorilla on campus.

I have to admit, though, he plays the part well. The other wrestlers are salivating to get at him. Party-goers are beginning to form a makeshift ring around them, and my guts are churning.

*Fuck. How can I stop this from happening?*

Gretchen emerges from the kitchen with straws that she's cut to various lengths. "Shorter straw fights Jeremy. Let's go." She winks at me over her shoulder.

*Gee, thanks, Gretch.*

Vlad draws short, and the two of them square off. I've never seen Jeremy's moves— at least not the wrestling kind— so I'm as nervous as a mother bird watching a baby jump out of the nest. He's a walk-on from a small town, for crying out loud. How good can he be? At least Vlad is a closer weight match for him than Truck.

Gretchen has retrieved the whistle from its wall hanger and slips it around her neck, pulling her long brown ponytail through it. Then she gives me a smile and a thumbs up.

*When did she become a wrestling official? Guess we've really rubbed off on her.*

"Ready, guys?" When they both nod, she gives a short tweet

on the whistle to signal the beginning of the match.

Jeremy drops to one knee and launches at Vlad in one of the fastest shots I've ever seen. Before Vlad can blink, Jeremy has struck like lightning, swept his legs and flattened him on his back. The entire fluid move is done before the crowd can even react, and by the time their gasps hit the air, Vlad is laughing.

"Fuck. I've had too much to drink." He takes the hand Jeremy offers, and Jeremy pulls him to standing.

"Yeah," I say. "Jeremy's got the upper hand on all of you guys there. He's sober."

"He's fast, though, I'll give him that." Vlad joins the other two, rubbing his ass and looking slightly sheepish. He's always been a good sport. And in his defense, he does appear to be off kilter tonight, and off his game as a result.

"You'll get him next time, Vlad." Gretchen offers an encouraging smile.

*Oh, now she's a cheerleader? She's acting totally out of character tonight.*

I'm standing off to the side with my arms crossed, biting my lip, trying to hide the fact that my nerves are getting the best of me. Jeremy is quick as hell, but as far as I'm concerned, he's still untried. Flipping a drunk guy doesn't really take a lot of skill, and now he's going to have to grapple with one of the best wrestlers in the school— and the heaviest.

Truck is anxious to do what Vlad couldn't tonight. As he passes me, he leans in close to my ear. "I'm gonna take this smart-ass little punk down." He's just talking smack, and I know it, but it still rouses my protective instincts.

"Just remember, we don't need any hospitals or lawsuits, okay buddy? Besides, I told Coach Roberts I wouldn't let you touch him."

He waves me off with a laugh, stepping onto the mat to face Jeremy, whose face is flushed with excitement. It's fascinating how his eyes sparkle as he contemplates his opponent. He's got so many different looks— every one of them intense, and every one of them hot as hell to me. I honestly don't think I've ever had such a strong physical attraction to anyone in my life.

Just before Gretchen sounds the whistle, Jeremy winks at me almost imperceptibly, sending a tingle dancing up the back of my neck.

When the match begins, Truck is expecting Jeremy to try the same double-leg takedown he executed so flawlessly on Vlad, and that is exactly what Jeremy does, lowering his level and attacking Trucks legs.

Truck sprawls hard - really hard, arching his back and hipping into Jeremy, putting all of his 240 pounds on Jeremy's upper body. Now Jeremy is stuck underneath the big man, with no hope of being able to salvage the shot and score a takedown. The look in Jeremy's eyes tells me he's never felt this kind of weight and power before. He's starting to realize that he might have bitten off more than he can chew, and I'm wishing like hell I'd honored my promise to Coach Roberts and not allowed this to happen in the first place.

Within seconds, Jeremy is lying flat on his stomach, arms extended and face planted firmly in the mat. Truck is laughing at him, taunting him. "Don't bring that shit here, little man," he growls, and the crowd erupts with laughter.

Truck eases up on Jeremy and lets him base up to his hands and knees before slapping a front-headlock on him and rag-dolling him in each direction. He wants to make sure everyone who's watching knows who the alpha male in this match is. After thirty seconds of humiliation Truck releases the front-headlock and spins behind Jeremy, chopping his near arm and breaking him down to his belly. Then he puts a hard crossface on Jeremy, forcing him to turn his face away in an effort to avoid the pain Truck is applying with his forearm.

When Truck tires of playing around with him, he uses the crossface to fold Jeremy up into a cradle. Once the cradle is locked up, Truck rolls Jeremy over on his back for the pin. Helpless and completely dominated, Jeremy stares up at the ceiling. I couldn't be any angrier with myself for letting this happen.

Gretchen steps onto the mat with a huge grin as Truck and Jeremy stand. She grabs Truck's hand and holds it up. He smiles back at her.

*Hmmm… Looks like I may not have to put in a good word for Truck with Gretchen after all.*

Truck and Jeremy bump shoulders, and Truck struts off to celebrate his win. The guy is a little more cocky than usual, and a little less thoughtful, because of the beer. And probably the girl.

Jeremy wanders over to me with an embarrassed shrug. "Knew that was coming, huh? That is one big motherfucker." He's out of breath, and his beautiful skin is flushed from exertion and being scraped across the mat.

I smile and grab him by the scruff of his neck. "There aren't many people who can beat Truck, you know."

"I'll bet you can." He gazes expectantly at me, waiting for confirmation.

"Yeah, I can. But I've been at this longer than you, and I've had college level training and experience. I can see a lot of potential in you, though."

"Really?" He beams with pride.

"Yes, really. I wouldn't say it if I didn't mean it."

I scan the crowd, suddenly feeling conspicuous. It can't be a good idea to stand here all night complimenting him like a jackass, and with him staring up at me like a lovesick puppy. What we've done here tonight breaks all of my rules, and I need to put everything on fast rewind and get my life back to the way it was yesterday.

*As much as I hate to do it.*

After explaining that I need to act like a proper host for a while, I leave Jeremy standing near the dwindling keg. The distance between us doesn't really solve anything, though. I can't stop following him with my eyes— watching where he's going, what he's doing, and who he's talking to. Mostly, he chats with Seth. There are a couple of cute girls in particular who keep hovering around them, and there's a lot of laughter exchanged. He hasn't laughed that way with me, so loudly and unselfconsciously. It's good to see him making friends so easily, especially after the not-so-warm welcomed he received from Caleb, though I'm feeling an inexplicable twinge of jealousy.

*Ridiculous. He's an easy fuck, that's all. A new hookup. Add him to the shortlist.*

But the fact that he's a wrestler is a huge kink, and I know it. I can't just compartmentalize him out of my everyday life like I've don't the other guys I've been with. Not to mention that jealousy is something I can't afford to feel. It's just not practical.

I'm still trying to talk myself into believing I don't care an hour and a half later, when I suddenly notice that Jeremy has disappeared. I run frantically down to the parking to find him stuffing his drunken roommate into a late model Toyota rust bucket.

"So did you have an okay time?" I ask, feeling like I'm fishing for a compliment but unable to come up with anything better to say to get his attention.

"Oh… yeah." He glances up, surprised to see me. "Except one of your goons beat the shit out of me and made me look like a little bitch in front of all your friends. Other than that, I had a great time."

"You can't win every time, you know." I lean against the passenger door of his car, fiddling with the hem of my shirt.

He smiles. "I know that. It still stings a little, though. It's stupid for me to feel bitter over a loss, especially at a party. Plus fighting Truck is kinda like getting plowed under by an avalanche."

"Or a Mack truck. Hence the nickname." I peer through the windshield at the figure of Seth passed out in the passenger seat. "Looks like you've got more important things to worry about tonight, anyway. Some designated driver he turned out to be. He's gonna be a bitch to drag inside the dorm. If I hadn't been drinking, I'd drive over and help you."

"Not a problem. He'll walk, or he'll sleep in the damn car. Makes no difference to me."

"He might puke in it," I point out.

"In this fine machine?" Jeremy gestures grandly toward his

car, imitating what I assume to be a television spokesmodel. "No worries. I'll just trade it in on a Rolls if that happens."

I laugh. "Maybe you want a nice Audi or Lexus instead."

"Hey, that reminds me…" Jeremy places a hand on my chest, right over my heart, and I'm sure he can feel it the moment my heart rate picks up. "You're supposed to be proving something to me, remember? Your bad-boyness, I think. Got any ideas yet?" He leans in toward me, and I watch in frozen fascination as his lips part and brush mine ever so gently. My whole body tingles with desire.

"No." I push him away a little too roughly and look around to make sure no one has seen. "Not here, okay? Too many people around."

"Oh, sorry. I forgot. It's too bad, though." He gives me a sexy smile that makes me want to take back what I've said. "You know, if there weren't people around, I'd love to kiss you. On the lips, on the neck, everywhere… I'd reach around and grab your ass, too. I haven't done that yet, and you have such a great ass."

I groan and back a couple of steps away from him and glance around again. "I want to. Really, I do." My dick is hard for him again, and he's making me consider doing things I never would have considered doing before today. It would be so easy to abandon reason right now and let him do everything he's describing. It's dark out, and everyone else is drunk. I could probably get away with spinning him around and bending him over the cool hood of his car, grabbing onto his trim hips and burying myself in him while the world moves around us and Seth snoozes in the front seat. "You are such a temptation for me, Jeremy. You have no idea."

He waves me away with a smirk. "It's cool. I understand.

You're worried that people around here won't understand if the big jock on campus is gay."

I shake my head. "No, that's not it at all. I don't care what they think. It's my fucking wrestling scholarship. I'm on the home stretch. This is the last year I have to worry about it before I'm officially done with the undergraduate part of my program. Then I go on academic scholarship for my post-grad studies. I've worked really hard and made it this far. I just don't know what the ramifications might be if I came out right now. It might screw up my whole plan. Not to mention, what if I ruin my chance of getting a Nationals title? That would break the coach's heart."

"You don't even know what might happen? Maybe it would be okay."

"Well, it's not something I can just ask. *Hey Coach, what would happen to my scholarship if I was gay? Just a hypothetical question. No basis in reality whatsoever.*" I huff out a humorless laugh. "If I'm gonna do that, I might as well walk into practice wearing a Gay Pride t-shirt and pink hot pants and see what happens."

"I see your point." He purses his lips. "Just for the record, though... I just pictured you in that outfit, and I've gotta say, you looked pretty hot."

"Yeah?" I grin and stare off into the night, listening to the random sounds of my party going down for the count. Music, a little talking, a car door slamming here and there, a girl's laugh. "Shit. What about you? You're not gonna come out, right? I didn't think about it before we were..."

"Seen together?" Jeremy snatches his car door open, and I have to jump out of the way to keep it from slamming into my hip.

"If it's that important, I guess you should have asked first."

*Damn. Is he pissed?*

He gives me a half-assed smile as he cranks up and pulls away in his noisy clunker of a car.

# 5

*(JEREMY)*

MY dorm room is quiet except for the sound of Seth snoring. If there was a chance in hell I could sleep, his wood-sawing would be really annoying, but right now it only serves to remind me that I'm up all alone with no one to talk to.

*Not that I could talk to Seth about this anyway.*

The problem is that Beck is buried so deeply in the closet, there's no way I'll be able to get him out. I recognize the signs, because I've been here in this very spot before.

I understand his reasons, but I'm just not sure what that means for me. Maybe I shouldn't even bother trying to pursue anything with him. There are probably plenty of hot gay guys at Southeastern State who would be proud to let people know they're with me. I just haven't had the chance to meet them yet. Hell, Seth might even be a contender.

I take a moment to check him out as he snores, mouth open, a thin stream of drool leaking onto his pillow. Okay, so not exactly his finest moment, but he's an attractive guy. Not the athletic type I prefer, but he's trim and healthy, with really nice hair. He reminds me of one of those alternative rock singers who are both cool and smart at the same time.

Oh, who am I kidding? I'm just not feeling it. And it would be icky somehow, because I've already compartmentalized him in my mind as my roommate and therefore off limits.

I sigh loudly, knowing no one will hear it.

Beck was perfection tonight when we were alone. There's no doubt we're hot for each other. I couldn't do anything else until I got my mouth on that gorgeous body of his, and he definitely didn't put up much of a fight. Once we got into his bed, we fell together like pieces of a puzzle.

Then he ignored me for the last two hours of the party and freaked out when it occurred to him that he's just been seen with a guy who might not be content to hide his sexuality.

*Dammit. College was supposed to be my big shining moment to come out. What am I doing messing around with this closet case?*

I cover my head with my pillow, an act which unfortunately reminds me of Beck earlier in the evening when he was talking to me through his pillow, so I immediately take it off again and just stare at the ceiling. The last thing I remember thinking is that maybe I'll meet some great guy tomorrow who's out and proud, and even hotter than Calvin Barnwell Becket III.

*Hey, it could happen.*

Next morning, there's no sign of Beck. I stand outside my class until everyone else is seated and the professor is calling roll. As soon as class is over, I'm out the door, scoping the students who are emerging from Beck's room. He's just not here.

Feeling shamefully like a stalker, I take a stroll out to the parking lot where Beck's truck had been parked the day before, wholly prepared to take a nosedive into the bushes if I'm in danger of being spotted. But he's not there, either.

Before I can change my mind I'm in my car driving to his apartment.

His absence doesn't necessarily mean he's avoiding me, right? What if he had a car accident, or got alcohol poisoning after I left last night? Or maybe he has the flu. There's even a chance he's been trying to call me, but I forgot to put my phone on the charger last night. When I got up, it was flatlined, so I had to leave it charging today. What if he's been frantically trying to reach me?

*Yeah, he's probably just avoiding me. But I'm going anyway, dammit.*

His truck is in the parking lot of his apartment building, and I don't know if that makes me feel better or worse. I take the outside steps two at a time to the second floor, but uncertainty jumps on me as soon as I'm standing outside his apartment. I study the white metal door, learning every scratch and ding, trying to work up the courage to knock. When I'm about a breath away from turning back, I close my eyes, take a deep breath and straighten my posture. No turning back now.

*Hell no. I'm Jeremy-Fucking-Miller, and I'm going to have an answer.*

I knock.

Truck swings the door open, bleary-eyed and scratching his ass through a pair of worn gym shorts. "Back for more punishment, freshman?"

"I don't have time to whip you today, old man. Besides, you look a little worse for wear. Where's Beck?"

"His room," he groans, jerking a thumb over his shoulder toward Beck's bedroom.

I blow past him like I have every right to be here, dodging crumpled snack wrappers and misplaced furniture from last night's party, and knock lightly on Beck's door. When he opens it, I have to catch my breath. He's all muscles and tan skin in nothing but a pair of gray drawstring pajama pants that ride low on his hips. The material is thin and slinky enough to insinuate everything he's got under them, and it's clear he's not wearing a stitch of underwear.

*Sweet baby Jesus, he's hot.*

After staring at me for a beat, he steps aside to allow me inside, and I close the door quietly behind me.

"Jeremy, I don't..." He can't seem to come up with the words he wants to say, but the look on his face speaks for him. He lowers his eyes, drinking me in, his face softening as if he sees something he really likes. "Fuck." With a resigned sigh, he slumps back against the wall beside his door, desire plainly etched on his handsome features.

I'm on him in a flash, so hungry for him I can't control myself, pinning him hard against the wall and crushing his soft lips

76

with a punishing kiss. I want to be on him, under him, in him... all at once.

My hands wander his hot flesh, running along the soft skin of his sides, feeling the ripples of his ribcage and the instant profusion of goosebumps when I hit a ticklish spot. I find his waistband, releasing the drawstring tie easily with two fingers, and his pants start to fall.

"Whoa... Jesus Christ!" Suddenly he's pushing frantically against me and grabbing for his pants, laughing as he ties the strings back.

"What is it?" I ask, bewildered. "I thought—"

Did I misread his signals? From the way he looked at me when I came in, it definitely seemed like he wanted me as much as I wanted him.

The sound of a throat clearing from behind me alerts me to the fact that we're not alone, sending an electric shock to my heart and throwing me into full-blown panic mode. I whirl around to find Gretchen sitting in the corner chair I'd tossed my shirt onto the night before, the look on her face one of intense amusement.

"Please don't stop on my account," she says with a grin. "That was way more entertaining than the Brat Pack movies we're watching."

"Fuck a duck!" I bend over, putting my hands on my knees and trying to calm my runaway heart and remember how to breathe. "Oh my God, I think I'm having a heart attack. Can't you people give a guy a heads up or something?"

Beck laughs and moves around me to take a seat on his bed, trying to hide his obvious erection. "As quick as you are? We would've had to bend space and time to give you a heads up,

Jeremy." He sits on the bed and leans back against the headboard, drawing his knees up to his chest and planting his feet on the bed shoulder-width apart. He pats the space on the bed between his legs. "Come sit over here with me. But make sure you lock the door first."

I do as he instructs, and soon I'm sitting with my back against his chest. It's really awkward at first, because I'm not used to being this close to someone when sex isn't involved. I find myself worrying that I'm too heavy or I'm in his way, but then the strangest warmth steals through my body, and I relax into him. When he reaches around me with the remote to resume the movie that's paused on the TV on his dresser, he props his arms on his knees, bracketing my body intimately. Even after the movie starts, he leaves them there, and I'm surprised at how good it feels just sitting with him wrapped around me like this.

I can't remember the name of the movie, but Gretchen is babbling and gushing over parts of it, especially when the guy asks the girl to the prom and they kiss like they want to eat each other's faces off. I think Beck and I kiss even better than that. Way hotter.

He's so quiet today, maybe because Gretchen is here. He's barely spoken to me, but his body communicates with mine through subtle touches— the gentle squeeze of his thighs at my hips, a rub of his arm against mine. Eventually, I relax enough to let my head fall back against his shoulder, and he nuzzles my temple with a stubbled cheek. God, it feels so good. His scent is all around me, like spicy body wash, spearmint, and pheromones. I keep having the urge to swivel around in his arms, close my eyes, bury my face in his neck and just breathe.

Once while Gretchen's especially engrossed in the movie, he

78

puts his hand on my jaw and turns my head enough to kiss me covertly on the side of the mouth, darting his tongue out for a quick taste before releasing me. It makes my whole body quiver.

*I don't ever want to move.*

As soon as the movie ends, Gretchen turns to me. "So Jeremy, you're the first guest Beck and I have had for one of our movie marathons. How do you like it so far? Not too cheesy, I hope."

"No, it's nice," I say, trying not to let on that I haven't been able to concentrate with Beck's body so close to mine. "I don't watch old movies all that much, but they're pretty good. How often do y'all do this?"

She muses. "Oh, about once every couple of months or so, maybe less. Just when we want to talk about relationship stuff."

Beck moves his face away from mine to mouth something to her behind my head, which of course I can't see. Whatever it is, Gretchen just laughs. "I'm flirting with someone, and Beck is dying to know who it is."

"Truck," he says.

"Shut up," Gretchen squeals, her face turning red. "How do you know that?"

"My amazing powers of observation," Beck says. "And the fact that Truck told me he's got the hots for you."

"Really?" Gretchen hops up out of the chair and bounces gleefully, the corners of her smile nearly touching her ears. "Oh my gosh. What should I do?"

"Hmmm..." Beck muses for a moment. "Next time he's watching MacGyver by himself, go drop down between his legs and give him a killer blowjob."

"Shut up!" she yells again. "That may be what you'd do, whore. But it's not my style." She leans over and hits him on the arm, but he's too quick for her. Laughing, he grabs her wrist in one hand and torques it until he's brought her to her knees on the carpet.

"I'm not a fucking whore, bitch. Take it back, or I'll keep you here all day."

"Ow," she squeals. "Okay, okay, I take it back!" When he releases her, she jumps to her feet, rubbing her wrist. "Dang, you're mean."

"Yeah, you'd better remember that next time you want to call me a whore." He glances at me as if he's just remembered I'm here, and then back at her. "We'll talk later," he tells her.

She smirks in my direction but doesn't say anything.

I feel very left out all of a sudden. Not that I have a right to be intimate with these people. They're roommates, old friends, and I just met both of them yesterday. I can feel the history between them, the secret looks they trade, the way they can communicate without speaking. It all just makes me feel like a stupid outsider. Like they're talking about me right in plain sight, and I don't even know what they're saying.

*They're probably going to talk bad about me after I leave. Might as well let them get started.*

"Well, guys..." I extract myself from Beck's loose embrace and stand up beside the bed, stretching and trying my best not to look at his half naked body or the way his package is outlined by the thin pajama fabric. "It's time for me to head out so I don't miss my next class. Thanks for letting me crash your movie marathon."

"No problem, Jeremy." Gretchen gives a little girly finger

wave. "Have a nice day."

"Yeah, thanks for stopping by." Beck doesn't bother getting up to see me to the door, or even looking at me. Instead, he fiddles absently with the remote.

*Thanks for stopping by? What, is this a convenience store?*

Truck and Caleb are watching TV when I pass through the living room on my way out, both of them looking excessively hung over, and Caleb gives me the evil eye. "So freshman, you want to hang with the big boys, huh? Like you're all buddy-buddy with our group now, or something? If you think you're gonna be able to suck up to Beck and get special treatment on the team, you're wrong. He don't play that shit."

"*Don't play that shit?* You already used that saying yesterday, Shakespeare. Might be time to work on your vocabulary." I don't even pause until I'm out the front door. If I do, there will be a fight, and right now that just seems like an inconvenience. Truthfully, I just want out of Beck's apartment, because I feel less than welcome.

Coming over here was stupid. I realized that before I even did it, but it was like a compulsion I couldn't control. I learned my lesson, though. If Beck wants to see me, he'll have to come to me next time. No way am I putting myself out there to get burned like that again.

After my last class, I wander campus aimlessly for hours trying to walk off my anxiety. I didn't expect to feel this way at college. I thought it would be all excitement, fun and freedom, with a little classwork peppered in. So far it's been boredom, then bullying, and now a heaping helping of sexual frustration.

The campus is nice, though. I shuffle along beside the pond for a long time, wishing I had something to feed the ducks that live here. A guy and a girl sit out on the dock, swinging their legs off the end and tossing breadcrumbs into the water between kisses. They look so happy, I find myself wondering how long they've been together, and how long it might take for two people to build something that special.

I've certainly never had anything even close to that— never even had a boyfriend. Secret hookups behind the gym or in the back of someone's car don't count. Especially when the guy has a girlfriend, and you're just the sex on the side.

*Fucking cheater. Screw him. Screw everybody. I'm gonna be happy if it kills me.*

Seth is just waking from a nap when I finally return to the room, and the sun is sinking below the horizon.

"You spend way too much time in this room," I tell him as I sling my messenger bag over my desk chair. "We need to get out of here and cut loose somewhere."

He looks at me like I've just spoken in Klingon. No, never mind. He's kind of geeky, so he'd probably understand Klingon. At any rate, he looks at me like I've just spoken in a language he doesn't understand, so I elaborate.

"Have fun. You know, like *fun*... F.U.N. What do you do for fun around here?"

"Oh." Seth sits up and squints his eyes in thought. "Um, how about going out to eat? Or a movie. Or a club."

"Club? That sounds like it would hit the spot. What club do

you go to?"

Seth laughs and tosses his long hair. "I don't think you'd be interested in the kind of club I go to."

"You don't know me very well. I'm telling you right now, whatever club is your favorite, that's where I want to go."

Seth's face splits into a wide grin. "Okay, you asked for it. I think I'd enjoy shocking your small-town sensibilities, anyway. We'll go to the Meat Market."

"Ew... Meat Market? That sounds awful."

"Well, the real name is Hoppers. But we call it the Meat Market."

"I shudder to imagine why."

"Yeah, you know what?" Seth huffs. "On second thought, maybe we should just go to the Collegiate. It's a pretty cool place, but tame. I'm sure it would be more your speed. Really, I don't think you would like my bar much. It's... different."

I run my hands exasperatedly through my hair. "Gah, Seth. I'm gay, okay? I want to go where you go."

Seth freezes, his mouth hanging open as if he was about to say something, only now it's so quiet I can hear crickets chirping. Then he's laughing and jumping up and down. "Oh my gosh, I can't believe it. What great luck that we got put together. Did they do that on purpose, I wonder? No, they couldn't have known. Or could they? Is this a conspiracy?" He takes a big breath. "Anyway, I'm so glad you're going with me, Jeremy. But you'll need to wear some different clothes. Oh, we've got so much work to do. How do you feel about eyeliner?"

"Whoa, Seth... Why do I feel like I'm suddenly your gay

Cinderella project? I do know how to pick up guys."

"I'm sure you do know how to pick up guys back on the farm, but this is a whole different world. You can't just grunt and bend some guy over your tractor. It takes a little finesse, and some fashion sense. Wait till you see me when I go out. I'm a different person."

Seth grabs his phone and starts jabbering ninety to nothing to someone on the other end of the line. "Dan, we have a new boy. Yeah, he wants us to show him around the Meat Market tonight. Do you have something he can wear? I think you two are close enough in size, but you'd better bring your biggest pants. He's slightly shorter than you, but he's got some really solid thighs and the cutest bubble butt you've ever seen." When I roll my eyes and fall heavily onto the bed, Seth winks at me. "My roommate. He's absolutely adorable. Dark hair, blue eyes, wrestler... I know how you feel about wrestlers." He puts his hand over the phone. "Dan says he'll let you wear his favorite leather pants if you'll save him a dance."

"Whatever." I shrug, thinking this is going to be a long night. Not only is Seth acting like my gay fairy godmother, but I get the feeling he's trying to set me up with his friend. His eyes are sparkling with excitement.

While we're waiting for Dan to show up, I run to the bathroom to get squeaky clean for my first night of clubbing. Before I'm even completely dry from my shower, Dan shows up.

The guy is beautiful, with curly blond hair and bright green eyes. His trim build is as close to perfection as you can get without working out. He's got an armful of expensive clothes and a Mac eyeliner pencil, which according to him is supposed to be the best.

We all work on getting ready together, dancing and cutting up in front of the mirror. They pull me away from the mirror to put the final touches on my new look, and when I finally see myself, I'm amazed.

My dark hair is tousled and waxed, and the smudgy eyeliner sets off the blue of my eyes in a way I didn't expect, making them impossibly paler and more vivid at the same time. Dan has loaned me a cool royal blue t-shirt that says, *Die wid yo boot on*, whatever the hell that means, and a pair of low-rise black leather pants. Seth was spot on in his prediction about the fit of the pants. They're too long, causing them to bunch at the bottoms, but the fact that they're a bit snug in the thighs and butt only makes them look better. Once I get my black jump boots laced, I'm ready to go.

"Wow," Dan breathes, checking me out from behind as I pose in front of the mirror. "Those pants look way better on you than they do on me. I'm definitely renewing my gym membership tomorrow."

Seth beams like a proud father. "It's that wrestler butt and thighs. I told you he was adorable. We're going to have to beat the men off with a stick tonight."

"Ouch." Dan smirks at him. "Being beaten off with a stick sounds painful. But speaking of that… How in the hell are you going to stand having a roommate this hot?"

"Mmmm…" Seth gives me a dramatic once-over that makes me very uncomfortable. "Now that I know he's gay, it's going to be really, really *hard*. Like twenty-four-seven."

"Hey!" I turn and give the two of them a dirty look. "You do realize I can hear everything you're saying? That's just creepy."

They both laugh hysterically, and Dan nudges my shoulder. "We're just fucking with you, Jeremy. You'll get used to our sick sense of humor. In the meantime, let's get going. I don't know about you guys, but I'm ready to shake my ass on the dance floor."

"It's party time," Seth says, and he and Dan do a booty bump.

"Oh, wait." I grab my black choker off the night stand and a handful of black elastic bracelets out of the drawer. "Gotta accessorize, ya know?"

# 6

HOPPERS, a.k.a. The Meat Market, is indeed hopping.

Edgy dubstep music primes us on the sidewalk before we even get to the door. On the inside, the club is a flashing wonderland of laser lights, blacklights, giant lava lamps, and strobe lights. The space is crawling with people whose faces are difficult to make out.

I've never been to a gay bar and never really thought about going to one, so it's a revelation to me that this is basically a buffet of mostly-available guys who would probably not be offended if I came onto them. Not that I'm planning on coming onto anyone, but it's nice to know it's an option.

"That'll be four dollars each," the mustached bouncer growls in an accent that sounds more Jersey than Georgia. "And I need to see some ID from you." He points a fat finger straight at my face.

Seth rolls his eyes. "He's eighteen, Raoul. Come on. We're roommates."

Raoul holds his ground. "Sorry, gotta see it. He looks young to me. You know how the boss is about that."

I fish my ID out of my pocket and hand it to Raoul, who looks repeatedly from it to me, scrutinizing with narrowed brown eyes. "Alright, kid. Four dollars."

He trades my ID for the money and stamps my hand in the shape of a rabbit that glows neon pink under the blacklights.

*Cool. My very first club stamp.*

Seth pulls me by the arm, winding us through the crowd toward the bar.

"Do I need a fake ID to get a drink?" I yell, trying to be heard over the thumping music. "Because I don't have one. Never needed one back home. We all hung out in fields or the woods or at someone's house, and everyone knew which stores would sell to minors."

"Chill, Jeremy," Seth yells back, showing me that the rabbit stamped on his hand is neon green. "I have friends in high places. What do you want to drink? I'm paying."

"Uh, just a beer, I guess."

"No mixed drink?"

"I wouldn't know what to order. Pretty much all I've ever had is beer, cheap strawberry wine, and my dad's Jack and Coke."

"You've got some living to do, man," he says.

"I've done plenty of living. Just not with a whole lot of alcohol variety."

A moment later, he hands me a tan-colored iced drink. "White Russian," he says, moving his hips to the music as he watches me take a tentative sip.

"Mmmm... tastes like chocolate milk." After three greedy swallows, I have to remind myself to slow down. I'm a total lightweight, and it would probably be a bad idea to get piss drunk my first ten minutes in a strange place.

"Who's your friend, Seth?" A tall guy in his late twenties approaches with a smile. He's got a long, dirty-blond ponytail, a well-groomed goatee, and a gleam in his eyes that tells me he's about three quarters of the way to smashed. I would know. Living with an alcoholic father has given me a skill set I'm not particularly proud of.

"Forget it, Farrell. His name is Jeremy, and he's off limits to you."

"Oh, Seth, you've got me all wrong, sweetie." Farrell draws his words out in one of the twangiest southern accents I've ever heard. Then he narrows his eyes at Seth. "Are you two... together?"

"God, no," Seth yells, glancing sheepishly at me. "But we're roommates, and I don't want your stink all over him."

"You little bastard." Farrell ruffles Seth's auburn hair. "Alright, why don't you guys at least come to the back room with me? I've got something for you."

Seth's eyes come alive, and he shoots a devilish smile in my direction. "Come on, Jeremy." He hands Dan a White Russian and motions for him to follow.

Farrell leads us to a cozy room in the back of the club, decorated with a cream slipcovered sofa, a couple of club chairs, a low table, and a refrigerator. Paper lanterns of various shapes and colors hang like makeshift stars from the ceiling, but what really catches my eye is the octagonal saltwater fish tank glowing in the corner.

"Oh my gosh, are these seahorses?" I stare in wonder at the

aquarium. "What is this place?"

"This place is my home away from home," Farrell says, shaking his straight hair loose from the ponytail and rolling the hair band onto his wrist like a bracelet. "I own the club, so I spend a lot of time here. Those are my pets. You know, in the seahorse world, it's the males that give birth to the babies."

"Really? I never knew that." I watch the toy-looking horses float awkwardly in the water, most with their tails wrapped around objects to anchor themselves. I don't think I could be more fascinated if I'd stumbled into a den full of dancing unicorns. "These are the coolest things I've ever seen. How do you get something like this?"

"I order them online. I can hook you up if you ever want to start a tank of your own. Give you some pointers."

"He's got three huge saltwater tanks at his house," Seth blurts, then he stares red-faced at Farrell for a tense few seconds. "Uh, that's what you told me, right Farrell?"

"Did I tell you that?" Farrell directs a secretive little smirk at Seth and winks. "Hmmm… guess I must've forgot."

Farrell sits on the sofa, pulling an old-fashioned serving tray from beneath it and setting it on the coffee table. There's a plastic bag of weed in the center, flanked by a pack of rolling papers and a green metal pipe. Seth joins Farrell on the sofa while Dan and I each take a chair.

"You smoke, Jeremy?" Farrell asks with a naughty smile.

I shake my head. "I have a couple of times before, but I don't know if the wrestling team does any drug testing, so I'd rather not chance it."

"Good deal." His long hair falls over his shoulder, curtaining one side of his face as he works diligently at packing a bowl. When he's finished, he hands the pipe and a lighter to Seth, who lights it, sucks on it, and barks out a loud cough of smoke. "Don't cough, don't get off, Sethy." Farrell grins at Seth, and there's a gleam in his eye that I'm thinking has nothing to do with his lack of sobriety. I'm really beginning to wonder if there's something going on between him and Seth. Or maybe it's just that Farrell has one of those personalities that makes everything he says or does seem heavy with innuendo. At this point, I'm thinking it could go either way.

"Hey, Farrell" Dan interrupts. "I don't want to smoke any either, and Jeremy owes me a dance. I don't suppose you'd have any little brown bottles, would you?"

Farrell laughs under his breath and walks over to the refrigerator. "As a matter of fact…"

He hands Dan a small brown glass bottle before reclaiming his spot on the sofa and taking the pipe from Seth.

"Is that what I think it is?" My mouth is hanging open, and I can't seem to shut it.

"Probably," Dan says. "You ever done poppers?"

"Um, no."

"I've only tried it a few times myself, but Farrell keeps some put back for special occasions."

Farrell laughs. "The real story is that I have a few patrons who pay me good money to get it for them. Otherwise you little shits wouldn't ever get your hands on them." He looks at me. "Jeremy, I do not condone the use of drugs."

Dan rolls his eyes. "Don't worry, these things aren't that bad as long as you don't make it a habit. The high only lasts a few minutes, and it doesn't show up in drug tests. Don't ever get it from anybody but Farrell, though. He's the only person I know who can still get the real shit. Imports it from somewhere. I tried some of that other garbage they make from rubbing alcohol once, and it didn't do anything but give me a pounding headache."

"And no Viagra while you're doing poppers." Farrell says, shaking his finger at me. "Shit'll kill ya."

"Um, I don't think I need any Viagra," I tell him.

"Good deal."

"Alright, Farrell, stop trying to scare the boy." Dan opens the bottle and holds it out to me. "Just take small whiffs, okay?"

Before I can talk myself out of it, I take a couple of whiffs, and Dan follows suit. Next thing I know, I'm lying on the floor giggling, and the other three are standing over me.

"That first step's a doozy," Farrell drawls.

I don't know what the heck that means, but it makes me laugh even harder. "Wow, I feel really good, guys. This stuff is cool."

Dan reaches down to help me up, and I notice for the first time that he's not just good-looking— he's downright sexy, with his curly blond hair, green eyes, and features that are so pretty they're almost effeminate. The fact that I'm wearing his clothes is suddenly a total turn-on. Why didn't I notice how hot he was before?

*Too busy obsessing over Beck and his muscles. Mmmm... Gah, everything is turning me on right now.*

"Let's dance," Dan says, snatching me up and dragging me along behind him.

When we emerge from the back room, Kerli's *Army of Love* starts playing. It's our anthem, the soundtrack to our grand entrance.

As the lights, sounds, and drug effects converge, the bass thumping and pumping through my entire being, I begin to feel something like a god.

*A freaking sex god is what I am. I was born for this life.*

I catch a glimpse of myself and Dan in the mirrors around the dance floor as we strut in strobing slow motion to take our places among the dancers. With our spiky waxed hair, eyeliner and leather, we look like models in a heroin chic photo shoot, or characters in a Warhol movie. We also look like a couple, and from the way he's looking at me with heavy-lidded eyes and that inviting boy-next-door smile… he's mine tonight if I want him.

He grabs my hand and pulls me to an open spot in the sea of sweaty, gyrating people. It's thrilling being able to hold hands with a guy in public, dance with a guy in public, flirt shamelessly with a guy in public… It's that freedom I've been dreaming of, and what a rush it is.

Or maybe that's the amyl nitrite. Either way, I feel amazing— like I'm in my element for the first time.

Dan is a great dancer. I've never done much dancing, but I'm very physical and can pick up on movements easily, so it doesn't take me long to get the hang of it. During the first verse we jump around with our hands in the air, pure energy flowing between us like a genuine electrical current, humming and connecting us in a surprising way.

When the chorus begins, things instantly turn naughty. Dan snatches my body up close to his and straddles one of my thighs, trapping it between his knees and grinding in an undeniably sexual way that makes me feel like I'm getting a lap dance. I glance around once to make sure that kind of thing is okay in here, and when I see there are other guys practically screwing on the dance floor, I'm all in.

In this moment I am pure sex. My inhibitions are gone, and I'm ready for whatever may come.

When I wrap an arm around his neck to anchor myself, Dan smiles and leans down to yell close to my ear. "Don't know if we should be doing this. Feels a little too good, you know?"

As he pulls back, I surprise him with a quick kiss on the lips.

"Fuck." He darts his tongue out to touch his bottom lip. The music is loud, but I don't have to be able to hear to read his lips— or his expression. He wants me.

The brown bottle appears beneath my nose again, and I inhale sharply, watching as Dan does the same before slipping it back into his pocket. He puts a bit of space between us when the second verse begins, still keeping my waist in his grasp, and my head lolls on my shoulders as the second wave of the drug hits my system.

Time stands completely still.

When it starts back up, everything is in super slow motion. The strobe lights flash, adrenaline courses through my body, and my heart pumps in time to the driving techno beat. People ripple and bounce around us like waves on an ocean of sex, sweat and light. It's like a big foreplay orgy in here, because even though no one is physically doing the deed, it's obviously on everyone's agenda.

An arm snakes around me from behind, banding across my chest. A warm body presses against me, hips grinding against my ass in a primal rhythm that is about as close as you can come to sex without getting naked. It's definitely not Dan, because he's in front of me. Honestly the way I'm feeling right now, I don't care who it is.

I just know whoever it is happens to be just as horny as I am. Dan looks happy to see the guy, so I know he must not be too unattractive.

From out of nowhere, I get a palpable memory flash of sitting between Beck's legs on the bed, and my chest tightens. It takes a moment to figure out what's triggered it. The guy behind me smells like Beck's signature blend of body wash, deodorant and pheromones that I was wallowing in earlier in the day. By the time I feel lips traveling across the sensitive skin of my throat and stubble scraping my jaw, and the distinct scent of spearmint reaches my nose, I know for sure it's Beck. I relax against him, letting him guide my movements with his strong arms.

A slow smile spreads across Dan's face as he watches in fascination. My eyes drift closed for a moment, abstract images of animal lust flashing in the darkness as I feel the two of them grinding against me, one in back and one in front. The unmistakable press of Beck's erection against my ass works me into a frenzy, and I reach back and wrap an arm around his neck.

My heart lurches when Dan leans over my shoulder and kisses Beck. From my close vantage point between them, I can see every detail as they suck at each other's lips, their glistening tongues touching only at the very tips. My dick presses painfully against the back of my zipper, and I know in this moment I'd let these guys do whatever they wanted to me right here, right now. They could throw me down in the middle of the dance floor and take turns fucking me bareback, and I'd be a hundred percent A-okay with it.

Unfortunately, their plans don't include mad sex on the dance floor. As soon as the song ends, they usher me to a shadowy booth off to one side of the dance floor, and I fall heavily into the seat. "God, am I hallucinating? Is this even real?"

Beck and Dan slide in on either side of me, trapping me between them, so close I can feel the heat coming off their bodies. Their arms cross behind my head along the top of the booth seat. "No, you're not hallucinating," Beck says. "It's very real."

For the first time tonight, I get a good look at him. He's delectable in a black button-up shirt, rolled at the sleeves and unbuttoned just enough to entice the eyes straight to his defined chest and the smattering of hair there. He's got the kind of masculine look that really flips my switch. Even in this light, his golden eyes seem to swallow me and hold me there in their depths, making me oblivious to everything but him and the way he looks at me.

Dan leans across me to kiss Beck, and they make out right in front of me again. I've never watched two guys together in person, and it gives me a funny feeling in the pit of my stomach. Especially since one of them is Beck, and he already turns me on so completely. I feel a slight twinge of jealousy, but mostly I'm just aroused at the sight of them together.

Beck reaches between my legs and rubs my dick through my pants while they continue to kiss. "Oh, fuck." I cry out and tense my thighs, trying not to go off. I've got a hair trigger tonight.

Beck smiles against Dan's lips before he starts to unbutton and unzip my fly.

"I'll come if you do that," I say through clenched teeth.

"That's the idea," Beck replies.

Dan looks down to see what's going on, and his eyes light up. "Is this okay with you?" he asks me.

"Definitely."

As soon as Beck has freed my erection, Dan leans down, ready to take me into his mouth. Before he can get there, Beck stops him, shaking his head.

Dan's brow creases. "Why not?"

"I go first." Beck pushes him away and leans down, taking my cock all the way into his wet mouth.

I smile to myself, because I know what he's doing. He's not about to let Dan go down on me before he does. He feels it's his right, like he's got some sort of claim on me.

*I fucking love that.*

Lifting my ass off the seat, I shove roughly into the back of his throat, mindless now except for the need to get off. And the need to own his mouth. I put my hands on the back of his head, holding him down, fucking his throat. He doesn't flinch at the abuse, but rather opens up gladly and takes me even deeper.

Dan reaches down under and grabs my balls, making me cry out from the dual stimulation. The sight of two hot guys pleasuring me at once is almost too much to handle, and I have to look away for a moment before I blow all in Beck's mouth.

"Open your pants," Beck tells Dan. While Dan does as instructed, Beck lifts his head and speaks quietly in my ear, stroking my cock the entire time. "Will it bother you if I touch Dan like this?"

"Um... no." To be honest, I'm not sure if it will or not, but my brain isn't its usual self right now.

"Okay, baby. Let me know if anything bothers you." He kisses me long and hard, sliding his tongue in for a taste before going down on me once more. With his free hand, he grabs Dan's dick and starts jerking him off. Dan leans in and starts kissing me, and I'm lost to the sensations.

After a moment, Beck slides to the floor under the table, and starts jerking and sucking both me and Dan, switching his mouth from one to the other of us until we're both moaning loudly against each other's mouths as we kiss. Fortunately, the noise of the club drowns us out.

"God, Jeremy, I'm about to come. Are you?" Dan can barely speak, and seeing him so close to the edge takes me there right along with him. "Maybe Beck will fuck both of us later."

As soon as the words are out of his mouth, I get a mental picture of Beck slamming both of us, and it's enough to take me all the way. I bite onto Dan's lip as soon as I start coming, and I feel him tense up with me.

"Fuck, that's hot," Beck yells from down below as he continues to stimulate us both, lapping the cum from our dicks and stroking us until we can't take it anymore.

"What the hell is going on here?" A voice startles us from our lazy post-orgasmic state. It's Seth, who's got a shit-eating grin on his face. "Guess I can't leave you two alone anymore, huh?"

"Um..." Dan begins, but then Beck pops up from beneath the table and falls heavily into the seat beside me, licking his lips.

Seth puts a hand over his mouth. "Oh my God!"

"What is it, Seth?" Beck asks, smirking as he stretches an arm behind me. "Never seen three guys having fun before?"

"I have. I'm just shocked to see the great and powerful Beck on his knees." He leans over and raises a hand in front of Dan and me. "High five boys. I don't know what kind of sex magic you used, but I'm in awe of you."

Beck laughs. "Who could resist Jeremy and Dan dirty dancing together? What can I say? I was overcome."

Dan looks puzzled. "How do you know Jeremy's name? I didn't tell you that."

"You didn't have to tell me. We're already acquainted." Beck grabs me and pulls me onto his lap, taking my ass in a bruising grip that makes me yelp. "Isn't that right, Junior?"

His words are enough to make my heart beat faster and my whole body heat up. I lean in to run my tongue lightly along the seam of his beautiful lips, and he hooks his index finger under my choker and pulls me closer. His lips part, allowing my tongue to venture inside for a leisurely tour.

"Wait a minute." Seth narrows his eyes suspiciously at Beck. I can practically see his brain working this whole scenario out. "Last night when you and Jeremy disappeared at your apartment… That really wasn't hazing, was it?"

I roll my eyes at Seth. "Dammit, I told you last night it wasn't."

"Yes," Seth agrees. "You told me what it wasn't. But you didn't tell me what it *was*, now did you?"

"He was protecting me," Beck says. "Besides, it's nobody's business but mine and Jeremy's, so let's just drop it."

"Well, excuse the hell out of me." Seth laughs. "But you could show a little appreciation, Beck. I didn't spill your precious beans to Jeremy, even today after he told me he was gay. So there."

"I believe that's called common decency, Seth. Not like it was a favor or anything. And besides, if you ever breathe a word about me to anyone without my explicit permission, I'll beat the hell out of you."

Seth crosses his arms in front of his chest and glares at Beck until Dan waves a hand between them like he's trying to wake them from a trance. "Okay boys, calm down. We're supposed to be having fun. Beck... to what do we owe the rare and immense pleasure of your visit?"

Beck automatically glances at me, and everyone at the table notices it.

Dan is clearly shocked. "You came here for Jeremy?"

Beck squirms and rubs the back of his neck, looking like he'd rather be eating razor blades than answering the question. "Uh... no. I mean not exactly." He avoids making eye contact with me, making it painfully obvious that Dan's guess is way off the mark.

*Oh shit. He didn't even know I'd be here, so why did he come?*

It's so obvious. When I replay the events of the day, the realization almost makes me sick to my stomach. I showed up at his apartment this morning and practically forced myself on him. Then he came out tonight hoping to hook up with someone else, accidentally ran into me, and took advantage of the situation.

*How fucking humiliating.*

All I can think of is redeeming myself and getting revenge on Beck at the same time, so I make a flash decision to do something risky. I just hope Dan will play along.

"Well, that's a relief," I force myself to say around the lump in my throat. In a bold move that could potentially prove disastrous, I hop off of Beck's lap and scoot over to Dan, resting my palm lightly on his thigh. "It would have been really awkward if you came here for me, Beck… considering I'm here with someone else. But I think I speak for both of us when I say thanks for the killer blowjob."

Dan raises his eyebrows but doesn't miss a beat, pulling me casually into his arms and slanting his head to plant a soft kiss on my lips.

When I glance over at Beck, he's shooting daggers with his eyes. "I'm not blind, Jeremy. It's pretty obvious you and Dan are hooking up. Especially with you wearing his clothes. You look like carbon copy sluts. I suppose you'll be side-by-side on your knees in the bathroom giving twin blowjobs to someone else before the night's over."

"Below the belt, Beck," Seth warns, shaking his head.

But Beck doesn't stop there. "You know, if your goal is to do a different guy every day, you're off to a perfect start."

The insult stings like a sonofabitch, breaking through the residuals of my drug haze and swirling up all that rage that's never too far from the surface. Beck starts to slide out of the booth, but there's no way I'm letting him get away without a parting shot. "Nice hit and run, asshole. You're nothing but a coward."

"If I'm a coward, what are you?" He leans on the table and looks me squarely in the eyes. "You were in my bed last night, then again this morning. Now you're here with Dan. That's pretty fucked up in my book."

"Whoa, whoa…" Dan grabs Beck by the wrist. "You know good and well this isn't what it looks like. We're not really together. Not in that way. He just said that to get under your skin."

I nearly fly off the seat. "What the fuck, Dan? You trying to throw me under the bus or something? You don't have a clue how I feel. None of you do. You don't even know me."

Ducking under the table like I haven't done since I was a little kid, I crawl out of the booth, banging my knee on the table leg in the process. There's no telling what's on the floor under this table— and some of it's probably mine. Once I'm out, I don't spare a glance at any of them as I make my way through the club and out the front door.

It's muggy outside. I'd hoped to get some fresh air to clear my head, maybe lose the headache that's just jumped me like a back alley mugger, but no such luck. I start toward the parking lot to find my car, and then I realize I rode here with Seth and Dan.

*Shit. Maybe it's not too far to walk. I should have paid more attention on the way over. I don't have a clue where I'm going.*

While I'm trying to figure out just how I've gotten myself into such a predicament, Beck falls into step beside me. "Jeremy, I'm sorry. I shouldn't have said what I said in there. I didn't mean it."

All the rage I've been fighting to control since this morning rears up inside me and spills out as I slam my fists hard into Beck's chest, sending him stumbling backward. With his strength and reflexes, it only takes him a heartbeat to recover, and he steps in front of me as I'm trying to walk away.

"Jeremy…"

"Why did you say it, then?" I stop and stare at him, trying to burn a hole through him with my eyes. "It was so cruel. If you didn't mean it, why did you say it?"

"I don't know." He looks at the ground. "You lied and told me you were with Dan, which didn't make me feel too great, by the way. What's the difference?"

I look away, embarrassed. "That was self-defense. You were so cold to me today when I came to your apartment."

"Cold?" He grabs my arm and spins me to face him fully. "Is that how you saw it? Because I kind of saw it as risking my fucking future to cuddle with you. Not have sex— *cuddle*. Which I do not do. *Ever*. And not to mention, just before you walked in the door, Gretchen had just been lecturing me on how utterly stupid I was for even considering dating you."

*Dating?*

I have a huge weakness, and he's found it. That one little magic word has the power to change everything for me. I stare into his face in disbelief. He sees the change and steps purposefully toward me, his face softening. I want to resist, but I'm too enthralled.

He reaches out to touch my face, and his fingertips have barely grazed my cheek before I'm glued to his body, kissing him with everything I've got. So much for not putting myself out there to get burned. I'm already on fire.

"I want you, Jeremy," Beck gasps between kisses, running a hand down my ass and cupping it, his fingertips slipping into the crack and spreading me gently, leaving no question about what it is that he wants to do. "Please let me take you home."

Instead of answering, I just kiss him harder.

# 7

*(BECK)*

THE moment I saw Jeremy dancing with Dan, I was toast.

At Gretchen's urging, I had gone to Hoppers. I wasn't planning on getting with anyone. I just wanted to get Gretchen off my case, and maybe get a little tipsy and dance. I needed something to take my mind off of Jeremy, to make me forget how badly I want to defile him.

How could I know what a cruel joke fate had in store for me? Not only was Jeremy there, and not only did he look freaking amazing in those leather pants and eyeliner and that damn evil choker, but he was dancing with a guy I've hooked up with on more than one occasion.

Yeah, I've fucked Dan.

We've been together a handful of times. He's someone I can

trust, he's good-looking, and there's very little drama with him. We're what you might call friends with benefits, but that's as far as it goes with us, and we both know it.

I have to admit when I saw him and Jeremy dancing all hugged up and grinding on each other, my dick jumped straight to twelve o'clock. I had some really dirty thoughts going through my mind involving the three of us. It didn't help that when I joined them on the dance floor, they both seemed totally down for a threesome.

Being with more than one guy at a time has always been a fantasy of mine, so I was surprised that I didn't want to snatch their asses out of that bar and take them somewhere we could do more. It was weird, but there's a reason for it. Something I don't like one little bit.

*I don't want to share Jeremy.*

That's why I went down on both of them. Seth was right; it was completely out of character for me. In keeping with my fantasies, I should have made them suck each other's dicks while I violated both their holes in turn. That would have been hot as hell, but I just couldn't stand the thought of Dan and Jeremy touching each other that intimately. The kissing turned me on like crazy, but when my imagination tried to take it any further than that, I started to get angry. Still, it seemed selfish to expect both of them to service me with nothing in return, so I did what I had to do.

I shake my head, trying to dislodge the unwanted thoughts. Thank goodness wrestling practice starts tomorrow. It always helps me get my head on straight, get focused. Tonight I'm going to allow myself to indulge in the pleasures of Jeremy's sweet body, then it's back to being responsible for the rest of the year. That's how it has to be. I have no choice.

"It feels weird being in your dorm room," I whisper. "Like I'm some kind of perv. I thought I was past all this dorm shit, you know?"

"You don't have to whisper. It's not against the rules to have another male student in my room."

I laugh. "It depends on what that male student is doing to you. I doubt the college would openly support what's about to go down in here tonight. Sex is strictly prohibited in the dorms."

"That just makes it more fun." Jeremy sits on his bed and leans back on his elbows, spreading his legs in a careless vee and looking up at me in a way that's got my dick fighting to get out. He and Dan got off at Hoppers, but I'm still about to die for some relief.

"You know, you look ungodly sexy in those leather pants. I've been so hard for you all night."

"Yeah?" He smiles.

"Yeah. You want to know how much you turn me on? I almost came in my pants while I was rubbing up against your ass on the dance floor."

"Oh. I just thought you were a really good dancer."

"Hmmm... am I?" I step between his legs. "You're in for a treat then, because I fuck way better than I dance."

Jeremy smiles and glances away. Even in the dim light I can see his cheeks color slightly.

"Ah, there's my shy boy," I tell him. "I've been waiting for you."

"I'm not shy." His cheeks stain an even deeper shade.

106

"Sometimes you are. I like that."

He balks. "You don't know me that well yet. I'm pretty confident most of the time."

"Yeah, about that… You know last night at my party, how aggressive you were?"

Jeremy nods.

"Well, that's because I let your cocky little ass take over. That's not happening tonight."

"It's not?"

"Uh-uh." I shake my head. "Do you normally top or bottom?"

"Depends on my mood and my partner, but usually I top."

"Well, you'll bottom for me." I pull a condom out of my pocket, rip it open, and drop it onto the bed.

"I will tonight," he says. "But last night, I totally would've mounted you."

"Don't count on it, Junior." I pull his shirt off over his head. "I'm not a bottom."

"I guarantee you'd love it if I topped you." Jeremy licks his lips and lowers his lashes, and so help me God, my heart drops into my stomach.

*Keep control, Beck.*

I clear my throat and steady my voice. "I'm Batman, you're Robin. I do all the fucking in this duo. Got it?"

His lips dip into a frown. "Can't we take turns being Batman?"

He runs his hand boldly between my legs, skimming over my balls and pressing a finger up into the crack of my ass. His firm touch

107

activates the sensitive nerves there and sends a jolt of pleasure from my asshole to my dick, and all the way into my stomach where it clenches and quivers deliciously.

*Oh my God…*

Laughter rumbles unbidden from deep in my throat, and I push Jeremy down onto the bed. "Sorry, baby, but I don't bottom for anyone."

He squirms as I kiss his smooth belly, licking and sucking my way down it as I unfasten his pants. His sweet moans spur me on as I inch lower with my mouth, pulling his pants all the way down and leaving them bunched at the top of his combat boots.

His cock juts proudly out of its bed of dark hair, and I wrap my hand around it, testing his sensitivity. He groans and his eyelids flutter shut when I start stroking.

"Do you have any lube, Jeremy?"

His eyes fly open. "Shit. No."

"Hang on." I rummage in Seth's bedside drawer, and it doesn't take long to locate a bottle of the slick stuff. "Hey, your smart-ass roommate's finally good for something."

He watches me from beneath hooded eyelids as I return and lean over him, working his cock again with my hand, bending to tap it on my tongue and suck the head into my mouth a few times. I can't stay down long, though. I'm too fascinated with watching the emotions play across his face while he writhes beneath me. Suddenly I'm so nervous I feel like a virgin, and that's not good.

*Stop acting like a bitch, Beck. Just fuck him and get it over with.*

Jeremy's in mid-sigh when I flip him over, slamming his angel face onto the bed and unzipping my jeans. Now we've both got our pants jammed carelessly around our ankles like this is some anonymous truck-stop fuck. *Exactly how I need it to be.* I don't need to look at his face anymore, that's for damn sure.

"Lift your ass, Jeremy." I roll on the condom and squirt lube onto his hole, working it around with my thumb and loosening the muscle, fitting first one then another finger in, taking my time until he's wiggling and pushing back against me. "I can hardly wait to get inside you. Are you ready?"

"Please," he whispers, arching his back and opening even wider for me.

I squat down and rest my knees on the edge of the mattress, burying my face between his cheeks and lapping at his hole before spearing it with my tongue.

"Aaahhh, oh shit, Beck." His legs start to quiver as I fuck in and out of him with my tongue, moving my lips all around him, sucking and tasting, working both of us into a burning frenzy. By the time I'm done eating him, he's wobbling like a colt and whimpering into the sheets, his breaths coming in quick succession. "I'm ready, I'm ready. Please, I'm ready."

A satisfied smile crosses my face. "For a top, you seem pretty eager." I press the swollen head of my dick firmly against his asshole without breaching it.

"Fuck you, Beck. Just do it already."

I push harder, battering against his opening a couple of times, and he shivers and arches his back. A little squeal of frightened anticipation escapes his throat, and I can't help but chuckle at how cute he is.

"You sure you can handle me, Junior?"

"Oh, hell yeah. Give it to me." He shoves his ass back toward me.

I bend and bite one ass cheek, making him yelp, before I begin to work my cock into him. He lets out a loud exhale as the head of my dick pops past the tight opening.

"Fuck," he cries loudly, his body pulling me in as if it has a will of its own.

"Are you okay?" I tense and go completely still inside him, leaning around to see his face. His cheek is on the mattress, his eyes squeezed tightly shut. "Jeremy, do you want to keep going?"

"God, yes." His voice is tight with a mixture of passion and pain. "You can move it. Feels so good."

I take in a ragged breath when he reaches back and grabs onto the base of my dick and twists, but he's only after the lube. As soon as his palm is coated, he grabs onto his own dick, squeezing it, keeping his hand still and dragging his shaft through it. Fucking his hand while I fuck him.

He moves his ass in that particular way that makes me want to lose my mind, rocking and thrusting like he's really sticking it to somebody, all the while changing up the angle of friction on my cock until I almost wonder who's fucking whom.

"Little slut," I whisper. "Christ." It's all I can do to keep from pounding into him until I see stars, but I'm not ready to finish yet. I hang onto his hips, fighting against him, slowing him, taming his movements, trying to hang onto what little bit of sanity I've got left.

It feels so right the way my hands and his hips fit together. I dig my thumbs into the dimples at the top of his ass, marveling that I've never even noticed they're like little thumb grips.

*Would my hands fit this perfectly on anyone else's body?*

"Harder, harder, oh Jesus... How can this... Mmmm..." Jeremy is more vocal than anyone I've ever been with. I'm almost tempted to shush him, because as usual I'm afraid of being found out. Only I can't bring myself to do it. He's trying but failing to be quiet, and his little grunts and moans and panting breaths are too damn adorable. I find myself fucking him harder just trying to make him cry out, and when he finally lets loose and yells, it absolutely destroys me.

"That's it," I growl. "Don't hold back, baby. Let me hear you."

Animal instinct takes over completely. I jackhammer brutally into his ass just as fast as my hips will go, heedless of his comfort and only dimly aware of the rickety headboard of the bed slamming a staccato cadence into the wall. I'm coming before I can get any control over myself, biting back my own cries as I jet cum into the condom inside Jeremy's hot hole.

When he feels my dick pulsating, his own movements turn frantic in response, his ass rhythmically squeezing me all the way through my climax as he finishes himself with his hand.

My arms are so shaky that my elbows collapse, and I fall heavily on Jeremy's back, flattening him onto the bed. His grunt turns to weak laughter as he squirms beneath my weight. I sink my teeth into the back of his neck, pressing him even harder into the mattress, subduing him.

"Ow, fuck," he yells, still laughing. "What are you doing?"

"Not letting you go." My dick begins to retreat slowly, uncomfortably. Jeremy whimpers when it makes its final exit, and I snatch the condom off and drop it into the wastepaper basket beside his bed.

He struggles, bucking me up a few times, but my weight and strength are superior. We're both at the same disadvantage with our ankles shackled by our pants. Finally, he succeeds in flipping me over and straddling my waist, his balls resting warmly in the notch at the bottom of my ribcage.

*God, I don't want to look at him. Not at his face. Not this intimately.*

"Hey, we could use a little cleanup here." I gesture toward his belly, where I wallowed him into his own cum on the sheets when he was crushed beneath me.

"What's the matter? You don't like it messy?" He wiggles his ass, rubbing slippery leftover lube onto my stomach.

"I'm serious, Jeremy. Let me up." I sit halfway up, almost cracking our heads together in the process, wondering why I'm getting so worked up over nothing. I've never felt awkward like this after sex before.

"Fine." The smile drops from his face as he rolls off of me onto his back.

"Excuse me," I mumble. "Need to... um... use the restroom."

As I step into the bathroom, I glance back over my shoulder to where Jeremy is standing up and repositioning his pants. He winces, and I wonder if maybe I was a little rough on him— both physically and emotionally.

*Maybe a little abrupt at the end? Maybe a bit of jerk?*

I check myself in the mirror. Yeah, I even look like a jerk.

Did I bring Jeremy back to his own dorm room with the intention of having sex with him just one time to get him out of my system?

*Yes, you did, asshole. But that's how it's gotta be, and don't you forget it.*

I run my palms along the sides of my face, down my throat, my chest, my belly, down to the waistband of my jeans that are still unzipped. I'm biting my lip, imagining him touching me again.

*God, I love the feel of his hands on me.*

What would it be like to feel that every day, any time I want it? Is it possible that I could… allow myself to have him?

A sound at the door snaps me out of my daze, but it's not the door to Jeremy's room. It's the door to the adjoining room in their suite. One of Seth and Jeremy's suite-mates enters the shared bathroom, and I realize that I was so preoccupied when I came in I forgot to lock that side.

The guy's eyes are wide with confusion at seeing a shirtless stranger in his bathroom.

"S-sorry," I stammer.

I don't live here, and I've just been feeling myself up in the mirror. Could this possibly look any creepier?

"Oh. Beck…" He glances at my unzipped fly, his face turning red. "Well, I'll just leave you to it, then. Just knock when you're done."

*Shit. He fucking knows who I am. Not good.*

Is there any halfway decent excuse for my being here in this state of undress? I don't think so. The fact is, I've just been caught shirtless in a guy's dorm room late at night. No way to explain that away, especially when Seth is openly gay.

*Oh God, Jeremy was so loud, and I was pounding the bed through the wall. There's no way his neighbors didn't hear that.*

I splash water on my face, clearing my mind, vowing to fix the situation I've created. Knowing I probably can't.

I pat my face dry with a hand towel, knock three times on the door to the adjoining suite, and scoot out the other side before I have to face the neighbor again.

Jeremy is lying on his back when I return. He's removed his boots and pants during my absence, and the sight of him lying there all displayed for me in his tight boxer briefs sends my heart straight into my throat, nixing my ability to swallow.

*Has anything ever looked so sexy?*

Music is coming from his laptop on the desk, something by Coldplay. Much too romantic for comfort, but I'm caught anyway.

After toeing off my shoes, I kneel on his bed and straddle his hips, leaning down to steal a brief kiss before flipping onto the other side of him and wedging my body between his and the wall. Even though the twin bed is far too small for us, he seems a million miles away. Probably second guessing himself just like I am, wondering what the heck we're doing.

*We're not doing anything, Beck. You're extricating yourself, remember?*

"Jeremy..." I run my fingers through his hair, loving the feel of it and knowing I shouldn't. "We need to discuss something."

He nods without speaking, so I continue.

"I like you. Way more than I should, if you want to know the truth. But—"

He nods again and turns his back to me. "I'm the sex on the

114

side, I get it. When you get bored with fucking your girlfriend. I know how it works."

"I don't date girls, Jeremy... But... I don't date guys either."

"Not even Dan?"

"Nope. Not even Dan." I close my eyes and take a deep breath, wishing like hell he didn't know about Dan. "Dating is not a realistic option for me right now, okay? Not in my situation. All I'm good for is an occasional fuck. It's nothing personal. I need you to understand that."

He's quiet for a long moment, and I don't think I take a breath until he answers.

"I do understand. It's just that I was kind of hoping to find a real boyfriend at college. I've never been able to have one before."

"I know," I whisper, rubbing his hair down and kissing the back of his head. "I'm sorry I can't be that for you. I wish I could."

*More than you'll ever know.*

Jeremy bends his knees and curves his spine into me. I fit my body to his, tucking my knees into the backs of his and wrapping an arm tightly around his waist. Catherine Wheel's *Black Metallic* comes over the laptop speakers, and I groan out loud.

"Do you have any music on your laptop that doesn't make me want to slit my wrists?"

He huffs. "This is supposed to be my sex playlist."

"Oh... well... I guess I can see that. If you want dudes to cry the whole time they're fucking you."

He elbows me in the gut, but he doesn't say anything else, and he doesn't look at me. He just lies in that fetal curl with his fists pulled up beneath his chin.

I close my eyes and bury my nose in his hair, just for a moment, just as a goodbye before I make my way back to my apartment.

*Just for this one song, and then it's over. I swear.*

As the hypnotic shoegaze ballad drones on, I float on the notes in a daydream-like state, allowing myself to indulge in a few innocent fantasies about what might have been if my stupid life wasn't so complicated. Fantasies like how it might be to have Jeremy as a boyfriend. A real boyfriend, like he said. I could touch him when I want, hold him, lean on him, share myself with him, tell him my dreams, hold hands with him, cuddle with him like this every night... Even without trying, he tempts me, silently daring me to believe in possibilities that just aren't there. God, it would be so much easier if I didn't... *want.*

My eyes fly open to the sound of a key turning in the lock. I have no idea how long it's been, but I'm pretty sure it's been a while, because a different song is playing now and I feel much too groggy to have only had a single-digit power nap. Jeremy is sleeping beside me.

Seth and Dan stumble into the room, shushing each other and laughing quietly. They both freeze when they see me.

"Beck..." Dan's face falls ever so slightly, but he recovers quickly and clicks the door shut behind them.

"Holy shit." Seth bursts out laughing. "Didn't expect to see this."

Dazed, I reach down and work the covers from beneath Jeremy's limp legs, arranging it to cover most of his lower body. He's wearing underwear, but it still seems rude leaving him exposed without his knowledge. And besides, I don't want anyone else to see him that way.

"Oh, lord." I roll onto my back, dropping my head onto the pillow and growling my annoyance. "Please tell me it's not midnight already."

Seth giggles. "Two minutes after. We barely made it in before they locked the doors, so guess what stud? You're stuck here till morning."

"You're slipping, Beck." Dan crosses his arms over his chest and shoots me a smug look.

"Fuck. I must have fallen asleep. What can I do? Are you guys sure there's no secret after-hours escape tunnel or something? A teleportation chamber? Someone we can bribe? I really do not need to spend the night here. Your suite-mate already caught me in the bathroom half naked, and he recognized me."

"You can always go out the window," Dan offers sarcastically.

"Yeah, I'm sure you'd love to see me plummet to my death."

Dan shrugs. "It's only three stories. You'd probably just break your legs."

"Alright, drama queens." Seth holds up his hands and takes a seat on his bed. "I don't need a lover's quarrel in here. Take it to your room Dan. I've got to get some damn sleep. Where's my Tylenol?" He digs around in his bedside drawer, and I cross my fingers that he doesn't notice his lube is missing and is now sitting on Jeremy's bedside table. That would just be a little embarrassing.

"This is not a lover's quarrel," Dan says. "I think you have to be in love to have one of those. But I do think that someone ought to point out that Jeremy seems to be a nice guy, and that he doesn't deserve the Beck Treatment."

"Are you kidding me?" I laugh. "I don't recall you complaining last time you got the Beck Treatment. Or any of the other times, for that matter."

"Kiss my ass. You know what I'm talking about. I know how to handle you. I'm more experienced, and I have much thicker skin."

"Are we speaking metaphorically here, or literally?"

Dan sighs in exasperation. "I mean that I'm aware of your noncommittal approach to fucking, and I accept it. But it's hard for me to stand by and watch you take advantage of an innocent, impressionable—"

"*Innocent?*" The word comes out much louder than I'd intended, so I immediately drop my voice a couple of notches and check to make sure I haven't woken Jeremy. "What makes you think he's so innocent? You obviously have no idea what he's like in private. He jumped me at my apartment last night. I'm telling you, I didn't stand a chance."

"Really?" Dan stares in disbelief. "The big, bad captain of the wrestling team couldn't fend off the little farm boy?"

"Hey, that little farm boy is strong." I burst out laughing, the whole situation striking me as incredibly funny. The other two look at me like I've lost my mind. Hell, maybe I have. It's certainly starting to feel that way. "Dan, don't you have your own dorm room to go to, or are you planning on busting my balls all night?" I'm laughing so hard tears squeeze from the corners of my eyes and run down my cheeks. Fortunately, my meltdown doesn't wake Jeremy.

Seth cuts his eyes at Dan. "Okay, he's officially lost it. Better call campus security."

"You deal with him. I'm going to my own room." He opens

the door to leave.

"Dan, wait," I call after him, instantly straight-faced. "I know where this is all coming from, and you'll probably get your shot at Jeremy. He already knows I don't date, and he's looking for a boyfriend, so it's pretty cut and dried between him and me."

He casts a dubious glance over his shoulder. "Yeah, I see. And you don't find it ironic at all that you're explaining this while spooning with him in his bed?" He slams the door.

Seth winces. "I need to be a hell of a lot drunker to deal with this." He slips off his shirt and jeans, pats down his pillow, and turns off the light.

We both lie in silence for a while before he murmurs, "You've got it bad, Beck. You know that, don't you?"

"Mmmm... maybe not so bad."

"Yeah, right." He snorts. "You look like a dog guarding his bone over there."

It's a long time after Seth starts snoring before I can go back to sleep. I just lie with my arm wrapped around Jeremy's sleeping form, the warmth of his body seeping into my skin and making me feel way more comfortable than I have a right to feel.

My mind works feverishly trying to produce a single brilliant idea about how I could date him and keep my scholarship at the same time, but every avenue I travel down in my imagination is a dead end. Like Gretchen said, it would be idiotic to risk my future over a guy I've just barely met.

# 8

*(JEREMY)*

I wake the next morning to find a note from Beck sticking out from under my alarm clock on the nightstand.

*Sorry*, it says. *Wish like hell it didn't have to be this way.*

It's unsigned. Written in all caps on the back of a stupid flyer announcing a party in the dorm lobby a week from Friday.

*A Dear John letter. How fucking romantic.*

I crumple the note and drop it into the wastepaper basket beside my bed. Then I scramble to fish it out again, flattening it on the bedside table and smoothing the wrinkles as best I can. Regret slices through my gut at the thought that I've damaged the sole keepsake I have from Beck— the only proof that he and I have ever been.

I slide the rumpled page carefully beneath my pillow like it's

Blackbeard's treasure map or one of those lost Dead Sea Scrolls, laughing at myself for being so damn pathetic.

*Hey, at least I'm not afraid to admit I like boys. Unlike some people I know.*

Beck isn't in the hallway when I get to my first class. I stick my head into his classroom to see if he's there, and the teacher surprises me.

"Can I help you?" she asks, lowering her reading glasses to the end of her nose and staring at me from across the room.

"Um, I was just looking for Beck... uh, Beckett." Everyone in the classroom turns to look at me, and I try to smile.

The teacher glances toward what I assume to be Beck's empty seat. "He doesn't appear to be here yet. Can I give him a message?"

"Oh, no, no, don't worry about it. I was just saying hey." I practically run from his classroom all the way to my own. I didn't mean to make a fool of myself or draw attention to Beck.

*If anyone tells him I was looking for him, I swear I'll die of embarrassment.*

The fact is, his note made it pretty clear that he doesn't want to see me, and there's just nothing I can do about it. No sense acting like an ass over the guy. I suspect he is going to be changing his schedule a lot from now to avoid me. Wrestling poses a bit of a problem, though. Our first meeting is today, and unless I drop out, there's no chance he and I can avoid seeing each other there. And there's no way I'm dropping out.

At least the cafeteria is one place I know I won't run into him. The crowd is a comforting distraction during lunch as I slide my tray along the silver runner and choose a turkey sandwich, a small side salad, baked sweet potato and milk. Seth and Dan are sitting together, and I take the seat beside them, hoping I'm welcome.

"Mr. Jeremy," Seth says in his chipper way. "How goes it, roomie?"

"Fine." I discard the top half of the bun and bite off a large chunk of what's left of my sandwich. It takes real effort to work the dry stuff down my throat, and I end up sighing and throwing the food back onto my plate. "I'd be better if this didn't taste like shit."

"I thought it was pretty good today," Dan says, casting a concerned look in Seth's direction. "You okay?"

"Yeah, just tastes like cardboard. I'm not hungry anyways."

"You know, maybe you and Dan should talk about some things," Seth says meaningfully. "Some things you kind of have in common."

Dan rolls his eyes at Seth. "You're the king of subtlety, as always."

"What good is subtlety?" Seth crosses his arms across his chest like a petulant kid. "Convince me that there's a need for it, and I'll start using it. Until then, I say what I mean."

"I don't need to talk about anything, guys. Seriously, I'm good."

I sense rather than see them exchanging skeptical looks.

Seth rests his hand on the table in my field of vision, not quite touching my arm. "Last year, Dan was where you are now. He's been through all of this with Beck. Everything you're going through and more. Moping, no appetite, depression, crying—"

Dan growls, flattening his palms on the table surface and lifting slightly out of his seat. "Dammit, Seth, are you trying to make

122

me look bad? I never cried, Jeremy. I'd like to set the record straight on that point. No tears whatsoever. But I'll admit I had a crush on the guy, and I was… disappointed when he didn't feel the same way."

"This is why Beck and I don't get along sometimes," Seth says. "We're friends, but I don't give him a free pass like everyone else does. Sure, he's gorgeous and popular, Dean's List student, wrestling star, all that shit. Everybody loves Beck. He can do no wrong. Well, I've seen how selfish he can be."

"Lighten up on him," Dan says quietly. "He's not so bad. It's just that he's got his priorities, and he's strong enough not to let anything get in the way of that. Yeah, it hurt my feelings in the beginning, but I think it was more my pride hurting than my heart. After a while I realized that he and I would probably never have been more than friends anyway, even if he was shouting he's gay from every street corner in town."

"Oh, yeah?" Seth looks confused. "If he's such a saint, why were you reaming him in my room this morning for taking advantage of Jeremy?"

"Because I don't know if Jeremy fully understands the situation. And I didn't think Beck spending the night all coiled up around him like some perverted anaconda was communicating a clear message."

"Anaconda." Seth snickers. "I told him he looked like a dog guarding a bone. Over there snarling and shit, covering Jeremy up so we don't see what he's got in his boxers."

"Wait a minute," I interrupt. "Beck spent the night? He said he couldn't stay, so I just assumed he left before midnight."

"Nope." Dan shakes his head. "He stayed all night long. He

123

was whining because one of your suite-mates saw him with his junk out in the bathroom or something."

That brings a picture to mind that I'd rather not imagine, but it does at least make me laugh. "I didn't know he stayed. When I woke up, there was only a note."

"Did it say he wanted to see you again?" Seth asks hopefully.

"Not even close." I push back from the table and pick my tray up, noting the matching sympathy grimaces on my friends' faces. "I'm gonna go on and head to class. Two more and then wrestling, and we all know how much I'm looking forward to that."

Coach Roberts paces in front of a set of bleachers at one end of the gym, while Assistant Coach Bradley stands to one side with his arms folded across his chest. The wrestlers, both current team members and candidates like me, fill half of the section. Everyone stares at me when I come through the door, and I suddenly wish I could vaporize into the air. Embarrassment does not even cover what I feel.

The last thing I wanted was to be late to my first day of wrestling, but I took my time getting over here, hoping to avoid any down time at the beginning of the meeting. The idea was to arrive exactly on time, so that there would be no chance of speaking to Beck, or of him speaking to me, or of us staring awkwardly at each other. In retrospect, it was a terrible decision, because now I look like an asshole in front of the entire wrestling team and the coaches.

*Who am I kidding? It's going to be awkward no matter what I do.*

Coach flattens his brow when he looks at me, but instead of shrinking, I paste on a big smile. The best one I've got in my arsenal, or at least I hope it is.

"Sorry I'm late, Coach," I call cheerfully. "Dang college girls."

*Let him make what he will of that.*

The guys near the front row— the ones who can hear me— laugh quietly, but the coach isn't impressed with my sense of humor. "Not a good start, Miller. Take a seat."

At least he remembers my name. Whether that's a good thing or a bad thing remains to be seen.

"Alright, as I was just telling our wrestlers who were on time, we're going to be doing some stretching and drills in a few minutes. Then we'll partner up and see what you've got. Coach Bradley and I will be walking around so we can get a look at each of you, try to recognize any areas where you need work." He scans the group purposefully. "You *will* need work. No one is coming in here perfect, so don't get your panties in a wad when I single you out for something. Understood?"

"Yes, sir," the group yells back.

Assistant coach Bradley rummages through a cardboard box and pulls out a school t-shirt and a pair of shorts and brings them over to me. They match the practice uniform all of the other guys are either wearing or holding.

"First set is on the house," Coach Bradley tells me. "But you're required to wear a clean set every day. So you'll have to buy more or wash these before every practice."

"Yes, sir."

Surprisingly, my hands are shaking when I take the uniform

125

from him. I don't usually let nerves take me over like that, but I'm really starting to worry about making the cut. Over the last couple of years, I've come to depend on the structure of being on a team.

The coaches start calling names from a clipboard, pairing each of us up with another wrestler in our weight class. I get paired with a baby-faced blonde guy named Mark, whose hazel eyes and friendly smile put me instantly at ease. He's skinnier and taller than me, which is good. I prefer taller wrestlers, because they're easier to get under.

*No pun intended.*

"Let's pace ourselves," Mark suggests. "We don't want to be worn out by the time they look at us."

"Sure," I agree, squaring off with him, looking him hard in the eyes like I do every opponent.

As usual, my shot gets him, and he's on his back before he knows what hit him. Every opponent doesn't fall for it. It's hard for me to get a really experienced wrestler down that way, but this guy is clearly not any more experienced than I am.

"You're fast," Mark says breathlessly. "Let's go again."

"Wait a minute," I whisper. "Here comes Coach Roberts."

We stand around for a moment until the coach approaches us. "Jeremy Miller," he says, clapping me on the back. "What's your name, son?" he asks Mark.

"Mark Allen, sir."

"Alright, boys. Let's see you." He gestures for us to continue, standing aside and resting his meaty hands on his hips.

I stumble a bit when Mark and I start wrestling, and he nearly gets the best of me. It's the nerves again. Now that the coach is standing over me, I'm having a hard time performing. My palms are sweating, and my thoughts are racing.

We struggle for about three minutes, and just when Mark thinks he's won, I go crazy on him. I give it everything I've got, ending the match by bringing him down hard onto the mat with a slam that I know good and well is illegal.

"Fuck, Miller, you trying to break my neck?" Mark jumps up with his hand pressed to his face. "And my nose is bleeding." Blood squirts out from between his fingers, falling onto the mat in a twisting trail of droplets.

"Go get cleaned up," the coach tells him, giving him a once-over to make sure he's not injured and then pushing him toward the locker room. "Put pressure on the bridge of your nose."

When the coach turns back to me, I notice for the first time he's got a mangled cauliflower ear, and my respect for the man instantly increases. There's just something about a wrestler's ear that screams dedication like nothing else. It's sexy.

"Well, Miller," he says, dragging my attention back from his ear to his face. "I see you've got a tendency to lose your cool under pressure. You know, you have a solid foundation and some natural talent, but if you don't get your emotions under control you're going to hurt someone. Or get yourself hurt."

"Yes, sir." I bow my head, ashamed that I've had to be called down on the first day.

"I'd better not see you doing anything else illegal just because you find yourself in a tight spot. If you're beaten, you're beaten. Breaking the rules isn't going to change that."

He stalks off, leaving me standing alone and wishing like hell

I'd made a better first impression.

I sit down on the mat and wait for the others to finish, and Mark eventually joins me again.

"No hard feelings?" I ask.

"Nah, we're cool."

The coach announces that we're going to get to watch some real college wrestling action. He brings out Truck and Caleb for a demonstration, and all I can think about is how Truck nearly bent me in half at the party. Even drunk, he totally dominated me. But I don't feel too terribly bad, because he beats Caleb as well.

Then Beck takes the mat with a gorgeous black guy named JoJo, whose body easily rivals Beck's in the hotness category. I'm mesmerized as I watch the two of them, and it occurs to me that as intimate as I've been with Beck, this is the first time I've seen him wrestle.

Their movements are quick and tight, almost unrealistically so, like they're on fast speed video— or one of those old Charlie Chaplin movies, but without the comedy. There's definitely no Chaplinesque clumsiness in this display.

Beck and JoJo are perfectly calibrated machines, rendering every wrestler I've ever seen in person until now sluggish and uncoordinated. Even my appreciation of my own quickness, which has always been my greatest source of pride, diminishes with every move they make.

They dodge and feint, clenching and releasing a number of times before they lock up in a show of strength that is so proportionate, it ties my belly into a knot. Rarely are wrestlers so talented and so equally matched that there is no way to predict the

outcome. This is the kind of stuff action movies are made of— high
excitement and high stress. I'm worried for Beck as he strains and
then flips the guy over, almost pinning him but being out-
maneuvered at the last second.

Even when he's being overpowered, Beck is beautiful.
Everything about him commands attention and respect, from the
intense look on his face, to the way his defined muscles ripple as he
rolls and lunges, holds and clenches. I doubt I could ever get tired of
watching him.

By the time JoJo pins beck for the win, I'm literally
breathless. Of course I wish Beck had won, but JoJo beats him so
beautifully, it's hard not to be impressed. And besides that, Beck
doesn't seem at all concerned with the loss.

Coach stands between the panting wrestlers and raises JoJo's
arm, an unnecessary but inspiring touch. My heart is still frantic from
their display. I didn't know it was possible for me to love wrestling
any more than I already did, but I find myself appreciating it anew,
fantasizing about someday being as good as Beck and JoJo.

Worse than that, I'm even more attracted to Beck now. I
think I'm being punished by the universe, because the guy I have a
huge crush on has turned out to be a wrestling god, and he doesn't
even want me. Looking at him standing there so awesomely in front
of everyone, admiring him and knowing everyone else is doing the
same, knowing how intimate we've been but not being able to tell
anyone— it all makes me feel so alone.

*He won't even fucking look at me. Third day of college, and I'm
already screwed.*

I sit moping for a while, only half-hearing what the coach is saying. It's probably important. *Oh well.* Against my will, I keep glancing over at Beck, who has taken a seat on the floor near Assistant Coach Bradley. A couple of times his eyes flick over to me and away just as quickly. I don't know when I've ever been ignored so purposely or so blatantly.

*Like he doesn't even know me.*

# 9

THE rest of my first two weeks of school are absolutely miserable. It's hard to enjoy what's happening when I'm so preoccupied with what's *not* happening. I've been struggling not to think about Beck. I keep telling myself to give it time, that it will pass. Classes don't do much to keep my mind occupied, because they're so boring I can barely stay awake through them. I've called Eric a couple of times, but his tech school Accounting degree program is a lot more rigorous than my core class load. He hasn't been able to talk for more than five minutes, and all I've learned is that he loves school and that he has a new girlfriend who's in the Dental Hygiene program.

When I think about Eric and his girl making a life together, an accountant and a dental hygienist, it sounds so stable it makes me · ache with jealousy. Looking out from the vortex of a tornado all the time has made me appreciate normalcy for the gift it is.

*I don't even know how to be normal.*

Seth has been keeping himself busy planning the dorm welcome party that takes place tonight.

"Apparently, they think all gay guys make good party planners," he says with an exaggerated eye roll as he heads down to make the final tweaks before the event begins in an hour. "I'm afraid they're about to find out just how wrong they are."

"I'm sure it will be great," I tell him, glancing over my laptop and offering a weak smile.

"What are you doing on that laptop? Seems like you've got your nose in it twenty-four-seven these days."

"Manga." I spin it around so he can get a look at the screen where two skinny anime guys are squirting bodily fluids all over each other's chests. "This one's pretty good. I'm on the fourth volume."

"Oh, Jeremy…" Seth shakes his head at me. "Yaoi? That's not manga, that's gay cartoon porn. One day soon, I'll show you some quality manga, but right now it's party time."

"Hey, I happen to like my gay cartoon porn. I only watch it for its educational value. It's taught me to stay away from dark-haired guys with rectangular glasses, how to date multiple guys without the others finding out, how to misunderstand everything the other person says—"

Seth grabs a dirty t-shirt off the floor on my side of the room and throws it at me, but it falls short.

"Don't fuck with me in a t-shirt war," I tell him. "I've got skills." I tie it in a quick knot and throw it right back at him, nailing him in the chest.

Seth grunts and stomps his foot. "I'm not playing with you,

Jeremy. If you don't come downstairs and meet some new people tonight, I'm going to call Beck and embarrass you. I'll tell him you're curled up on your bed in a bathrobe eating jelly beans and crying over cartoon guys fucking."

I hug my tub of gourmet jelly beans to my chest. "I'm not crying."

I'll tell him you refuse to shower, and that all you do is sit around muttering his name over and over with a wild look in your eyes, and—"

"Okay, Seth. I'll go if it will shut you up. Just let me grab a quick shower. I can't go to a party smelling like jelly beans and tears." I snap the laptop closed and grab a slightly used towel off the back of my desk chair as I head for the bathroom. "And just for the record, this is not about Beck. I'm just trying to get used to college, that's all. You didn't have a hard time adjusting in the beginning?"

Seth looks thoughtful for a moment. "I suppose so, but you've sulked long enough, farm boy. Hang with me, and by the time this night is through you'll be wearing a smile... and possibly nothing else."

"*What?*" Being naked is not really something I want to be discussing with my roommate.

Seth angles his brow Jack Nicholson style and lets out a diabolical cackle. "See you downstairs."

He closes the door and leaves me standing with my mouth hanging open. I'm not even sure if I want to go to this party now. Beck was right about Seth. He can be a real pain in the ass, because you never know what the little red-haired bastard is going to do next.

The lobby is nearly full of people when I finally make it down after my shower. I feel surprisingly refreshed and ready to enjoy myself, and I suppose I have Seth's pep talk to thank for that. He made me realize that I haven't been taking advantage of my college experience. I had forgotten I was here to start a new and exciting life, not wallow in depression like I've done so often in the past.

*College life, here I come...*

Attractive maroon and gold streamers line the walls of the lobby, and matching balloons are everywhere, even on the floor. Every now and then, someone steps on a balloon with a loud pop, followed by squeals from the girls. A large wall hanging dominates one wall, with the words *Welcome to Spangler Hall & Southeastern State U* written in spray paint. A perfect likeness of our school's mascot — a tiger — has been painted in the center. Similarly painted tiger heads and *SSU* logos dot the walls here and there.

"Seth, this place looks fantastic," I tell him when I finally spot him by the snack table. I grab a cup of soda and lean against the edge of the table. "I don't know what you were saying about being a terrible party planner."

Seth beams with pride. "All I did was coordinate things and do a little bit of painting. Jenna and Simone did the rest."

"Wait, are those girls? Last I checked, we don't have a coed dorm."

"Yeah, Jenna and Simone are friends of mine from our sister dorm, Gray Hall. That's how these parties work. Every dorm is having one tonight— like an open house. Each male dorm has a female sister dorm, to facilitate a coed experience when it's convenient. We kind of work together on the decorations and planning. Then everybody just kind of visits around from dorm to dorm partying until curfew. You need to check out Gray Hall before the night's over. I did some paintings over there, too."

"Well, I must say you're quite an artist, Seth. I had no idea. Why don't you do some pictures for our room?"

"Firstly, all you've seen are some simple cartoons I've done. And secondly, I don't like to display my own work." Seth looks at the floor. "I guess it just feels like bragging or something. My parents pay for a storage unit nearby, and that's where I keep all of my paintings."

"Paintings? I'm totally embarrassed to ask you this, because a good roommate would know the answer already, but... are you an art major?"

He nods. "Don't feel too bad, Jeremy. I haven't even asked about your major. I just assumed you were the typical undecided freshman."

I laugh and drain my soda cup. "I decided to major in business a long time ago. Figured it was the most marketable major, and I really need to be marketable when I get out of here. I don't want to live in a trailer park all my life, you know?"

"Yeah," Seth agrees. He looks a little uncomfortable, and I wonder if I've shared too much. I don't want my new friends to think I'm white trash... even if maybe I am.

"So, can I see your paintings sometime?" I ask.

Seth beams again. "Of course you can, roomie. We'll go tomorrow, since it's Saturday."

"Okay, it's a date."

We both stand there trading goofy smiles, and I have to

admit it feels good. I haven't been the most attentive roommate so far, but I plan to change that starting now.

"Hey, look who finally made it." Seth points toward the entrance, and Dan is there, his blond curls sparkling beneath the fluorescent lights. He really is magnificent-looking, with his high cheekbones, bright green eyes, and lean body. The black V-neck shirt he's wearing tonight contrasts with his coloring for a startling effect. Both Seth and I accidentally sigh at the same time, and then we break down laughing at ourselves.

"I swear," Seth says between laughs. "All that boy needs is a pair of wings, and he'd be an angel."

When Dan spots us, he makes a beeline to where we're standing.

"So what's the plan tonight?" he asks. "Start up a rave in here? Drink till we puke? Dance till we pass out?" He grabs a crustless pimiento cheese sandwich quarter off the table and eats half of it in one bite.

"'Fraid not, Danny-boy," Seth says, snatching the other half of Dan's sandwich and scarfing it down. "Tonight is straight-up college partying. Hell, I don't even think anyone's spiked the punch yet. I might have to do it myself."

Dan grabs a cup of punch and takes a swig, swirling it in his mouth like he's at a wine tasting. "Needs some coconut rum," he says quietly. "I'll do it. Jeremy, you wanna come with me to get a bottle?"

"Uh, sure."

Dan's ride turns out to be a really nice Harley Davidson. I don't know anything about motorcycles, but it looks new, and it has an awesome green and black tribal style paint job. He drags two helmets out of the saddle bags, handing me one. As soon as they're on snugly, he speaks. "Can you hear me okay?" His voice comes through a speaker in the helmet, and I gasp.

"Wow, that is so cool. I can hear you in my head."

Dan chuckles. "Wrap your arms around my waist and hang on tight, Jeremy."

I nod and link my hands together at his belly, feeling the hardness of his abs beneath my arms and the warmth of his back against the front of my body. It feels better than it should, and I try to come up with something to say to take my mind off of it. "You got a fake ID to buy alcohol, Dan?"

"Nah, I'm twenty-one. Finally legal."

"I wish I was twenty-one. I've still got almost three years to go."

Dan laughs under his breath. "You want to drink that bad, or what?"

"No, I just feel so young compared to all of you, that's all."

"Aw, no need to feel that way, kiddo."

"Shut up, asshole." I nudge his arm with my shoulder, hard enough to get my point across, but not hard enough to make him lose control of the bike and smash us into oncoming traffic.

"Hey, there's nothing wrong with being young. Trust me."

Dan maneuvers expertly through traffic while I hang on, still trying to ignore the feel of his body within the circle of my arms.

"Now sit tight while I grab the booze," he says once we're in the liquor store parking lot. I wait for a moment, but he comes back so quickly I almost wonder if he's stolen the bottle.

When we're on our way once again, Dan asks the question

I've been dreading. "So, have you talked to Beck lately?"

"No. He's kind of avoiding me, I think."

"Ah…" Dan pauses as he turns onto the road in front of the school. "You know, he's only avoiding you because he likes you. Otherwise, he wouldn't care. I've known him for two years, and I've never seen him act this way before."

"What way?" I ask.

"I don't know, it's subtle. You don't know him as well as I do, so you don't see what I see. Just trust me when I say he likes you a lot. You've got him running scared."

I laugh, but there's nothing funny about what he's said. "I think Seth's right. You give Beck more credit than he deserves. He's just a horny, closeted jock who uses people to get what he wants. He acts like he feels something, but then he pretends he doesn't even know you."

"Well, I don't see it that way, and I've been with him several times. He was never anything but honest with me about what he wanted. The fact that I read more into it at first was my fault. I take full responsibility for that. But hey, I was young and stupid, and I had a crush."

"He said he wished he could be my boyfriend. That I was a temptation for him."

"Did he?" Dan sounds surprised. "Wow. That doesn't sound like him at all. Can I maybe give you some advice?"

I shrug. "Whatever."

"I say if you want that, go for it. You seem to have really gotten to him. Believe me, I wouldn't say that if I didn't mean it. But he's cautious; that tree's not going down without a little push. You know what I'm saying?"

"No!" My voice is shrill, and I instantly regret yelling at Dan. Especially since it's coming out of a speaker in his ear. "I mean I'm done with him. He doesn't want me. He's made that very clear, in more ways than one."

"Okay, I'll shut up." A quiet chuckle comes through the speaker.

*Time to change the subject.*

"So, uh…" I take a deep breath, realizing I shouldn't be asking what I'm about to ask, but knowing I'm going to do it anyway. "You've slept with Beck multiple times. That means you bottom, right?"

He lets out a surprised laugh that blasts my eardrum through the speaker. "Yeah, Jeremy. I bottom."

He may as well have just said *Abracadabra*, because magically, I'm hard. It's just that it's been so long since I've fucked anyone. Without even a stray thought of stopping myself, I flatten my palms against his abdomen and press my dick into his ass, letting him feel my erection.

"Oh, God." He groans through the speakers, wiggling subtly against me. "Jeremy, I…"

"You what?" I run a hand down his belly, onto his zipper, where I can feel him responding to me.

"Uh, I need to hurry up and park this thing." He laughs, whipping the Harley into a space and shutting it off. "Hop off and hold your horses." He hands me the rum, digs in the saddlebag and pulls out a thin cover, and stretches it over the motorcycle.

"You're cool with this being just sex, right?" I ask.

"Yeah, it's cool." He grins. "In fact, it's *very* cool."

Once we're back in the dorm lobby, Dan grabs the paper bag of liquor from me. "Gonna take this to Seth. Wait for me at the bottom of the stairs, then we'll go to your room. No telling when my roommate might show up."

I watch Dan cross the lobby, looking around for Seth but failing to spot him. I scan the other side of the room for Seth, but when I locate him, I almost wish I hadn't.

He's sitting on one of several beige sofas, talking animatedly with a group of girls. Beck is sitting beside him on the arm of the sofa, smiling and nodding as if he's totally into the conversation, looking yummy in a white school logo t-shirt and jeans.

The girl nearest him giggles and puts a hand on his thigh, as if unconsciously, which pisses me right the fuck off. Before I can look away, Beck glances over and catches me staring.

*No way to pretend I didn't see him now.*

Without missing a beat, he winks at me, says something to the group, and starts walking toward me. I look frantically to the other side of the room, hunting Dan, feeling like I'm about to be caught with my hand in the cookie jar.

*What will Beck do if he finds out I've just propositioned Dan?*

Over at the food table, Dan is busy working the cap off of the bag-covered rum and pouring every bit of it into the punch bowl. He doesn't even bother trying to be discreet about it.

Meanwhile, Beck has made it over to where I'm standing.

"Hey, Junior." His voice and smile set my stomach to fluttering, as always. It's really not fair that he should be able to have this kind of effect on me, especially after leaving me a *Dear John* note

140

and then ignoring me for almost two weeks.

*Bastard.*

"Hey," I say casually. "How have you been?"

"Shitty. I wanted to see you again."

I hold my hands out to the side, palm up. "You're seeing me now."

He leans in close, his voice almost threatening. "That's not what I mean, and you know it."

"Really? What exactly do you mean? That you want to see me naked again? You want to see me come again? You want to see me take your cock in my ass again?"

"That's a little harsh," he says. "But yeah, I would like that. Among other things."

Dan walks up at that moment and throws his arm casually across Beck's shoulders. "I see the gang's all here."

Beck shrugs out from under his arm and glances around, no doubt paranoid that someone might see him getting too friendly with the queers of Spangler Hall.

"Dan, I've just been informed that Beck would like to see me naked again. Among other things."

"Hmmm…" Dan taps his chin, pretending to contemplate.

"Fuck." Beck runs a hand over his buzz cut, looking agitated as hell. "I knew I shouldn't have come here."

Before either Dan or I can react, he's spun on his heel and crossed the room toward the front door. I just stand in shocked silence as he leaves, wishing I hadn't been so stupid. I've been dying to see Beck, pining for him, wanting him to stop ignoring me and show me some attention. When he finally does, I act like an asshole.

"Well, that didn't go well," Dan says. "You want to go after him?"

Tears well up in my eyes for a second, but I quickly wipe them away. "No. It can't work between us anyway, can it? I mean, he doesn't even want to be seen with me."

"I don't know." Dan shrugs. "He did just show up at a cheesy dorm party. That is so totally not Beck. He doesn't do that kind of thing."

"Oh my gosh, I know," a strange girl says, leaning into our conversation that she's overheard in passing. "I couldn't believe it when he walked in. We were all trying to figure out why he would be here."

Her friend nods. "We thought maybe he's dating someone from Gray Hall."

"Or wanting to..." the first girl adds with a grin.

"Yeah, he was sitting over there beside Simone, and they looked pretty darn cozy."

"So you think he came to see Simone?" Dan asks. I don't like the mischievous twinkle in his eye.

"I don't know," says the second girl. "What do you think?"

Dan smiles ear to ear. "Oh, I think he had to have been here to see someone." I give him a warning look, but he keeps right on talking. "There's no way Beck would come to a party like this unless there was someone here he had the hots for. Now who did he talk to tonight?" He makes a big show of looking thoughtful.

"Simone," the second girl says. "And I think I saw him talking to Ashley."

The first girl jumps up and down. "Ooh, what about Jenna?

PINNED

She was over there with him and Simone. And Tasha... was she with them?"

"Well, there you have it." Dan snaps his fingers. "It must be one of them. I'll bet you girls can figure out which one if you really put your minds to it. Have you had any punch yet? I heard it's really good." He grabs me by the arm. "Jeremy, I need to talk to you for a minute."

We make our escape, and Dan pulls me into a dark slot beneath the stairs, breaking into a fit of silent laughter once we're there.

"Dan, what the hell is the matter with you?"

"Sorry, dude. Just having a little fun. Did you notice that I asked them who Beck spoke to while he was here, and they didn't mention a single guy? I just thought it was funny."

"I thought it was kinda mean."

"Those two girls are just gossip hounds. Ask Seth, he knows them." Dan taps me gently on the arm and gives me a worried look. "Hey, cheer up. He came looking for you; that's a good sign. Blowing him off like you did might not have been the best thing, but at least now he knows he's gotta work for it if he wants it, right?"

I nod, unconvinced. "I shouldn't have acted like that. I just got pissed all of a sudden."

"Well, maybe you can control that when you see him again. In the meantime, I don't think it's a good idea if you and I hook up. You're clearly still hung up on Beck, so I'm not the one you really want to be with. Besides, I don't know how he would react if he found out we were together without him. He might go to the bar to blow off some steam occasionally, but I can tell you right now—

143

Beck is so morally uptight, he's like my freaking grandmother."

"So you're saying he might not respect me if I sleep with you?"

Dan laughs. "No, I'm saying I think he'd fucking kill *me*."

# 10

*(BECK)*

WEEK three of wrestling, and I'm finally starting to feel a little like my old self. The familiar routine really helps to ground me, and the restlessness of summer begins to fall away.

"Alright, men," Coach Roberts says, doing his best imitation of a drill instructor. "We're going to be trying something new for a while. Something I think will better prepare our new guys. I'm going to pair each incoming wrestler with a mentor. Every Monday after we run drills, we'll split off into pairs, and each mentor will train his recruit. I've already compiled a list of partners, so Coach Bradley if you'll read off the list..."

Coach Bradley clears his throat. "Once you've heard your name, you can go to the locker rooms and get dressed out, then come back out here and choose your spot. For simplicity's sake, this will be your spot every week. Got it?"

Everyone nods, and Coach Bradley starts reading off names. I'm on pins and needles, because I don't want Jeremy to be partnered with anyone but me, but I damn sure don't want the awkwardness of being his mentor. I honestly don't know which would be worse.

My name is called third in the alphabetical list. "Calvin Beckett and Jeremy Miller," Coach Bradley announces, and my heart sinks and soars at the same time.

*Holy crap. How did this happen? Is there even a remote possibility this could be a coincidence?*

I can't look at Jeremy at all as we make our way to the locker room and drop our duffel bags onto the bench in front of a row of lockers. Should we act like we barely know each other? What would normal be? How would I act if I'd gotten paired with one of those other new guys?

*Think, Beck! What is normal?*

And then normal flies completely out the window when Jeremy gets undressed. He's wearing a jockstrap, which isn't unusual in itself. A lot of the guys wear them. But instead of the usual white, gray or black, Jeremy's got on this brilliant canary yellow one. The color complements his skin beautifully, and the back straps form a perfect frame for his smooth ass. The fact that I already know what that ass feels like under my fingers makes it a hundred times worse.

I groan and turn to walk away, though I have no idea where I'm going, and I run smack into Caleb as he escorts his own newbie into the locker room. "Damn, Beck. Watch where you're going, dude."

"Sorry," I mutter, sitting down hard on the bench, wishing I could have some privacy to think about all of this.

"Hey, I see you got paired with your little pet. How convenient is that?" Then he glares at Jeremy. "Don't think Beck is going to be able to protect you forever, dude. My guy is gonna trounce you. See?" He grabs his bewildered boy's collar and shoves him toward us before dragging him toward the back row of lockers.

Both Jeremy and I break into laughter as soon as Caleb is out of ear shot, but I sober quickly when I get a good look at his jock again. I grab the nearest thing, which is Jeremy's t-shirt, and pull it over my lap.

"Why the fuck would you wear something like that?" I ask quietly, making sure there's no one close enough to hear.

He pulls his shorts up, covering the article in question.

"You should be grateful. Can't have my junk going all haywire when you're holding me down on the mat. Certain positions might, you know... *arouse* me." He puts the rest of his things in his locker and closes the door. "Now get ready, senpai. I'll go claim a good spot for us."

"Senpai?" I groan. "Don't tell me you read that manga shit. What does that even mean, I'm your mentor or something?"

"More of a social thing, really. Like you're a hot upperclassman, and I'm the little peon who worships you." He pulls his t-shirt on and smiles over his shoulder as he leaves the locker room. Once he's gone, I can almost focus again, and I make quick work of getting dressed.

Jeremy is waiting patiently for me on the mat, and I immediately get us right down to business. We work on shots first, which is definitely a strong point for him. Then I run him through a few exercises to test his form in top, bottom, and neutral positions.

He's itching to do some fancy stuff, but it's too early for that. I keep reminding him that, while speed and strength are important, a strong foundation and perfect form are crucial and can make the difference between a good wrestler and a great one. He rolls his eyes at me, but he does exactly what I tell him to.

Surprisingly, it's not that difficult to focus on the work rather than our proximity and sexual attraction. I find that I really want to shape my little student into an exceptional wrestler, and that desire keeps my baser instincts in check.

"How's it going, fellas?" Coach Roberts comes up beside our mat, and we immediately stop what we're doing. "Beck, I took the liberty of putting you two together without asking, because I knew you'd want to put your stamp on this one. I hope that's alright."

"Uh, yeah Coach. It's fine. This guy has a lot of potential, if I can curb his enthusiasm just a little bit."

Jeremy smiles proudly. "Yeah, I'm kinda hyper, Coach Roberts. But Beck is slowly and methodically boring that right out of me."

Coach stifles a smile. "Good. Maybe he can bore some of that smart-ass attitude out of you while he's at it."

"That's my number one goal," I assure him.

"Good luck with that," he chuckles. Then he leans in and drops his voice. "Listen, if the other guys get their tails on their shoulders about favoritism or conflict of interest, I'll handle it, okay? There's no rule that says you two can't train together." He stuffs his hands into his pockets and winks before moving on to the next group without waiting for a reply.

"What did he mean by that?" Jeremy asks under his breath, still eyeing the coach suspiciously.

"I don't have any idea. Why would anyone have a problem with it? As far as anyone else knows, we barely know each other."

We share an awkward moment of silence as our eyes meet, and it's clear both of us are thinking about just how well we do know one another.

"What the coach just said was pretty creepy, though," Jeremy says. "It's almost like he knows about us. Do you think he does?"

"Of course not." I reach down to help Jeremy to standing and quickly change the subject before things get any weirder. "Here, we'll finish up with something fun. I'll start teaching you how to master an explosive double-leg takedown from almost any position. It's almost guaranteed to work every time. At least until you get to the last round of the championship, when you're the best guy fighting the other best guy. Then nothing fucking works except luck and miracles."

"Wow, you're gonna teach me your signature move?" The look of awe on his face makes me laugh.

"Yeah, some people call it my signature move. I borrowed it from Jordan Burroughs. I do use it a lot, but only because it works and I'm good at it. How did you know?"

"Um..." Jeremy looks at the floor. "I kinda watched some competition videos of you online. You're practically a celebrity."

"Oh, so you've been cyber-stalking me."

"Kiss my ass," Jeremy says. "But yeah, I have."

As we practice some more, I can't help being concerned about the coach's comments. Jeremy's right. It was pretty creepy, as if he knew something he wasn't saying.

I ate dinner with the coach and his family recently, and he did ask how Jeremy was doing. I told him he was doing fine as far as I knew, but that we hadn't talked much over the last couple of weeks. It was a random question that seemed to come from out of the blue, but that's all that was said. All I can figure is that he paired me with Jeremy because he knows we've hung out together, and he sees potential in him like I do. That's enough reason for him to think I might want to put my stamp on him, right?

When practice is almost over, I've got Jeremy down on all fours, covering him with my body. We're both breathless and sweaty by this time, ready to call it a day, when suddenly he turns and looks over his shoulder at me with a smile. "Does this remind you of anything?" He nudges his ass back up against my dick, and I immediately start to get hard.

I push him down flat onto the mat. "Don't you ever do that shit to me, Jeremy. Not here." I jam my knee into his back hard enough to force the air out of his lungs. "And I'd better not see that fucking jockstrap in here again."

He nods, but it's too late for me. He's done what he set out to do. Now all I can think about is subduing him and making him pay for turning me on. I already think about him all the time— in class, during practice, while I'm working out, every time I jerk off. Hell, he's the first thing on my mind when I wake up in the morning. It's an obsession, and I'm being eaten alive by it.

Funny thing is, he's still trying so hard to get my attention. He has no idea he's already got me.

*And I'd like to keep it that way.*

Back in the locker room after practice, he struts around in

that yellow jockstrap longer than necessary, torturing me. It's so hard to keep my eyes off of it that I literally have to turn my back to him to get stripped and wrap my towel around my waist.

Guys are crawling all over the locker room, and as usual some of them stop by to talk. I'm on auto-pilot, responding politely, trying to pretend everything is normal, forcing my eyes not to search for Jeremy in the fray.

Once I'm in the shower, letting the cool water run over my hot skin, I'm able to clear my mind and reset. Fortunately, Jeremy has enough sense to stay away from me.

# 11

*(JEREMY)*

IF I thought Beck went crazy over the yellow jock strap I wore last Monday, it's nothing compared to the reaction I get when I strip my sweaty shorts off to reveal the neon pink one I'm wearing today. His lips fall so slack I think he's going to drool all over himself. Beck is like a love god in my eyes, so the fact that I can do that to him fills me with an unbelievable sense of power.

"Fuck you," he mouths silently from across the room, flipping me off with his middle finger. He looks like he might be genuinely angry, but that doesn't stop me.

*Playing with fire, Jeremy.*

I just grin and turn my bare ass toward him, running my thumb up under the strap and snapping it. Then, knowing he's still watching but trying not to, I take my time getting things situated in my locker and duffel bag.

The other wrestlers are all rushing to get out, not paying me much attention. I can feel them passing one by one on their way out the door. To them, I'm just another dude getting dressed in the locker room. They have no idea I'm trying my best to seduce their team captain.

"Jeremy, can I ask you a favor?" I look up to find one of the other freshmen, a cute boy with sandy hair and pale freckles, standing beside me. He stares at the pink jockstrap with a look of wide-eyed amusement, but he doesn't comment on it.

"Sure, Chris." I say, hoping I've gotten his name right. "Ask away."

"I was wondering if there's any way you could give me a little private coaching on my Granby rolls? Coach Roberts is really riding me, and you're supposed to be so amazing and all."

"I appreciate the vote of confidence, but I think you've got the wrong guy. I'm probably on the verge of getting cut because of my recklessness, aggression, and— what did he say?— oh yeah, smart-ass attitude. That's literally word-for-word what the coach thinks of me, so I'd say you're probably in better shape than I am."

Chris drops his voice and leans in closer, practically whispering in my ear. "Last Wednesday, I overheard Beck and the coach telling Assistant Coach Bradley you were a little Houdini— fast as hell and way stronger than you looked. Then the coach said he could probably wrangle you a scholarship for next year if you can control your temper."

"Are you for real? Beck and the coach were talking about me?" I glance over at Beck who is chatting with Caleb, packing up his things and totally ignoring me. In fact, Beck has barely given me a second look since we trained together last Monday.

"Ha." Chris rolls his eyes. "Like you have no idea you're one of their little pets. People talk, dude. Everybody knows it but you. Most of the rest of us don't have a guaranteed place, or the coach just dying to give us a free ride, so we're sweating the cut."

"Well, I definitely don't mind helping you out sometime, Chris. Let me give you my number." Chris drags out his phone and types in the digits as I dictate them. "Call me, and we'll set up a time."

"Thanks, man." Chris slips his phone into his jeans pocket and grins. "Nice strap, by the way."

After Chris leaves, Beck and Caleb and I are the only ones left in the locker room. I still haven't gotten dressed, and neither has Beck. While I'm digging in my locker for my jeans, I hear Beck telling Caleb he'll see him later at home. I don't even look his way. I think I've made enough of a point already today, and honestly now that we're alone, I'm feeling a little apprehensive. I had meant to show my ass and get the hell out of here, but Chris waylaid me just long enough to get stuck alone with Beck.

"You gave that guy your number?" Beck asks the question from all the way across the room at his locker.

*So he was paying attention, after all.*

"Yeah." I nod without looking at him.

"You gonna fuck him?"

"What?" Now I turn to stare at him. "Jesus. He was just asking me for help on his Granby's."

"That's not what it looked like from over here. Looked like he was eye-fucking you and your pink jockstrap. Is there anybody else?"

I put my hands on my hips. "Excuse me?"

"Don't play dumb, Jeremy. Have you been with anyone else since me?"

"Not that it's any of your business, but no. I have not."

Beck moves the few paces from his locker to the main locker room entrance, closing the heavy door with an echoing bang. Then he punches a code into the keypad and the lock clicks into place.

When he turns to face me, he's deadly serious. "I told you not to dress like this in front of me anymore."

"Actually, you told me not to wear the yellow one."

"Why are you fucking with my head, Jeremy?" He comes toward me, wearing nothing but a pair of black briefs and a grim expression.

I take an involuntary step backward.

"You know I'm attracted to you. You also know that I can't be doing this shit, especially in the locker room, and yet here you are prancing around in this thing." He reaches around behind me with one hand, sliding his finger down under the strap and cupping my ass warmly in his big, rough hand. "You're doing it on purpose, trying to get a rise out of me. Aren't you?"

I look down between us, where his dick is straining to break free of his underwear, the head peeking over the top of the waistband. "Mmmm... looks like I succeeded in getting a rise."

He threads his fingers through my still-damp hair and snatches my head toward him. I yelp from the shock, but he covers my mouth with his, muffling the sound with an angry kiss.

I moan against lips, returning his kiss and leaning into him as he caresses and squeezes my ass cheek.

"I'm sorry, Beck. I just wanted to get your attention."

"Well you've got it now," he growls, pushing against my chest. He backs me up until he gets me to a blank wall, then pushes me roughly against it. This is a side of him I haven't seen before— unrelenting, dominant, almost cruel. *Angry.* He slips his underwear down his thighs and kicks them away. "If you want lube, you'd better produce some quick, because I'm going in."

My mouth waters as I look down at his massively hard cock. I bend and spit on it, getting it as wet as I possibly can. I'm dying to have Beck inside me, but I don't particularly want to be dry fucked with that big dick and have to limp home. And in his current state of mind, there's no chance he's going to go easy on me.

He reaches down with both arms and hoists me up the cold block wall, resting my thighs on his forearms and bracing his hands against the wall. Then I feel the wetness as his cock head presses against my opening, and desire twists in my gut.

"I love how strong you are," I say, rubbing my hands from the top of his shoulders, down over the swell of his delts and his bulging biceps. "You throw me around like I weigh nothing. That is so sexy."

"You've got my adrenaline pumping. I could bench press a dump truck right now." He lowers me onto his cock, and my head falls forward to rest on his shoulder. A strangled cry rips from my throat, and I bite down hard on his shoulder to divert the pain of his rough entry.

"Ow, fuck!" He adjusts so that my knees are bent over his arms, dropping my ass down farther onto his cock at the same time he thrusts all the way up into me with a grunt. "Is this the kind of attention you wanted?" He doesn't give me time to answer, instead kissing me over and over as he slams into me.

The reserved wrestling captain is gone now, regressed into some primal thing, his fierce eyes darkened to a burnished gold. It's frightening and exhilarating at the same time to see him this way, to know I'm the one who's made him lose control.

All I can do is hang on while he batters my body, channeling all of his aggression into me.

I reach down and pull the jockstrap to the side, releasing my erection, but when I grab on and start stroking myself, he growls. "Uh-uh. No touching, little tease. This is punishment."

"Best punishment ever."

I throw my arms around his neck and kiss him, pushing my tongue deep into his mouth as he drives his cock up into me again and again, simultaneously tearing me apart and making me whole. I'm starving for him, needing more and more, even as he's giving me everything he's got. His breathing is harsh, broken, ripping out of his throat along with animal grunts and little moans that mingle with my own.

I put my face right next to his, my lips near his ear, and I thrill to the rasp of his stubbled jaw burning my cheek. "Come inside me," I say. "I want to feel it all."

With my fingers clasped around his neck I lean back, forcing Beck to hit just the right angle to get me off. His cock swells and gets even harder inside me as I buck my hips and shoot ribbons of cum all over my own chest.

"Take it..." Near mindless now, Beck crumples my body

against the wall. "Take me... Christ."

I can feel him emptying inside of me, all warm and slippery, grinding his hips up with shocking strength, as if he can push his seed even deeper into me. It makes me feel so close to him— like he's marking me permanently.

*Making me his.*

Only he's not mine, and he doesn't want me for anything other than sex. I know it. He doesn't date, and he's made that perfectly clear. The thought brings me crashing back down from my post-coital high, and I extricate myself from him, squirming to get out of his grip.

As soon as my feet hit the floor, I slide my jockstrap uncomfortably back into place, the fabric smearing the fluids I seem to have everywhere. I'm a mess now on top and bottom, but I'm also beyond caring.

What was I thinking baiting a guy who's completely unavailable? Dressing provocatively, flirting with him, forcing him to react...

*I just literally begged a guy for sex.*

He gave it to me alright, but at what cost? My respectability?

At the time I was baiting him, it had seemed irresistibly naughty and fun. And yeah, I'd hoped it would end well for Beck and me, like some cheesy-ass romance novel. Now it just seems like poor judgment. Instead of feeling powerful, I feel more pathetic than I've ever felt in my life.

If I hadn't thrown myself at him, Beck probably never would've had anything more to do with me. That knowledge is gnawing a hole in my gut.

Without even bothering to clean myself up, I snatch my clothes on and rush the locked door with my shoes in my hand. "Crap. Gotta get out of here. I'm late to meet Seth." Sounds like a plausible excuse, right?

*Not at all like I'm running away.*

Beck's brow creases as he pulls on his jeans. "Wow. You're just gonna—"

"Sorry to bang and run." I interrupt him before he can call me out on it. "Look, I know you don't want anything serious. I get that, and there's no pressure here, okay? We were just having a little fun."

*Am I talking too much? Can he see through me?*

"Yeah," he says, looking a little embarrassed as he walks over to unlock the door to let me out. "Thank goodness nobody tried to come in, huh? What the hell was I thinking?"

He runs a palm absently across his pecs, down his sternum and all the way to his belly, drawing my eyes to that sexy trail of hair. Suddenly it seems like there's less oxygen in the room. He looks so irresistible, I know I've got to get away or I'm lost forever.

"Yeah. Thank goodness." My half-assed attempt at a laugh falls flat as I dart out and leave Beck standing shirtless in the doorway.

# 12

*(BECK)*

JEREMY is what I want. After losing my cool and taking him in the locker room, I know it for sure. Funny how giving in to my baser instincts and doing something incredibly stupid and risky has clarified things for me in a way that being careful never could have.

It was the first time I've been able to let go and admit to myself that I have desires that may not fit into my carefully laid plans. I can't keep treating them like simple inconveniences and trying to ignore them in the hopes that they'll go away.

If I had given in to my desire for Jeremy in the first place, I wouldn't have felt so out of control in the locker room. I wouldn't have taken such a risk.

*But why him? Why now?*

In the past I would find myself trying to yearn for more, watching committed couples together and attempting to slide into their place in my imagination, if only for a moment. It's what we're all programmed to shoot for, right? The soul mate, the happily ever after… Somehow, I couldn't relate. The romantic movies Gretchen forces me to watch have a certain charm, but I never truly understood what would make a person give up freedom, individuality and choice just to have someone. In theory I wanted more, but in reality I just couldn't feel it.

But that was before Jeremy. Now I can't even remember what it felt like to *not* want him. That scares the shit out of me.

Practicality still rules me, as always. I keep reminding myself that I don't know Jeremy very well, and that I'm not in love with him. Thinking I'm in love would be absurd at this point, but I do very much want to get to know everything there is to know about him. I want to hear about his past, his family, and his aspirations. I want to know what his favorite toys were as a kid, if he had a special place to go when he was upset, and what he did for fun with his friends. I want to sleep with him all night, feel his smooth body pressed against mine as the first rays of sunlight coax me from sleep, kiss his hair and wrap my arms around him before we roll out of bed and get ready for class.

I don't know what you'd call all of that, but it's what I want. Question is, how much am I willing to risk to get it?

The more I think about it, the more things my imagination has me hypothetically giving up. That's why I'm sitting in front of my laptop staring at a web page about student loans. It doesn't seem too terrible an option, really.

The trust fund my grandfather left me pays for my living expenses, and I've got a pretty strict budget that should make it last through the entire six years of the fast track Sports Medicine program I was fortunate enough to get into. The fact that my academic scholarship doesn't go into effect until I start the fourth year of the program is a pretty big hitch, but now I'm wondering how bad it would be to have one year's worth of student loans to pay off after graduation. Not a travesty, right? With the money I'll be making, I'll be more than able to afford it.

If I'm honest with myself, the scholarship isn't the only thing I'm worried about, though. I know how those guys on the wrestling team can be. I've heard them making crude fag jokes, sneering at guys they perceive as being less masculine than they are. As the team captain, they look up to me, and that leadership role gives me a sense of purpose. The possibility of having it snatched away because of narrow-mindedness scares me. At the same time, it turns my stomach to be put on a pedestal by those very same narrow-minded people, especially when the entire structure beneath the pedestal is built out of lies and false assumptions.

*Shouldn't I be a better man than that?*

I groan and snap my laptop shut, leaning back in my desk chair and running my hands over the three-day stubble on my face.

"What is it, hon?" Gretchen is curled up in what she's now calling *her* chair in the corner of my bedroom, reading an autobiography of some engineer for a personality class she's taking this semester. She's been boring the crap out of me with it for hours, insisting on pausing every couple of chapters to fill me in on the details of his divorce, his work on the atomic bomb, discovering nanotechnology. Blah, blah, blah… Okay, so the guy's life is not boring at all, but I've got too much on my mind today to be interested.

"I'm just looking into student loans and stuff," I tell her.

She splays the book out on her stomach to keep the page and fixes me with a serious look. "Why are you doing that, Beck? You have a scholarship."

"Well…" I hesitate, knowing she's not going to like what I'm about to say. "I'm thinking some things might happen. Things that could potentially cause me to lose my wrestling scholarship, or be forced to quit the team. Maybe have to quit because of, you know… hate… or something. You never know how people will react."

Gretchen's eyes stretch to the point of bugging out of her head. "Are you planning on making an announcement sometime soon?"

It's weird that even in the privacy of my own room we still feel the need to talk in code.

"No, not exactly. But I've met someone I like, and I want to see if we can go out. Like for real."

"Oh, Beck," Gretchen turns to face me fully, her book sliding to the floor. "Are you talking about Jeremy? I don't want to come off sounding mean, but he's beneath you, hon. Sure he's cute as a button, but he doesn't have much class, even for a jock. Even worse than that, he's too wild— like he doesn't have a governor on his little motor."

I smile and close my eyes for a moment, remembering what he looked like up against the wall in the gym with his legs slung over my arms. "Yeah, I know. That's what I like about him. He's kinda raw, huh?"

"Raw?" Gretchen rolls her eyes. "That's putting it kindly."

"I fucked him in the gym yesterday," I blurt, smiling uncontrollably. "Right there in the locker room after practice. But he left before I could tell him how I feel. He— well, he played it off like it was just sex, but that's only because that's how he thinks I want it. How do I tell him I've changed my mind?"

"Oh my lord, Beck." Gretchen leans forward, looking appalled. "What are you thinking? You've been so careful all this time, and now that you're nearing the end, you're just gonna blow it?"

"Don't look at me that way." I jump up from my chair, pacing to the door and back again several times. "That look of disappointment on your face is so fucking offensive to me right now. It's not fair, and you know it. You've got it so easy. You could be dating a serial killer, the two of you murdering babies in your spare time, but still no one would bat an eye if you French kissed right in the middle of downtown rush hour. As long as one of you is a girl, and one of you is a guy, that's all that matters. You have no idea what it's like to have to deny what you feel just because it doesn't match some people's idea of what's acceptable."

"Beck—"

"You know, we were all born into the same world, with the same human rights. What the hell makes you right, and me wrong, huh?" At this point, I'm not interested in hearing her side or even arguing mine further. I don't get angry very often, but when I do, there's only one solution. "If anyone needs me, I'll be at the gym wearing myself out until I can't think anymore." I slam out of the room before Gretchen can respond.


Rarely have I required such a vigorous workout to get my head right. By the time I get home, the sun has gone down, and my muscles are quivering globs of Jell-O.

Gretchen is nowhere to be found now. Her room door is closed, and there's a pale light coming from beneath. Looks like she's settled in for a night of reading by the bedside lamp.

I feel a little guilty about getting so angry with her earlier. She may be a little obtuse sometimes, but she's only looking out for my well-being. During my post-workout shower, after I was pretty well numb and incapable of having a strong emotional response to anything, I'd decided to apologize to Gretchen as soon as I made it back to the apartment. Instead, I close myself up in my own room and fall out on the bed, the down pillows puffing up around my head the way I like. My roommates joke that they're going to come in and find me suffocated one morning with all of these pillows, but I think it would be a pretty comfortable way to die.

I'm relaxed to the point of weakness, and I could definitely fall asleep with no trouble, but that doesn't stop me from sliding my cell phone out of my pocket and dialing Jeremy's number.

"Hello?"

"Hey. Guess who."

"Beck." His voice is breathless, excited. That's a good sign.

"Yeah, it's me. What'cha doing?"

"Trying to hang this awesome painting Seth gave me today. I finally conned him out of one, but now I can't seem to get the dang thing straight."

I laugh and switch the phone to my other ear, settling deeper into the pillows and closing my eyes.

"I like you." The words come out of my mouth surprisingly easily.

"Oh-kaay." Jeremy chuckles quietly. "That was random."

"It may seem random to you, but not to me. I've been thinking about it all day. In fact, it's all I've been thinking about."

"Well, I don't know what to say. I like you, too, but..."

I think I can guess what's coming, but I have to ask anyway. "But what?"

"But you said you don't want to date, so where does that leave us? I don't want to be your boy toy."

"Boy toy?"

"Yeah, Beck. Your booty call. Your late-night hookup, drunk dial, fuck friend, whatever you want to call it. I don't want to be that. Call me crazy, but I'd like to feel special to someone for a change. I need to know there's someone out there who even gives a shit if I wake up in the morning, or if I even live and breathe at all."

His voice has reached an alarming shrillness by the time he clicks off the line and leaves me in stunned silence.

*What the hell just happened?*

I call him back, but he doesn't answer, so I text instead. *I don't want to be your fuck friend, Jeremy. I want to get to know you. Please pick up the phone.*

Then, as an afterthought, I send a second message. *Give me a break, okay? I don't know how to do this.*

After giving him a moment to read the messages, I lift the

phone to call him back, but he's already calling me.

"I'm sorry," he says as soon as the call connects. "I got a little carried away."

"No, you're right to tell me how you feel, and to give me hell. I've been an insensitive prick. And I know there's no reason for you to trust me, but I'm asking you to give me a shot. Overall, I really don't think I'm a bad guy. Not too awfully bad, anyway. I care about people, try to help out where I can, volunteer for charity work and whatnot. I'm pretty good at wrestling. But when it comes to this— to you— I truly fucking suck."

Jeremy laughs. "Don't be too hard on yourself. Your ability to suck is one of the things I like best about you."

I pull the phone away from my ear, gape at it, then put it back to my ear. "What the hell, Jeremy? I'm being all serious over here, trying to put you at ease about my intentions, and you're the one making dirty comments. Talk about sending mixed signals."

He laughs even harder at that.

"Well, listen…" I stifle a yawn. "I worked myself silly in the gym this evening, and I need to pass out."

"Okay."

I pause, not quite ready to hang up.

"Hey, Jeremy… what was your favorite toy when you were a kid?"

"You sure are full of random comments tonight."

"Just humor me, alright? Here, I'll go first. I think my favorite one was my second skateboard. The first one I got was pretty lame, but that second one was sweet! My parents took me to a good skate shop, and they taught us all about how to build a quality board.

167

It had this really disgusting zombie picture on it. That skateboard changed my life, because it got me outside and active. Before that, I was a video game geek who rarely saw the light of day."

"Um…" Jeremy thinks silently for a long moment. "I guess mine was a slinky."

"Really? A slinky?"

"Hey," he cries in mock outrage. "What other toy can walk down stairs alone or in pairs?"

"And make a slinkety sound?" I finish. "Could you have chosen a more ancient toy?"

"The slinky is timeless, Beck."

I chuckle weakly, running only on fumes of energy now, my eyes nearly drifting shut. "I'll call you tomorrow—"

"Mr. Floppy," he blurts before I can finish.

"Excuse me?" My eyes are wide open now, and I'm praying he's not trying to give me the most offensive nickname ever.

"That was my favorite toy. He's a floppy blue dog with long, skinny arms and legs. A blue tick hound, I guess. When my dad was on one of his drinking binges and I didn't know how bad things might get, I used to curl up in the bed and wrap Mr. Floppy around me like he was hugging me. He always fought off the fear, helped me sleep. Sometimes when it was really bad, I'd tie his arms around my neck so he wouldn't let go after I fell asleep." He chuckles as if he's lost in the memory. "Guess he was always more of a friend than a toy."

"Wow." The word comes out garbled, and I have to clear my throat before I can continue. "I totally do not have a tear in my eye right now, or a lump in my throat." I'm dying to ask more about his

168

dad, but it feels too soon to press. "So how old were you when you quit sleeping with Mr. Floppy?"

"I didn't. He's lying beside me right now."

Jeremy's cute little laugh on the other end of the line makes my stomach do a lazy somersault.

"Hmmm… I think I'm jealous of Mr. Floppy."

# 13

(JEREMY)

WHEN my phone rings at almost nine o'clock, I nearly break my neck trying to get to it. I haven't talked to Beck all day, and when I looked for him after wrestling practice he was nowhere to be found.

Maybe I'm just being paranoid, but I'm beginning to wonder if he's having second thoughts again. I don't know if my heart can take any more of this back and forth. I've already got emotional whiplash.

When I see that the incoming call is from him, I work to slow my breathing and sound casual. "Hello, senpai."

"Stop calling me that," he growls.

Seth looks up from his sketch pad and gives me a smiley thumbs-up.

"Beck, you have no sense of humor." I flop down onto my bed with a pout that he can't see. "So where did you disappear to after wrestling?"

"I had to get away. Some hot guy has been wearing these insanely sexy jock straps in the locker room. He was wearing a yellow one today, and I was afraid I was going to jump him right there in front of everyone."

"Really?" I can't help but smile.

"Yeah, really. You can't keep doing that, Jeremy. It's not easy for me to... not look. And if I look, something is going to happen."

"You mean you're going to get hard?" I ask, baiting him on purpose.

Seth snatches his head up and stares at me with his mouth hanging open. "Sorry," I whisper, covering the mouthpiece.

Beck doesn't answer. Even through the phone, I can sense his exasperation.

"Okay," I sigh. "I'll stop. Only plain white jock straps from now on, or compression shorts. And I'll dress and undress quickly, so as not to call attention to my awesomely hot body."

"Thank you," he says. "And besides, you don't know who else might be looking. That guy Chris seems to be getting his eyes full. I'm about ready to body slam that motherfucker."

"Nah, he's just trying to get me to tutor him, and we haven't been able to set up a time yet."

"Private lessons, huh?" Beck laughs. "You know there's a rule that the team captain has to be present at all tutoring sessions involving freshmen, right?"

"Crap. I didn't know that."

"That's because I just created that rule. And it only applies to freshmen named Jeremy."

"Uh-oh, someone's jealous."

"Hell, yes." Beck says. "And don't you forget it."

His voice gets distant, and I hear him mumble something to someone before he continues our conversation. "So Jeremy, how would you like to go on a vacation with me and Truck and some other people? We've gotten access to a mountain house for the weekend."

"Are you serious?" I yell, unable to contain my excitement. "That sounds so amazing! I've never been on a vacation before."

"Never?"

"Yeah. I mean I've been on a few school trips with the wrestling team and stuff, but not anything major like going to the mountains." I know I'm making myself sound pathetic, but I can't seem to help it. It's the truth, after all.

"Well, I'd be honored to take you on your very first real vacation. It'll be a lot of fun."

"Who all is going? Is Caleb going?"

Beck sighs loudly. "Unfortunately, yes. Caleb is going. It's hard to do anything without him knowing, since he lives with us and all. He and Stephie are going, Truck and Gretchen are going, because they're a couple now. Vlad is taking his girlfriend Melina, whom you've never met, and Truck's cousin Anna is going. I think maybe a couple of her girlfriends, too."

I pause for a moment, mentally sorting the guest list. "So you're going with Anna, and I'm one of the extras."

"No!" Beck yells. "Hell, no. Why would you even say such a

thing?"

"Well, there are three established male-female couples, plus you and Anna, and then me and maybe a couple of her girlfriends. Seems pretty obvious to me. I know I'm not going with Anna, because I've never even met the girl. But you have, and I told you that night she was a slam dunk. I'm telling you, Beck. She likes you."

"What is this, jealousy night? *Fuck.*" From the sound of Beck's voice, I can almost see him running his hand over his short hair the way he does when he gets exasperated. "There's no possible way she could think I'm interested in her. I barely spoke to her, okay? Her family owns the house. She agreed to let Truck use it if he would introduce her to me, but I guess she wants to come along to keep an eye on things."

"She bribed Truck to introduce you? Jesus, Beck... There's something very wrong with this picture. You may not see it, but I do."

"Look, Truck assured me there were no strings attached. He said she didn't expect me to like her or whatever. I think she's just a fan."

"A fan? Really?" I laugh. "What, are you Hulk Hogan now?"

"I don't know, I see myself as more like The Rock." He laughs half-heartedly. "You know, I may not be a pro wrestler, but there are people who follow me."

"I know that, Beck. I didn't mean to make it sound like you were a nobody." I pause, try to will myself to change the subject, and fail. "Do you have to pretend to like her? Sleep with her? Will you be sharing a bedroom?"

Seth has completely abandoned his sketch and is listening

intently. I know I should take this to a more private place, but my passion is running high.

"Jeremy, you and I are going to be together. *We're* the fourth couple. The others may not know that, but that's how it is. Truck promised he wasn't pimping me out to his cousin. I cleared that up with him before I said I'd go. He even suggested that I invite you."

"He did? That's kinda weird, isn't it?"

"I don't know. Is it?"

"Depends on how he said it."

Beck thinks for a moment. "Well, he said he wasn't pimping me out, and that I could invite you. Then I asked if he was sure she wouldn't get mad if I brought you. He said that she thought I was dreamy or whatever, but that he had made it clear that she wasn't my type."

"Um, yeah. Beck, I hate to be the one to break this to you, but Truck knows about us."

"No he doesn't," Beck scoffs. "How would he?"

"I don't know, dude. But he couldn't have said it any clearer. *He knows.*"

Beck doesn't say another word about Truck. I've rendered him speechless on the subject.

# 14

THURSDAY and Friday take forever to get through, with lots of boring classes and homework. At this point in the season, we're only having official wrestling practices on Mondays and Wednesdays, so I don't even have that to keep me occupied.

Things will pick up significantly next month and hit full swing by October, but for now I get precious little Beck face-time. He's got much heavier classes than I do, and he believes in getting plenty of rest. I suppose I should be glad he's not a partier like Seth and Dan, who stagger in stoned or drunk every few nights. They've told me I have a standing invitation to go with them, but I'm not really interested.

I always just stay in, do homework, and read a little manga before bed. True to his word, Seth has emailed me links to several online comics, and I have to admit he was partially justified in calling the stuff I was reading garbage. Though most of the sites he's recommended are much tamer than the yaoi porn stuff I'm used to, they feature higher quality artwork, more engaging story lines, and much more readable translations. My only complaint is that one of the comics is ongoing, and they only post one new page a week on Wednesdays, which has me pulling my freaking hair out. At least it gives me something to look forward to every week.

When Beck comes to pick me up on Saturday morning, I am so ready to get away from my routine. His suitcase is strapped into the bed of his pickup truck with a bungee cord.

"Is this all you have?" he asks.

"Guess so." I shrug and hand him my duffel bag, and he tosses it behind the seat.

It's an hour-and-a-half drive to our destination in the North Georgia mountains, where we'll spend two nights, and then it's on to Blackwood for the annual Labor Day party in Ryan Wilson's field. It may be shallow of me, but I can't wait to show Beck off to all of those fuckers I went to school with. There's no better way to come out in style than by showing up at a party with the hottest date there. Not to mention I won't be scared or worried at all about doing it as long as he's by my side. He gives me courage.

Introducing him to my family is a different matter, and not one I'm particularly looking forward to.

We start our road trip by listening to music and indulging in a bagful of beef jerky and soda. We're both hyper as hell, and I'm talking ninety to nothing about classes, Seth and Dan, and whatever else pops into my mind. About halfway there, I start to stress.

"Are you sure it's gonna be cool that I'm coming?"

Beck levels his gaze on me as well as he can while driving. "Of course. I want you here, and everyone is fine with it. This is our vacation— yours and mine."

I want to slide across the seat and touch him, but I can't. Not yet.

"Beck, there's something that's been bothering me." I look out the window, because I can't make eye contact with him while I'm saying this. "We haven't had sex or even kissed since that day in the locker room. I was just wondering if maybe you're not attracted to me anymore or something."

Beck laughs so hard that after a moment I start to worry about him. "Hang on," he says through his laughter. "I've gotta pull over." After a couple of minutes we come to an exit with a rest area. He pulls into the empty parking lot, shuts the truck off, and turns all the way around in his seat to face me.

"If I remember correctly, it was you who said he did not want to be my booty call, fuck buddy, etcetera. That's why I've been calling you on the phone so much and trying to avoid being in the same room with you. I've been trying to prove I want you for more than sex, and it's really hard to do that in person. Was that not the right thing to do?"

"Well, apparently there's a fine line between wanting me for more than sex and not wanting me for sex at all." I cross my arms over my chest and look out the window again.

There's a little voice in my head telling me I'm pouting like a spoiled child and making an ass of myself, but I don't listen to that voice very often. It's way too soft compared to the other voices I've got in there.

"Is that really what you think? That I don't want you?

Jeremy, my entire life is being redefined by what's going on between you and me. And yeah, it's fucking scary. I feel like I'm tightrope walking without a net, and I don't know if I'm gonna make it to the other side in one piece." He slams his head back onto the headrest and stares up at the headliner of his truck in frustration. "I want you, okay? God... I want you so much."

I lean slowly across the center console, reaching out a hand to touch his cheek, and he rewards me with a wistful little smile that melts my heart. I touch my lips to his, but it's not a sexual kiss. I don't want it to be that. He's just bared his soul to me with the sweetest words I've ever heard, and I want to let him know how much it means to me.

I tickle his lips with mine, running only the tip of my tongue back and forth across the seam between them before sucking gently on the plump swell of his bottom lip. He returns the kiss in the same lazy style.

"So sweet." he whispers.

After we've played like that for a while and both of us are sufficiently breathless and floating in a hypnotic cloud of endorphins and pheromones, I trail tiny kisses across his cheek until my lips are right next to his ear. "No one's ever said anything like that to me," I whisper before sucking his earlobe into my mouth.

Soft laughter rumbles deep in his chest. "Does that mean you liked it?"

"Mmmm... can I show you how much I liked it?"

"Yes, please." His voice breaks.

I can sense that he's suddenly feeling vulnerable again, just like that first night at his apartment. Like he's barreled fearlessly to the edge of a cliff but then stopped short, too afraid to jump. He needs me to take control from him… and right now I am so ready to do that.

"Open the door and get out," I tell him in a quiet but firm voice.

He clicks open the driver's door and slides out, and I jump from my side and come around to meet him. Without prelude, I reach down and undo his jeans, pushing them to his knees. His cock is hard and waiting for me when I grip it tightly and start stroking it. I kiss his lips without stopping the motion of my hand.

"You like it when I take control sometimes, don't you?"

"I don't know." He doesn't try to stop me. Instead he leans back through the open door and onto the truck seat, squeezing his eyes closed.

I bend over and take the head of his dick in my mouth, swirling and sucking over and over until I coax a ragged moan out of him. Then I take my mouth off of it, leaving it slippery wet.

"Jerk off for me, Beck. Let me see how you do it when no one's around. When you're alone in your room. I want to see that. Think about the things you like to think about, whatever gets you off."

He starts moving his hand up and down his shaft, cupping the head in his palm every few strokes. "You," he says. "That's what I think about."

When I've watched for a moment and learned his rhythm, I add my mouth to the mix, sucking roughly on the head whenever he's not palming it. I reach down to cup his balls, and he growls and bucks up into my mouth.

179

"Oh, fuck…" He looks down at me with lust-fogged eyes, and I can tell he won't last much longer at this rate.

"Keep doing that," I tell him, forcing his body around so that his back is to me and he's leaning over the seat of the truck. He's so far gone, I'm fairly certain I can get away with what I'm about to do. "It's so fucking hot watching you get yourself off." I squeeze his ass cheek hard, then I bend and shove my tongue right in to rim his tight little asshole.

He tenses immediately, but I push down on his back before he can rise up, keeping him bent over the seat.

"Jeremy, I don't—" He whimpers. "What if someone comes up and sees us?"

"Shhh…" I keep working his ass with my tongue until he's relaxed again and pressing back, silently begging for more. Then I know he's ready for the next step.

Quickly, I rise up and undo my pants, pushing them down onto my thighs. "Keep on doing what you're doing," I tell Beck, who seems more than happy to comply.

I pull my dick out and nudge it gently into the crack of his ass, dripping saliva from my mouth into the space to lube the way. This time he tenses even more and nearly rares up straight like a spooked horse.

"What the fuck, Jeremy?"

It takes some strength to push him back down, but I can tell his resistance is only half-hearted. "Calm down." I rub his back gently with my hand. "I'm not going to fuck you, okay? I'm only pretending. Going through the motions. Will you let me do that? Will you trust me?"

He doesn't answer, but he relaxes back down onto the seat and resumes working his dick with his hand. Through all of this, he's remained rock hard. I know he's as turned on as I am. He's just so afraid of losing control.

He lets me run my dick up and down between his cheeks for a while, both of us getting more and more worked up. Eventually, I slide the engorged head up into the crevice and nudge against his opening repeatedly while I run my hands up and down his back, establishing a tantalizing rhythm I could easily get lost in.

My stomach knots up with need, and with the knowledge that if I nudged any harder, I'd go in. It's a temptation that's almost too strong to resist. It would be so easy, so quick. If I got a little overzealous, I'd probably slide in by accident. Then it would be too late to stop me, and he'd love it. I know he would. Christ, we both would... so much. But I promised him I wouldn't.

"Are you ready to come, Beck?"

"God yes," he gasps, pulling his dick harder and biting his lip as he looks up at me over his shoulder. "Are you?"

"Definitely. I'm gonna shoot all over your back, okay?"

He nods, and I drop more saliva into the channel at the top of his ass and move my cock into position. With my hand pressing down, holding it against the top of Beck's ass, I slide my shaft frantically back and forth until I hear his breath hitching in his throat, warning of his impending orgasm.

"Coming," I gasp, spurting ropes all over Beck's spine and the back of his hair, some of it arcing over his head to land on the truck seat.

"Oh. Fuck. Yeah." Beck shudders beneath me, still watching

me over his shoulder as he squeezes out the last bit of his own milky cum onto the black asphalt between his feet.

Beck works his truck up the steep dirt drive with ease. The nubby tires stay well within the established tracks as he darts back and forth between trees. Having lived in rural South Georgia all my life, I'm accustomed to off-road situations, but there are some very distinct differences between the area I'm from and the mountains.

For one thing, I don't get car sick riding on dirt roads and fields, but these zig-zagging switchback roads have nearly gotten the best of me. At one point, I plead with Beck to stop and let me stand beside the truck for a moment to recuperate. He just laughs and assures me that we're almost there.

Sure enough, just before I heave second-hand beef jerky all over his clean interior, we hit the gate leading to Anna's property, and my stomach and head gradually calm down from there. The only thing that bothers me is that we've got to drive back down that hellacious road to get home. Maybe someone has some Dramamine.

"Judging from the number of cars, I think everyone else is here," Beck says as we come around the last bend in the drive.

I don't even know how he can see the cars with that amazing house in his line of vision. It's a three story monstrosity made from red wood, glass and stone. Exactly what you'd expect to see in the mountains, only way bigger and nicer.

"Oh my gosh," I breathe, leaning forward to see the top of the house through the windshield. "Is this a house or a hotel?"

Beck chuckles. "A house. It's pretty amazing, huh? Truck said it's got an indoor/outdoor pool and a huge hot tub." He wags his eyebrows suggestively.

"Yeah, that sounds like tons of fun. Sitting in a hot tub with three other couples and pretending we're not together. I'm afraid this is going to be the most awkward weekend ever."

"We'll deal." Beck leans over the back of the seat and grabs my bag, then he gets out and unties his from the bungee cord in the back.

He thoughtfully carries both bags up the steep walk to the front door while I twirl around and gawk at the scenery— trees as far as the eye can see, broken up only by gorgeous blue sky. I'm in love with the mountains already.

"Beck!" Anna greets us at the front door. "And..."

"Jeremy, this is Anna," he says.

"Nice to meet you, Jeremy. I saw you at the party. You were the shy little wallflower playing with your phone."

What is it with these chicks calling me *little puppy dog* and *little wallflower* and shit? I open my mouth to defend myself, not knowing exactly what I'm going to say, but Beck beats me to it.

"Shy little wallflower?" He laughs. "Jeremy can be very dominant when he wants to be. And he may not be tall, but he's definitely not little."

*Damn. Too bad she probably didn't understand all of that innuendo.*

"Oh, I didn't mean anything by it, sweetie." She pats me on the shoulder. "If you guys will follow me, I'll show you to your rooms."

"Thanks," Beck says. "I'd like to put these bags down and

freshen up."

She starts up the wide, curved staircase, and we follow. The others are in the living room, most of them sitting on a huge sectional sofa that must be custom made from the size of it. They watch us as we ascend, dodging the dozens of deer antlers that line the walls. I make a mental note to never go down these stairs half asleep in the middle of the night. They'd probably find me impaled and bled out the next morning.

"Oh, wait." Anna pauses halfway up and gestures down toward a couple of twin girls with long dark hair who are seated together in an overstuffed recliner. "Beck and Jeremy, that's Lacey and Tracey. I believe you know everyone else."

The four of us who have been introduced nod and mumble pleasantries before Anna leads us the rest of the way up the stairs.

"Alright, Beck," Anna announces, pushing open a door at the end of the hall on the third floor. "This is your room."

She touches him on the arm, wrapping her fingers around his impressive biceps and squeezing gently. She thinks she's being subtle, but I know exactly what the bitch is doing. She's copping a cheap feel while letting him know she's his for the taking. Beck acts like he doesn't have a clue what she's doing.

*Mine,* the voice in my head growls, though I have no idea how to go about staking my claim when our relationship has to remain a secret. *Gah... I fucking hate it.*

"All rooms have a bathroom and balcony overlooking the mountains behind the house," she continues, speaking only to Beck. "I saved this one just for you, because it's got the best of everything... besides my room, of course. Anyway, get settled in and join the rest

184

of us downstairs. There's plenty of alcohol and party games, and we've got a wild night planned." She laughs, then glances over at me like she's just remembered I'm here. "Jeremy, follow me and I'll show you to your room."

Beck hands me my bag, and I glance back over my shoulder at him as Anna leads me away. He's standing awkwardly in the middle of the room watching me leave, looking just as lost as I feel.

My tour is not nearly as personal or friendly as the VIP treatment Beck got.

"This is your room," she says, opening a door all the way at the opposite end of the hall. It's half the size of Beck's room, and though there couldn't possibly be a bad room in this entire amazing house, I get the feeling I'm as close to being stuck in the basement as it gets around here.

When she leaves, she makes a beeline straight back to Beck's room. I know this because after I take a quick piss and rush back over there, she's already inside chatting with Beck. The smile slips from her face as soon as I show up in the doorway.

"Come in, Jeremy," Beck says before turning back to address Anna. "If you don't mind, I'm going to freshen up before I come down."

"Sure. No problem," she says. "See you in a sec."

Both of us are standing like goofballs with our hands shoved into our jeans pockets, but as soon as the door clicks into place we make a mad dash for the bed.

I leap onto it and roll to my back, and Beck is instantly on top of me, laughing and kissing me like he can't get enough. I feel exactly the same way. In a romantic setting like this, our first official

185

date is a dream come true.

*Except that our hostess is trying to seduce my guy.*

I grab him around the back of the neck and pull him down for a deep kiss, simultaneously arching up to press my budding erection into his hip. "Let's fuck." I suggest, looking up at him from my nest in the puffy down comforter. "Right now. Let's do everything we can think of to each other, until we're so worn out we can't move and our dicks are shooting nothing but air."

Beck smiles indulgently down at me and grabs my cock for a thorough grope through my pants. "I'd love to, but we need to get downstairs before they send out a posse. None of the other couples are having mad sex right now, so we can't either. We have to use proper etiquette."

I sigh and roll out from under him. "Fine, then. I'll do the etiquette thing, but only until dark. Then you and I have a date right here under these covers."

We both stand and straighten our clothes. I pat my hair into place.

"Wild horses couldn't keep me away from that date." He nods his head toward my crotch and smiles. "Make that thing go down before we join the others, please. I wouldn't want anybody getting the wrong idea."

I wrap a hand around the back of his neck and pull up onto my toes, pressing my erection against him as I whisper in his ear. "If you want it to go down, you're gonna have to stop staring at it."

The afternoon crawls by in a haze of mountain air,

meaningless conversation and liquor. Lots and lots of liquor. I'm assuming beer is too ghetto for this venue. There's rum, scotch, vodka, mixers, fruit juice, energy drinks, and God knows what else. The kitchen is set up like a bar, with a couple of blenders pulled out onto the island and ingredients strewn from one counter to the other.

"I don't want to get drunk," I whisper to Beck when no one's paying us any attention.

"Me, neither. Just sip along. They'll all be schnockered before long, and then we can sneak off to my room."

The thought fills me with such glee, I can't stop smiling. This will be the first time we can just go crazy on each other all night with no one sleeping in the next bed.

Gretchen comes up next to us while the other girls are mixing drinks in the blenders and shakers, making a sticky mess on the countertops. "Having fun, boys?" The question means something totally different coming from her than it would coming from anyone else in the house.

"Bucket loads," Beck says, raising one eyebrow and taking a sip of his Jack and Coke. "How about you and Truck? Are you two slapping skins yet?"

"Shut up, Becky," she teases, pinching him on the arm. "Stop trying to embarrass me. I could ask you the same question."

"You already know what my answer would be, and it doesn't embarrass me one bit." He looks at me and winks, and for some strange reason I can feel my face heating. I think it's because Beck's intimacy with Gretchen still intimidates me. I always feel like an outsider when those two are together.

"Okay Jeremy, here's your Sex On the Beach," Anna

187

announces in a sing-song voice, handing me a large glass filled with a pink-orange iced liquid. "Most guys won't drink girly drinks like this."

*Wow. Did she really just say that?*

"Interesting," I say, trying to ignore my irritation at what feels like a thinly veiled insult. "I don't know as much about mixed drinks as you do, but then I'm not an alcoholic. Sex On the Beach just sounded like something I'd enjoy, even without the alcohol."

Anna giggles. "I like Sex On the Beach, too. How about you, Gretchen?"

"Oh, yeah," Gretchen says in a vague way that makes me suspect she's never actually had sex on the beach. Or the drink.

Anna turns back to us and touches Beck's chest briefly with her index finger. "How about you, Beck?"

*Okay, that was very definitely a flirt.*

Beck levels his golden gaze on her and smiles. "I've never had it, but I'd love to try Jeremy's."

He reaches for my drink, and I hand it over without hesitation, fighting an overwhelming urge to stick my tongue out at Anna.

We all watch Beck, his Adam's apple bobbing as he drains half of my drink. I'm about to come out of my skin waiting to hear what he'll say next.

"Damn, that's good. Best I've ever had." He passes the glass back to me with a wink. "Hope you don't mind putting your mouth where mine has been."

"Not at all." I turn the glass and deliberately take a swallow from the same spot.

188

Anna doesn't get the joke. I think she's already had a few too many drinks, or maybe she's just not that sharp to begin with. Gretchen has her hand in front of her mouth trying to hide the fact that she's laughing, but the shaking of her shoulders is a tell-tale sign.

When Anna runs off to join her twin friends, who are calling her from the living room, Gretchen gives Beck a stern look. "Do not terrorize the hostess, Beck. What the heck is wrong with you? Are you trying to give yourself away?"

"So what if he is?" I step closer to Beck, our arms close enough for me to feel the heat of his skin, but not quite touching. "If it's what he wants, then what's wrong with it?"

"Who the hell are you to say what he wants?" Gretchen flips her ponytail over her shoulder and glares at me with open hostility.

"Well, I'm pretty sure he doesn't want *her*. What's he supposed to do? Flirt back and pretend he likes her just to make everyone else happy?"

"Oh, now you're speaking for Beck? He's a responsible guy who's making a life for himself. You're only temporary, and after you're gone, he's the one who has to live with the choices he's made. Wake up and stop being a selfish, manipulative little prick."

My whole body turns hot at her words, and it's all I can do to keep quiet. I don't even know if I *should* keep quiet. Maybe I should be as forthcoming about my feelings as she's been about hers— point out that I already know Beck in ways she never will. That I'm more than just a casual hookup.

*Aren't I?*

Angry words boil up to the surface, but before I can speak them, Beck covertly presses a hand to the small of my back. His warm fingertips run up under my t-shirt, calming me instantly, drawing lazy circles there while he leans over to whisper in Gretchen's ear. I have no idea what he's saying to her, but it takes a good thirty seconds, and her face is absolutely scarlet by the time he pulls away from her and drops his hand from my back.

"Jeremy… I apologize," she chokes out before making her way silently back to the living room.

"What did you say to her?" I ask, unable to keep my curiosity at bay.

He shrugs. "I'll tell you sometime… but not now."

I put on an exaggerated pout like I always see girls doing to get their way with their boyfriends. I don't think I'm very good at it, though, because Beck still doesn't tell me what he said to Gretchen.

"Just try not to be too angry with her," he says. "She's a little drunk and a lot jealous. It's hard for her to see me spending so much time with someone, caring about someone… Things are changing, and it's got her a bit freaked. She's like a sister to me, you know. And sisters can be really annoying."

"I wouldn't know," I say. "I'm an only child."

"Well, I've got a real brother and sister, and they're just as annoying as Gretchen. The difference is I don't have to see them every day."

"I'll try to keep calm, Beck, but it's hard. Especially for me, and especially today. It may sound crazy, but I feel like everyone is being hostile to me. I keep telling myself it's not as bad as it seems, but I think maybe it is. Do you really not see it?"

"Yeah, Jeremy, I think some people are being a little aggressive toward you. But it's only because of me." He bumps his

190

hip into mine and smiles. "You don't regret going out with me, do you?"

"I don't know. Let's wait and see how bad it gets."

He laughs and glances around to make absolutely sure we're alone. When he confirms that everyone else is in the living room, he moves in front of me, pushing me against the counter, pressing his dick hard into my belly as he leans in to speak softly next to my ear. "I'll take care of you, baby. Don't ever doubt that." He trails kisses slowly along my jaw until he reaches my lips.

I sigh against him, letting him kiss me silly. At the moment, I truly believe that this strong man— *my* strong man— can make everything in the world right for me.

The feeling lingers long after the kiss is over and he's pulled me into the living room to join the others. I wish we could be alone for this entire trip, but Beck is right; we were invited here as part of a group for a party weekend, and we need to act accordingly.

Soon everyone moves into the game room, where there are even more animal heads covering the walls. While the girls giggle and talk and sip their drinks on the floor in front of a flickering fireplace made of stone, the guys drag out the poker chips and sit down at the fancy felt-covered table in the center of the room.

"I think I'll go sit with the girls," I say. "I don't really feel comfortable—"

"Look on with me." Beck pulls my chair closer to his. So close it makes me feel conspicuous.

"Yeah, Jeremy," Truck says. "Look on with Beck at first. He's great at Texas Hold 'Em. And we're not playing for a whole lot of money."

I nod and settle in beside Beck, resisting the crazy urge to rest my head on his shoulder. I'd rather be in front of the fire than sitting at a poker table, but there's no way I'm turning down the chance to sit this close to Beck and watch him play. Besides, you can learn a lot about a person by watching how they bluff other people.

Caleb wins the first hand, but Beck wins the second. I can already tell just by observing that Beck has more skill than the others. Of course, he's not as tipsy, either.

On the third hand, Caleb turns to me. "Alright, enough looking over your daddy's shoulder. You ought to have the hang of it enough to play now."

"If you call him my daddy one more time, you'll be carrying your ass home in a paper sack," I tell Caleb in a smooth, unperturbed voice. Then I tap the table in front of me. "Now go ahead and deal me in."

Vlad wins the third hand. He had great cards, plus I can tell Beck is so preoccupied with worrying about me that his concentration is compromised.

"I got shit cards that hand," Caleb announces to no one in particular. "Nothing I could do, man."

"No need to make excuses to us, Caleb," I tell him. "Everyone has a bad game every once in a while. I'm sure you'll do better this time."

He gives me a suspicious look, but he doesn't say anything. He's probably trying to figure out why I'm being so nice to him.

I win the next hand. And the next. And then the next. I don't always have the cards, but I can bluff like a sonofabitch.

By the end of the third hand, Caleb is vibrating with anger.

He stands and stalks out onto the back deck. It's easy to hear him growling and cussing even through the storm windows. He punches the wood siding on the outside of the house, and one of the lights falls from the wall and crashes to the deck floor.

When Caleb comes back inside, he casts an apologetic look in Anna's direction. "Sorry I busted your light. I'll pay you back for it."

"Don't worry about it," she says with a sour look. "You probably couldn't afford it anyway."

"Bitch," he mutters under his breath as he returns to the table. Then he addresses Beck. "So Junior's a fucking ringer. Did you know about this?"

Beck shakes his head, fighting a grin. "No idea, man. I was over here making an ass of myself giving him pointers like he was in kindergarten."

# 15

*(BECK)*

ANNA slips down into the water, submerging her trim body and her flattering couture bikini, the white fabric blurring beneath the surface. She twirls around in the middle of the hot tub, nearly losing her balance. "Wow, this feels amazing. Nothing better than a hot tub party with plenty of pretty girls and hot guys in bathing suits."

Everyone else nods in agreement. I'm only vaguely aware of what she's saying, intent as I am on Jeremy as he climbs into the water. Anna reaches over and flips a switch to turn on the motor, and the surface of the water comes to life with rolling bubbles.

"You know," she continues, "usually we just get in naked. I think this is the first party hot tub we've ever had with clothes on. Do you guys not like to get wild at Southeastern State?"

"Hell, yeah, we do," Caleb yells, determined not to be outdone by UGA. He leers around at the group, his glassy eyes at half-mast. "That's what I'm talking about." He bounces around beneath the surface of the water before tossing his trunks behind him onto the edge of the hot tub.

Stephie gapes at him. "Caleb, what are you doing?"

He pulls her into his arms and kisses her, even though she's pushing at his chest. "Take your suit off, baby. We're all friends here. It'll be fun. I've always wanted to have a naked hot tub party, haven't you?"

"Um, no." She looks uncertainly at him.

He leans close and whispers in her ear. I don't know what he's said to her, but it works. When he pulls back, she slowly unties the strap of her bikini and slips her top off, making sure to keep her breasts submerged.

For a girl who used to seem overly flirtatious, Stephie's gotten very reserved. I suspect it has to do with Caleb's controlling personality.

Now I'm ashamed about judging her for being her former happy-go-lucky self, because as far as I know she never cheated on Caleb. Seeing her this way just makes me feel sad.

"Yay," Anna cries, shedding her own bikini and tossing it onto the stamped concrete floor. Unlike Stephie, she doesn't bother to hide her breasts.

I glance at Jeremy, and he's staring at Anna with a look of disgust.

Through all of it, Truck and Gretchen are looking around with bewildered expressions.

"What do you think, babe?" Truck asks her. "You wanna go for it? I don't think it's fair that I've got to look at these girls' boobs but not yours."

That decides Gretchen, who starts dragging her top off before he can say another word. She's pretty far gone from the looks of it, with glassy eyes and perma-grin like I've never seen on her before. I resolve not to let my eyes wander in her direction again, because if there's anyone here I absolutely do not want to see naked, it's my best friend. I'm afraid I'd never be able to get that image out of my head.

"Oh, yeah," Truck says, smiling and pulling his trunks from under the water as he admires his new girlfriend. I'm thrilled that they found each other, because they make such a nice couple. Not to mention I care a lot about both of them.

Lacey and Tracey have both tossed their identical lavender suits to the side and are squealing and bouncing in the water, breasts bobbing in and out of view. With their long chocolate locks clinging tendril-like to their pale shoulders and breasts, they could easily pass for a matching pair of mermaids.

Vlad and Melina remove their suits slowly, staring intently at each other. Once they're unclothed, they start making out like they're the only two people in the hot tub. They've been together for a long time and are clearly very much in love.

"Wow, I didn't expect this," Jeremy whispers from beside me.

"Me, either."

I have to admit I'm shocked at my friends' willingness to party naked. I'm not exactly a prude, but these folks are drunk as hell and showing it. We're in for some awkward moments when we get back to school.

I can already hear Gretchen whining, *Oh my God, did I really do that?*

"Looks like we have some shy guys in our tub," Anna says, smiling toward me and Jeremy, who seem to be the only ones not participating in the group striptease.

Caleb laughs. "Don't be a chicken shit, Beck. Take it off. Unless you're worried you won't measure up to the rest of us."

"Haven't you seen enough of it in the locker room?" I roll my eyes at him and prop my elbows on the side of the hot tub, refusing to be goaded.

I should have known my little firecracker Jeremy would respond, though. Now that he associates himself with me, he considers a challenge to me a challenge to him. I only know this because I can relate. I'm known for being laid back, but he brings out my protective nature like no one ever has.

"Fuck you, Caleb," Jeremy says. "Everybody knows you're just jealous of Beck."

"He doesn't bother me, Jeremy," I say calmly.

I take my trunks off anyway just to avoid any further show of aggression. I know from experience that neither Jeremy nor Caleb will let it rest until they feel vindicated.

I toss my trunks over to Caleb, and they land on top of the water, splashing a few drops into his face.

Surprisingly, he only laughs and throws them back at me. "That's more like it, man." Then he sets his sights on Jeremy, giving him that same challenging look he gives him every time he looks his way. "What about you, Junior? Afraid the ladies are gonna laugh if you take off your shorts?"

"Not hardly." Jeremy hoists himself smoothly onto the side of the tub, revealing that he's already stripped down without anyone noticing. His trunks are lying on the concrete behind him.

He struts naked to stand right beside Caleb, spinning in a slow circle with his arms outstretched, showcasing that beautiful body that has become my addiction. Everyone stares blatantly, the girls not even bothering to pretend to be offended. I'm the only one in the group who's blushing, and it's because looking at him has given me an instant erection, and I feel like everyone is going to know.

I just can't help responding to the smooth perfection of his compact body, and the way he moves with that springy, athletic grace, every muscle primed and ready to do what it's meant to do.

"Is this what you want, Caleb?" His voice is dark with challenge and undisguised sexual innuendo. "Do I pass your inspection? You're a brave guy, bullying people while you're hiding in the water."

Caleb smiles and climbs out of the water to stand like a dripping hulk in front of Jeremy, displaying his unnaturally muscled physique. Jesus, the guy's got muscles on top of muscles.

*How did I not notice how much he's grown over the summer?*

Coupled with his recently ramped-up aggression, the sudden growth is a clear indication of steroid use. I can't imagine he'd be dumb enough to try it with the NCAA piss tests, but maybe he's planning on stopping in time to pass.

"You want to push me, little man?" Caleb looks down his nose at Jeremy, crowding him slightly. "We can take it there if you want, but I think everybody here knows who'd win."

Of course Jeremy doesn't back down at all, which is exactly

why he's going to get himself killed someday. If there were a plus for Caleb threatening to pound my date into the concrete, it would be that it's instantly deflated my embarrassing erection.

I jump out of the water and rush around to them. Truck and Vlad follow my lead, as always. Now all of us guys are standing naked in a group, and all of the ladies are staring. It occurs to me in a totally unconceited way that they're getting an eyeful of five of the best built guys at Southeastern State. If the situation wasn't so volatile right now, it would be hysterical. But the problem is, it could go anywhere from this point, and I want to make sure it doesn't end badly.

"Hey, no need to step up," Caleb says directly to me, holding his hands up in surrender, his eyes barely slits. "I was just playing. Didn't mean to offend your boy. He's got a hot little temper on him, don't he?"

"Yes, he does," I agree. "And he's also got backup— a hundred percent guaranteed backup. You need to remember that in the future."

"It's cool," he says. "I just like yanking his chain, that's all." He lowers himself back into the water beside Stephie and gives her a quick peck on the forehead. "Now would you guys get back in the hot tub so we don't have to all stare at your hairy asses?"

We return to our respective places, and I try to ignore the way Anna's eyes drop to my groin as I'm lowering myself into the hot tub. And the way her twin friends are devouring Jeremy with their eyes. It's as if there's been a division of ownership discussed without our knowledge; Anna gets me, and it's open season on Jeremy for the other two single girls.

Maybe I should have paid more attention to Jeremy's

assessment of the situation, because at the moment it appears he was right on the money.

Anna smiles. "Guess we should have expected something like that tonight with a house full of hot wrestlers. There's a lot of testosterone floating around in here."

"Does that bother you?" I ask, trying to make conversation, not thinking about exactly what I'm saying or what it might sound like to her.

"Oh, no," she assures me in a low voice, wading closer, her nipples hovering just below the surface. "I love it. Big, muscular, manly wrestlers totally turn me on. Especially national champions. Or future national champions in your case."

When she runs a hand through her blonde hair, a breast pops into full view. I think she's done it on purpose.

I'm aware of Jeremy moving in the water behind and to the left of me, and I'm praying he hasn't heard her last comment. How did we suddenly get to this place, where Caleb is baiting Jeremy and Anna is openly flirting with me? Not to mention we're all simmering in a pot of naked ass soup.

*Damn, I'm beginning to hate partying.*

Even though Jeremy and I have had only a couple of drinks apiece, the rest of the crew is hammered. They're all just a little too brave right now, and I'm worried that something messed up is about to happen. I lean back against the side of the tub, stretching my arms out as if I'm relaxing. Truthfully, I'm just trying to think of a subtle way to get Jeremy to meet me upstairs, but before I can do it, things go awry.

"I'm really flattered that you decided to come this weekend,

Beck," Anna says in a slightly slurry voice, bouncing up directly in front of me and smiling in a way that says she's about to put me on the spot.

*Flattered? Why would she be flattered? Shit, what is she thinking?*

"Uh…" I've just gone dumb.

"You know, I've had a crush on you ever since we met at Nationals last year."

"We met last year?"

"Yes, silly." Her laughter deteriorates into pouting. "Remember? After seeing you destroy that brute from Ohio, I told you that you were my absolute favorite college wrestler. You said you were going into Sports Medicine, and I said I was going into Veterinary Medicine, and we joked about going into business together and working on those Vegas show animals, or all of the Uga dogs… You really don't remember that?"

I try to smile, but I'm too disturbed to pull it off. "Your memory is a lot better than mine."

"It's okay. At least you came this weekend." She moves to stand beside me, much too closely, her back pressed up against the side of the hot tub right next to mine. "I have a confession to make." She blushes. "I've never had a naked hot tub party before. I just said that so I could see you. Plus I'm a little drunk, if you couldn't tell. Drinking makes me very brave."

She reaches over and touches me on the hip, sliding her hand around to grab my ass. Before she can get a good hold on it, I seize her thin wrist and stop her from touching me.

"What the hell, Anna?" I lean close, keeping my voice low so as not to cause a scene and embarrass both of us. "I think you're right. You've had too much to drink, and things have gotten a little confused. We need to step back and start over, okay?"

"But I thought..." Her forehead creases as her tipsy brain tries to work out what's going on.

Out of the corner of my eye, I see Jeremy pass by, wading across the tub toward the twins. The girls exchange a triumphant look when they notice he's coming their way.

"Jeremy," I call without thinking, grabbing his arm as he passes. "What are you doing?" Now I've got his arm in one hand and Anna's in the other, so I drop hers into the water with a splash.

Too late, I realize what it probably looks like to him— me holding Anna's arm and speaking softly in her ear. He still doesn't trust me not to sell out just to stay under the radar.

He turns and glares at me over his shoulder. "I'm damn sure not going to be the only guy who's not getting laid here tonight." Snatching his arm out of my grip, he continues across the hot tub toward the girls.

*Fuck.*

When he reaches the twins, they immediately start chatting and laughing. Jeremy doesn't laugh back. His face looks like pure retribution, and it turns my stomach. If I don't stop this right now, he's going to do something that will probably destroy our relationship, and I can't have that.

*It's now or never, Beck. Decide. Jeremy or the closet.*

"Beck, what's wrong?" Anna asks. "I'm sorry if I upset you. I thought you and I were supposed to be together this weekend."

"Really?" I stare at her in horrified shock. "Whatever gave you that idea?"

"Well..." She's unable to make eye contact with me, stepping back and sitting on the underwater bench so that she's completely submerged to the chin, a miserable expression on her face. "I told Truck to tell you I wanted to be with you, and he said he would. He also said that he didn't think I was your type and that you were probably bringing someone. But when you didn't bring anyone, I just assumed you wanted to be with me, too."

"Didn't bring anyone?" My voice is so loud that everyone stops what they're doing and looks our way. "How do you figure I didn't bring anyone, Anna? Did I walk through your door alone? No, I did not." I glance at Jeremy, who is now looking our way. "Dammit, I'm sick of people and their fucking dim assumptions. Now Jeremy's over there about to revenge fuck the mermaid twins just to get back at me, and I haven't even done anything. *Fuck!*"

I grab my shorts off the side of the tub and slide them on underneath the water. Then I look over to where Jeremy and the twins are staring open-mouthed at me. "Come on." With a flick of my wrist, I gesture for Jeremy to join me, and he sloshes eagerly through the bubbling water.

As soon as he reaches my side, I hand him his trunks, determined that these people aren't getting any more free shots of our junk. I already feel like we've been violated by the whole situation, both as individuals and as a couple.

"Beck..." Gretchen calls to me, but I hold up a hand to silence her.

"Don't worry about it, Gretch. This has been a long time coming."

"K, hon," she says quietly.

I hop out of the tub with Jeremy following closely behind. We each grab a towel from a stack in the corner of the room and make our way toward the door.

I pause on the opposite edge of the hot tub, looking back and forth repeatedly between Caleb, Vlad, Truck and their girlfriends. "This is my fucking business," I tell them, vibrating from the adrenaline coursing through me. "If one single person at school finds out about it, I'll know who to come looking for. And rest assured... I will Fuck. You. Up."

Vlad shakes his head. "Not me, bro. I'd never say anything if you didn't want me to. Melina either, right babe?" Melina nods, her eyes wide.

"Beck, I'm offended." Truck crosses his arms over his broad chest and scowls. "I've never said anything before. Why would I start now?"

*Truck knows?*

I raise a brow at him, but now is not the time to quiz him, so I file it away for another day.

"Caleb..." I bend low over him, staring him straight in the eyes.

"I won't say nothing, Beck. I swear it."

"Good," I reply in a voice too low for anyone else to hear. "Everyone has secrets, and I'd hate for anyone to find out how you've put on twenty pounds of muscle in two months."

He swallows hard. "You don't have to threaten me, Beck. I told you I won't say anything. I'm not a bad guy. I know you think I am because I like messing with Jeremy, but it's just because he keeps his cool and he never backs down. He doesn't act like a little bitch. I like that, you know?"

"Well, tone it down or someone's gonna get hurt."

I stand up straight and try to muster all of my dignity to walk out of here, wishing I was wearing something more respectable than a pair of wet swim trunks. More than that, I wish I could absorb any pain or embarrassment Jeremy may be feeling. This whole thing is on me, and I cringe to think that he may be hurt by it.

"Come on," I tell him again, reaching out and urging him forward with a hand at the small of his back. "Let's go upstairs and watch a movie."

After we leave the room, I hear Truck bellow at Anna, "I told you not to mess with him, dammit! Now look what you did."

I just ignore it and lead Jeremy up to my room to privacy, and hopefully some peace. I don't care what the rest of them do now as long as they leave us alone.

As soon as I close the door behind us in the room, Jeremy breaks ranks and starts jumping up and down. "Oh my God, Beck. Do you realize what you just did?"

A slow smile spreads across my face. "Yeah, I guess so."

"Does it feel good to you? Cause it feels fucking awesome to me." He paces around in erratic circles, bouncing on his toes like he does when he's excited.

"Are you kidding? It feels terrible."

Jeremy stops pacing and stares at me in shock, but when he sees that I'm grinning from ear to ear, he hops over and throws his arms around my neck. "You're so full of shit, Beck." He kisses me on the side of the neck. "You feel it, too, same as me."

I just laugh quietly and hug him back. "Let's cuddle up naked in bed and watch a movie, okay?"

I drag my laptop out of its case and set it up on the bed. Jeremy sits between my legs, exactly where I like him, but he chooses to watch some of my home videos of wrestling trips instead of a movie.

"How did you know you wanted to wrestle?" he asks as we watch.

"Hmmm…" I try in vain to recall any early feelings on the subject. "I guess it all started when I was in middle school. Pretty typical story, really. Some of my friends wanted to join the wrestling team, and some of my friends wanted to play basketball and football. I started out trying all three, but wrestling was the one that was a perfect fit for me. I love the fact that it's just me and another guy out there competing. No question who wins. It's a clean competition. Mano a mano, you know what I mean? It just feels pure."

"Pure, yeah. I know what you mean." Jeremy is quiet for a moment. "Don't laugh, but the reason I got into wrestling at first was because I wanted to be able to defend myself."

I lean around to look him in the eyes. "I wouldn't laugh at something like that, Jeremy. Jeez. Who did you want to defend yourself from? Bullies?"

"Yeah, bullies. People who hurt me."

I wrap my arms around Jeremy's upper arms and chest, giving him a bear hug. "I wish I'd known you then. I would never have let anyone touch you. Not a hair on your sexy little head."

206

"Why do people always have to call me little? I'll bet no one's ever called you little."

I laugh and squeeze him even harder. "No, you're right; people don't call me little. But I have a confession to make that might make you feel better." I run a hand down Jeremy's chest and abs, feeling every contour along the way, until I reach his dick beneath the covers. It responds immediately to my touch, filling out in my hand as I stroke it. "Everything about you... your height, your compact frame, your defined muscles, your thick neck, your perfect cock, even your feet. Every fucking thing about you drives me wild. All I have to do is look at you, and I get a raging boner. See?" I nudge my dick into the small of his back, making him laugh and squirm against it. "When you're in front of me like this, or spooning, we fit so perfectly. Like our bodies were made to go together."

"Well gosh when you put it that way..." Jeremy spins around with in my arms, turning toward me and placing a kiss on my nose.

We make love slowly and sweetly, taking our time, learning each other's bodies by heart. For the first time, we have all night. No one bothers us... lucky for them.

The rest of the weekend is more of the same. Anna pulls me and Jeremy aside and apologizes for what happened.

"I don't know what I would've done if some girl had come up flirting with my date right in front of me," she tells Jeremy. "I'm really embarrassed, and I hope you can forgive me."

Jeremy gives her a big fat hug. "You didn't know. And you were drinking. Plus, Beck is pretty irresistible."

They both laugh at that, and I can feel my face getting warm.

Besides that, no one mentions the big blowout in the hot tub

Saturday night, and the atmosphere is surprisingly relaxed.

We hike, enjoy the scenery, watch movies, and socialize a bit. Between it all, we make love. Overall our first vacation together is a great success, and I feel like it's just the beginning of something wonderful.

By the time we pack up our things in my truck and head out toward Jeremy's hometown, it's Labor Day, and we've got just enough time to get there before the party starts.

# 16

SO I'm lounging on the tailgate of my truck with Jeremy seated between my legs, both of us clutching a beer can and watching a wide stream of bonfire sparks float up into the nighttime sky. I'm thinking I've never felt so content in all my life.

"Happy Labor Day," he says.

I laugh quietly. "You know, this is the first time Labor Day feels like something to celebrate."

We're hidden in a large dirt clearing surrounded by tall pines on the edge of the woods behind a field. From the looks of the scorched earth, ashes and debris, it's obvious this is not the first time a bonfire party has been held here. Vehicles continue to arrive and leave, bumping along a winding trail that skirts the edge of the field, their headlights bouncing and illuminating narrow swaths of trees.

Someone's got their truck doors open and their high-end stereo system pumping out classic rock from the seventies. Not my usual music choice, but I'd be hard pressed to come up with a better soundtrack for a redneck get-together in a field.

With the scent of grass, dirt and pine filling my lungs, I take a large swig of beer and drape my arms possessively around Jeremy's shoulders. It's so awesome to be able to be openly affectionate like other couples. This weekend has been a real eye-opener for me. It's so liberating, I swear it feels like my lungs have expanded, making it easier to breathe.

"So how does it feel?" I ask him.

"How does what feel?"

I shrug. "I guess bringing a guy back home to meet your friends and family. Are you nervous at all?"

He turns in my arms and gives me a sweet smile that makes my heart soar. "No, Beck, I'm not nervous. I'm proud of you. I've been dying to show you off. See all these people here tonight? They're all saying to themselves, *How the hell is Jeremy Miller going out with the hottest guy in the state of Georgia? I didn't even know he was gay!*"

He leans his head back even farther and lands a little kiss in the cleft of my chin before laughing and facing front again. His body melts against me, his back to my chest, and I tighten my hold on him.

I don't know what's going to happen with us in the future, or when we get back to school on Wednesday, but right now feels so right.

*I don't want to go back.*

"Besides," he adds, "I've been waiting a long time for this. To be free to be myself."

"If it's so easy for you now, why couldn't you before?"

He looks at me as if I ought to know the answer. "Because it doesn't mean anything to anyone here now. High school is a mine field, you know? There's no fucking way to get out. You just have to keep showing up every day, tiptoeing around all the bullshit, hoping you don't make a wrong step and blow yourself up... and take all your friends down with you."

He sips the last of his beer and crushes the can, tossing it over our shoulders into the bed of the truck. His eyes lock on a group of people across the clearing who are partying around a bright red truck, but it's as if he's not really seeing them, only staring through them.

I kiss the back of his hair. "You want another beer?"

"Yeah," he whispers, snuggling back into me a little closer.

I reach back, grab a cold one out of the cooler, and pop the top for him, surprised at how damn good it feels to do little things for him.

While he's chugging half of it, a girl stops in front of us. She's about his age, black pixie hair, cute. She's only about the fifth person who's dropped by to speak since we've been here. They all seem to be keeping their distance pretty well.

"Hi, Jeremy." Her eyebrows draw slightly inward as her gaze drops to my arms wrapped around him, then back up to his face.

"Mindy, great to see you." He gestures toward me with his beer can. "This is Beck. I met him at college. Beck, this is my good friend Mindy. We've been friends since fourth grade."

"Um, sorry I didn't call you over the summer, Jeremy. I was at my grandmother's in the mountains, and time just got away from me. How's Southeastern State?" Her eyes flick suspiciously to me again, and I smile at her.

It's almost fun watching her try to figure out if this is really what it looks like. I have the urge to lay a big kiss on Jeremy just so she can quit wondering, but I wouldn't do that to him. This is his party, and I'm letting him run the show.

"SSU is great," he says. How's Atlanta?"

"Great," she says. "Well, I'm gonna go stand by the fire for a while. It was good seeing you."

"You, too, Mindy."

As she wanders off to the fire, I have to stifle a laugh. "I think she was a wee bit taken aback, Jeremy."

"Yeah," he sighs. "We've been getting some strange looks all night. It's just people trying to work it out in their heads, that's all."

"If you don't mind me asking, what exactly do you hope to accomplish here? I mean, what would be your ideal outcome?"

Before he can answer, there's a commotion in the center of the clearing as a kid backs a small pickup truck near the fire, and I see that it's about half full of watermelons. "Alright, guys. Last of the crop. Grab one and enjoy."

Jeremy leaps off the tailgate and makes a mad dash for the truck, returning with a medium-sized watermelon in his arms and a huge grin on his face. "You like watermelon?"

"Love it. But I don't have a knife. I left my camping gear at the apartment."

"No problem," he says. "Country boys don't need knives. We use our bare hands, baby." He throws the watermelon down onto the ground and it splits open just enough that we can break into it.

I laugh as he retrieves the melon and sets it on the tailgate. "I just got turned on from watching you throw a watermelon. Does that make me a country boy, too?"

"No, Beck" Jeremy replies. "I think that just makes you easily impressed."

At the side of my truck with the watermelon broken into large chunks, we eat it the way it was meant to be eaten— bent over at the waist, faces buried in it, juice running down our forearms. After a while, we're laughing hysterically at our own slurping sounds and the mess we're making.

"I think the sugar is going to our heads," I mumble around a juicy mouthful.

Jeremy casts his rind into the woods at the front of my truck with a satisfied grunt. "I'm sticky as hell, but it was worth it. Mr. Wilson always has the best watermelon. Is that not the sweetest stuff you've ever tasted?"

I toss mine into the same spot before giving in to a sudden urge to push Jeremy against the passenger door. "I think you've spoiled me," I say. "Now nothing tastes as sweet as you." I cover his mouth with mine, pushing my tongue in deep and coaxing his to come out and play. We both taste like dizzying mix of watermelon, beer and lust, and I don't care who sees us devouring each other.

Jeremy grabs my face with both hands and stills my movements. "How do you make me want you so much?" he whispers. "We probably won't get a chance to do it again until we get back to school, but I don't want to wait."

He lifts up onto his toes and bites my lip playfully, pulling it into his mouth and sucking gently, relentlessly on it until I startle myself with a growl.

I push away from him, slamming his back roughly against the

213

door in the process

"Open your pants," I gasp. "Fold them down for me the way you did that first night."

"Here?" He casts a dubious glance around the clearing, where everyone is busy eating watermelon, drinking, dancing, or making out.

"We're between the truck and the trees, Jeremy. No one can see us unless they physically walk around here. But I understand if you're scared…"

I feel kind of guilty daring him, because it always works so well on him it almost seems like cheating.

He grabs the front of my shirt and snatches me to within inches of his face. "I'm not scared." He licks my lips and releases me, then unbuttons his jeans and folds them down that sexy way that drives me so crazy.

"You have no idea how hot you look like this." I reach around and run a finger slowly up and down the exposed crack of his ass, watching in anticipation as his cock grows before my eyes. When his lips part and his head falls back, I drop to my knees and take him into my mouth.

My one goal is to get him to come just as hard and fast as I can. I cup his balls with the palm of one hand while reaching back with the middle finger and pressing firmly against his sensitive hole. I take his dick deep into my mouth, using my intimate knowledge of him to suck it the way he likes it best.

He shudders from the sudden sensory overload, grabbing onto my head with both hands and guiding my movements. The frantic noises he's working to keep at bay in the back of his throat are like a siren song to me, making me painfully hard. I want to make him so hot he has no choice but to cry out loud.

"Oh my God, Beck, that feels so good. Don't stop." His knees tremble with the strain as he strives toward his climax, every muscle tense. "Yeah, just like that." He looks down at me with fevered eyes, barely able to keep the lids from dropping shut. "I want to fuck you so bad... Please."

I know what he means. He's been dying to top me since the day we met, and now when he's in the throes of intense passion, that's what he's fantasizing about. It makes me feel a little bit guilty.

The thought of bottoming has never done anything for me. On the other hand, the control that comes with fucking someone, from owning them in that moment, has always been a total turn-on for me. In my fantasies, I'm always topping. When I watch porn, I'm zeroed in on the bottom, watching his facial expressions, enjoying the taking of his body. That's how it's always been, and it never really occurred to me that there was a flip side to that— another way of looking at it.

But now, with Jeremy standing over me giving me that pleading look that says he'd do anything to get inside me, to own me like I've owned him... It seems different. Especially after he teased me with it on the ride to the mountains.

He has no idea how close I came to pushing back onto him in that parking lot, especially when he really got his rhythm going and I could feel him almost breaching me. In that moment, my whole body felt what it might be like to have him there, and it was fucking amazing. Earth-shattering. I wanted it so much it scared me. He also has no idea that I fantasized about it over the weekend while we were making love. Now just the thought of giving in to him makes me so hot I could probably come at the slightest touch.

Feeling really vulnerable, I gaze up at him, pulling my mouth off of his dick just long enough to nod. "Okay." My voice is husky with desire. "I'll let you. Just not tonight."

Suddenly he's got my head in a crushing vice grip, steadying me while he fucks my mouth with frightening intensity, jamming his cock into the back of my throat over and over, stretching and bruising the tender flesh until I think I can't take any more. I push his hips away, trying to get air, just as he shoots what feels like a gallon of cum all over my face. Ribbons of the stuff drip down my cheeks and chin, cooling and thickening in the night air.

I pull the tail of my t-shirt up and use it to wipe my face clean, knowing I'll regret that decision in about three minutes. For now I'm horny enough not to care. Besides, I have a spare shirt in the truck.

I stand with a little help from the running board as Jeremy stuffs himself back into his jeans and zips up. He falls back against the truck door and lets out a huge, contented sigh.

"God, I love you," he groans. Then he tenses and stares wild-eyed at me, like he's just been shot. "I... Uh... I mean I love the way you suck cock. Shit. You know I didn't mean it that way."

He slumps, so adorably shamed by his own words I can't help but chuckle to myself. I wrap a hand around the back of his neck and pull him close, resting my forehead against his.

"Don't worry about it, Junior. I think it's sweet."

He grunts and pulls away abruptly, heading around to the tailgate, leaving me to wonder if I've said something wrong.

I take a moment to change into a slightly wrinkled but clean shirt and drop the cum-soaked one onto the floorboard.

"Let's get another beer," Jeremy says.

"I have to drive, so I'm not drinking any more. I'll have another when we get back to your parents' place if you want, alright?"

"Oh, okay." He looks disappointed.

"But here, you have one." I pull a can out of the cooler and pop the top for him.

"Are you sure it won't bother you? I don't want you to feel like my driver."

"It's already open. Go ahead, I don't mind. As long as you don't get sloppy drunk and puke all over my truck."

We sit for a while, listening to the music and swinging our legs, chatting idly about the antics going on around us and what the guys from school might be doing right now.

After a while, I start noticing that one of the jocks in the group crowded around the red truck directly across the clearing has got his eyes trained right on us. It strikes me as odd not only because it's the second time I've caught him staring, but also because his drunk girlfriend is on his lap, swinging her hair across his face and gyrating her hips in time with the music. If Jeremy was riding my lap like that, there's no way I could pay attention to anything else. So why is he staring so intently at us?

*Maybe he's gearing up to do a little gay bashing.*

Somehow, I don't think that's it. In fact, I'm starting to suspect it's got everything to do with Jeremy, and that I'm not going to like it one bit. Especially because the guy is totally Jeremy's type— a jock with killer muscles and boy-next-door good looks. My stomach

217

sinks at the thought of them being together, but curiosity gets the best of me, and I decide to test out my theory.

Staring unflinchingly at the jock, making sure he knows I'm looking at him, I reach over and run my hand slowly up Jeremy's thigh and all the way to his dick. It's such a direct and obvious challenge; I know Caleb would be proud. Jeremy looks surprised, but he recovers quickly and leans in to me with a smile, letting me have my way with his sweet mouth.

If anyone is watching, and I know for a fact that at least one person is, they don't have to wonder anymore if Jeremy and I are having sex. I've just answered that question beyond a shadow of a doubt.

I continue to watch the jock out of the corner of my eye, searching for a reaction. He doesn't disappoint.

Even from this distance, I can see his muscles tense. He stands abruptly, dumping the girl off his lap in the process. She squeals, but he doesn't pay her any attention. Instead, he levels a murderous glare at me before turning and throwing his beer bottle toward the woods, where it smashes against a tree and sends glass and rivulets of beer raining down onto his screaming friends.

"Hey, watch it Matt," one of his buddies yells, jumping up out of his lawn chair and shaking himself off. Most of the group is so drunk they just laugh and swipe at their clothing, several of the girls still squealing.

"This is bullshit!" Matt stalks away for a moment to collect himself, pacing the edge of the woods with his head in his hands. His girl approaches cautiously, touching him on the shoulder, but he shrugs her hand off, and she goes back to stand with some of the other girls.

"Damn," Jeremy remarks casually. "He seems pretty wasted, huh?"

"Appears so," I agree, wondering why he doesn't just come out with it. His vagueness only serves to make me suspicious.

*What if he only asked you here to make someone else jealous?*

The thought turns my stomach. Jeremy wouldn't do that, would he? He couldn't fake the kind of passion he has for me, could he?

I sit mulling over the disturbing thoughts for a while, getting more and more agitated with each passing moment. After a while, Jeremy grabs another beer from the cooler. "Open this for me?" He jumps off the tailgate. "I gotta go take a piss."

He's gone before I can even think to object, trotting off toward the woods. Would it have been crazy to insist on chaperoning him?

And then the unthinkable happens. Matt the pissed off jock follows Jeremy into the woods. Jealousy, hatred, suspicion and worry all combine inside me, a volatile mix that will explode if I don't get off my ass and do something about it.

I'm on my feet, making my way steadily toward the spot in the woods where the other two were heading. I'm half afraid of what I might find there, but I have to go. Dammit, I'm not some schmuck who's just going to sit around while this asshole tries to edge me out. And in a dark wood, no less.

*Fuck that.*

The woods are creepy, but I'm used to camping so it's no big deal for me, even with the sound of coyotes yipping in the distance.

They're probably just voicing their displeasure at being driven out of their territory tonight. At least there are no panthers screaming. Besides rattlesnakes, water moccasins and copperheads, the panther is the only indigenous animal that truly scares me. Their scream is so evocative of deranged desperation, like a crazy ghost lady haunting the woods looking for her long lost baby.

The mere memory of the sound sends goosebumps racing across my skin as I sneak through the pines, trying my best not to snap twigs under foot. The last thing I need to do is give myself away before I figure out what's going on between Jeremy and Matt.

When I spot them, I stand stock still and strain my ears to hear what they're saying. Fortunately for me, Matt's using his cell phone flashlight app for illumination, and their voices carry on the still night air.

"But I thought we'd hook up over the holidays." Matt's voice is pleading, which surprises me after the display of aggression he put on for the entire crowd. "I haven't seen you since graduation."

"We're both with someone, Matt. You brought a girl, and I brought a guy. That's the difference between you and me. You will never be out, and I am now. I'm sorry if you're unhappy—"

"What the fuck makes you think I'm unhappy, Miller?" His voice is angry, defensive. "I'm on the football team at Georgia, dating a smoking hot cheerleader, I'm in a frat... It's everything I ever wanted. What are you doing? Wrestling for a lame second-rate school and prancing around in public with some fag? What the hell happened to you?"

Jeremy shrugs. "I got what I wanted too, I guess. You and I just wanted different things, which was the whole problem from the start."

Matt wraps his arms around Jeremy's shoulders, his phone light shining down Jeremy's back and making it difficult for me to see anything but a swath of shirt and the ass of his jeans. "So after all we had, you can forget me just like that?"

"All we had?" He peels Matt's arms from around him and takes a step backward. "You had a popular girlfriend, and I had a dirty little secret to keep. You had the fucking homecoming crown and a beach party. I went stag and had a late-night breakfast with Eric at the Huddle House. Do I need to go on? *We* didn't have anything, Matt. *You* had it all."

"Don't be that way, Miller. You know what I'm talking about." He makes a move toward Jeremy, and Jeremy backs up again, brushing against the side of a tree and knocking a chunk of bark off.

I'm impressed with the way Jeremy's been handling this goon so far, but now it's time to step in. It only takes about three seconds for me to come up directly behind Jeremy and put my hands around his waist, dropping a kiss into the curve where his neck and shoulder meet. "Do you have a problem?" I ask Matt.

"This is between me and Jeremy." His face is smug, and it's obvious he thinks he's got some sort of right to be doing what he's doing.

*He thinks Jeremy will choose him.*

Jeremy looks up at me over his shoulder. "I can handle this myself, Beck."

"I know you can, baby." I tighten my grip on his waist. "But what kind of man would I be if I didn't make it clear to this asshole that you're with me now?" I look daggers at Matt, enjoying the sudden twitch at the corner of his mouth and the uncertainty in his eyes. "If you don't go back around to your side of the fire and quit bothering Jeremy, I'm going to beat the shit out of you. Then I'm going to make sure everyone here knows you're gay— including that smoking hot cheerleader girlfriend you're so proud of."

Matt backs away with a smirk, holding his hands up like I've just pulled a gun on him. "Hey man, I'm not gay."

"Then you should have no problem not trying to fuck my boyfriend." Not waiting for a response, I tug at Jeremy's waist just enough to get him moving, and we head back the way we came in. "Did you still have to take a piss?"

"Oh yeah," he says with a laugh. "Forgot about that."

"Yeah, I'll bet you did," I say humorlessly.

"Hey, I didn't plan on doing anything with him, Beck. I promise. I just—"

"Wanted to rub it in his face," I finish for him. "I get it, okay? And I don't blame you. He hurt you... used you."

I lead him to a tree and stand aside, doing a little impromptu stargazing to the familiar sound of urine spattering across dead leaves and puddling into the dirt. It sounds like he's evacuating about a twelve-pack of beer, though he's only had a couple.

When he's done, he jumps at me, throwing his arms around my neck and causing us both to lose our balance. We end up on the ground, and he covers my forehead and cheeks with sloppy kisses, laughing all the while. When his lips finally find mine in the dark, I roll him beneath me and kiss him back, wishing like hell we were somewhere else. Someplace we could do every last thing we want to each other, without fear of being caught or getting attacked by wild animals.

"Thank you," he says quietly, his lips touching the side of my throat. "You didn't have to do that. I owe you one."

"Why would you owe me anything? I did that for myself as much as for you."

He lifts his head and looks at me, his face obscured in shadow. "I figured you were just putting on. You know, trying to give him a good show for me. Make me look good."

"What?" I move my head to the side so that he's not in my shadow, letting the pale moonlight illuminate his face. "I meant what I said, Jeremy. Every bit of it. Why would you think I wasn't serious?"

He tries to look away, but I grasp his chin in my hand and gently force him to make eye contact.

"Because you called me your boyfriend."

"Well, I just assumed we were…" I wrack my brain trying to come up with the exact words that have passed between Jeremy and me about the nature of our relationship, and I realize that although I consider us to be officially dating, I've never actually said the words to him.

*Time to fix that.*

I push up, flipping my legs under me and straddling Jeremy's chest and upper arms, my hands resting on the ground on either side of his head. From the strangled sound of his laughter, I can tell I've got his chest constricted, so I ease up on it just a little, still keeping him immobilized.

"What the heck are you doing?" he asks, trying to squirm out from under me.

"Jeremy Miller…" I invoke my most serious tone. "Will you go steady with me?"

He kicks his legs, laughing all the while. "Stop fucking around, Beck. You're embarrassing the hell out of me."

"I'm not letting you up until you say yes." I scoot slightly lower, bending at the waist until my mouth is touching his, kissing him over and over until we're both breathing heavily.

"Yes," he whispers, the laughter forgotten. "Yes, I'll go steady with you."

"Good." I hop to my feet, grabbing him by the hand and helping him up. "Now we're officially boyfriends."

# 17

THE trailer park Jeremy grew up in is pretty depressing, with a crumbling laundromat and a cracked pool that should have been filled in long ago. A couple of dirty bums are sitting inside the laundromat, probably just to get out of the cold.

"The house has gotten a lot worse without me here," Jeremy whispers over his shoulder as we enter the front door of the trailer.

When I step across the threshold, my foot sinks a couple of inches with a crackling sound, and I hop quickly into the room to keep from going through the floor. The place smells like cigarette smoke, dust and mildew, with an unrecognizable chemical scent underlying it all.

Mounds of clothes, boxes and papers line the walls with no apparent organizational pattern. It's quiet except for the clicking of an ancient cuckoo clock hanging on the kitchen wall behind a folding table. A couple of lights burn overhead, but the low wattage bulbs illuminate very little. I think I'd be less creeped out in the pitch dark than in this sickly amber glow.

Jeremy looks back at me with a pained expression on his face, and I work hard to keep mine pleasant. He's been brave enough to bring me here, so the least I can do is not make him feel even shittier than he already does. As an afterthought, I grab his hand, lacing my fingers through his.

"Jeremy, baby? Is that you?" The nasally female voice comes from a darkened corner, and I have to do a double-take to see the woman sitting on the couch. Thin, frail, gaunt... Any weak adjective could probably describe her. She looks like she's about a breath away from disappearing altogether.

"Mama," he says, moving in to give the little woman a careful hug. "Um... this is Beck. The one I told you about. He's my—" He looks at me, as if for confirmation. "He's my boyfriend."

"Well, tell him to come over here and let me see him," she says. "It's too damn dark in here. Turn on some lights."

Jeremy flips a wall switch, brightening the room only marginally, and I inch closer to his mother. She's much younger than it would seem from her voice and posture, and her face is almost pretty beneath the smattering of sores and scabs across her cheeks. When she speaks, I can see that she's missing some teeth.

"Hi, Mrs. Miller." I reach out to shake her hand, my fingers trembling slightly. "Nice to finally meet you."

"Oh, he's so good looking, Jeremy." She raises her eyebrows, making him blush several shades of red. "And you're going to be a doctor?"

"Yes, ma'am. I've got four more years of school, though,

including this one."

"Wow, my little boy did good." She smooths a lock of graying hair back from her eyes. "I'm so proud he's finally found somebody who's good for him. This place, the people here… it's all a dead end for my sweet son."

"Mama, please." Jeremy stuffs his hands into his pockets.

"Really," she continues. "That Eric was nice enough, but he never did quite accept Jeremy for who he was. Always kept him at arm's length. And don't even get me started on Matt, the football player who thought he was God's gift to women. And apparently men, too. I never did like that boy. He's just as fake as his daddy. Using people for what they can do for him, but when it comes time to return the favor, where are they? Nowhere to be found. The bastards."

"Mama, we really don't want to hear about whatever creepy things you and Matt's dad have in your past."

Mrs. Miller grunts. "You know, adults have lives, too. You don't stop existing after thirty."

"I know that, Mama." Jeremy cuts his eyes in my direction. "I just have company, and I thought it was a little awkward with you talking about Matt and his dad, that's all. We kinda had a run-in with Matt tonight at the party."

"Oh yeah?" She leans forward. "What happened? Did you boys fight? I hope you gave that little shit what's coming to him."

"Ma, *please*…"

"Alright, fine. I'll behave." She smiles at me, tightening her lips down to hide what's left of her teeth. "Are you boys hungry? I think I've got some noodles in there, maybe some corn dogs. Or a peanut butter sandwich, if the bread's still good."

"No, thanks, Mrs. Miller." I rest a palm against my belly. "We ate dinner at the Huddle House, then we had a ton of watermelon."

"Still sticky." Jeremy laughs, pressing his hands together and pulling them apart. I resist the urge to lick his fingers to see if they still taste sweet.

"So… your dad's working tonight," Mrs. Miller tells Jeremy. "He may not come in at all."

"If we're lucky," he replies.

She frowns at him but doesn't say anything.

"Well, I think we'll go on back to my room. Goodnight, Ma." Jeremy takes me by the arm and pulls me all the way to a room halfway down the uncomfortably narrow hallway. Once inside, I can hear his sigh of relief. He clicks on a small lamp at the corner of the bookcase headboard, and that same dull yellow light washes over an unmade bed that nearly fills the room. "Okay, so that wasn't too terribly bad, right?"

"Not bad at all." I wrap my arms around him, feeling the tension drain from his body as he melts into me. "Calm down, Jeremy. Everything's good."

"Yeah?" His eyes are wide, his face hopeful.

"Yeah. Better than good. You know I'm crazy about you, right?" I sit down on the edge of the bed, but instead of being supported, my ass sinks down and the mattress sloshes up around me. "A freaking waterbed? Really? I haven't seen one of these in years."

"It's a hand-me-down from one of my mom's hippie cousins." Jeremy jumps into the bed, laughing as the mattress rolls beneath us. "Sorry about the sheets, man. They haven't been washed since before I left home. It's all how I left it, except my mom has stacked some boxes in here. Guess it's gonna be a storage room now."

"Does that bother you?" I ask, trying to read his face.

"Hell, no." He climbs up out of the mattress and straddles my lap, draping his arms over my shoulders and looking into my eyes. "I need to tell you something, now that you've been here." His voice sounds sad, and it's got me worrying about what he might say. "The truth is I don't ever plan on coming back here again. I wanted to say goodbye to my mom."

Just like that, tears well up in my eyes. "Jeremy, you can't mean that. She's your mom."

"Did you see her? She's half gone, strung out on meth. She doesn't even know what's going on most of the time. I think she sleeps with the dealers in the trailer park to get her drugs, because she sure as shit doesn't have any money. This place is falling down. My dad is a fucking bastard, Beck. Hopefully, you won't ever even have to meet him. He's nothing but a drunk. Plays poker for a living, but he doesn't know when to stop. People have come here looking for him. People with guns. He's hardly ever here, though, and when he is, he usually finds some reason to beat the shit out of either me or my mom. Usually her, because I haven't hung around long enough since I hit sixteen. I don't expect you to understand where I'm coming from, because you have a normal family, but I've been waiting for the chance to get out for a long time. When I leave here in the morning, I don't care if I ever see this miserable place again. It drains the fucking soul out of me."

When he stops talking, I'm speechless. My eyes are full of

229

unshed tears, but Jeremy's are dry. He's so matter-of-fact about the whole thing it's almost scary. How much hell do you have to live through before you get to the point that you can discuss your mom whoring for meth and your dad beating you like it's nothing?

*He's numb.*

"I'm glad I got to show you where I grew up," he continues in that same bland way. "But I don't want you to think of me this way, okay? I don't want you to picture me in this place. I'm starting a new life, and pretty soon it will be as if this part of my life never existed."

"How did you stand it?"

"I stayed gone a lot. Spent a lot of weekends at Eric's house. I got a job down at the dollar store and saved up enough money to buy a car when I turned sixteen. Hell, sometimes when the weather was decent, I even slept in that car just to keep from coming home." He's thoughtful for a moment. "My mom said Eric never truly accepted me... Maybe she's right. Probably is, I don't know. But it was better than this."

I nod silently. There's not much I can say without coming across as condescending, so I just roll back into the bed and pull him with me.

"Fuck!" Every muscle in my body spasms when my back hits the water mattress. "Why is this bed so cold? Even through the covers, it's like sleeping on ice."

"Yeah, the heater goes in and out. Mostly out. We'll just have to bundle up." Without looking, he reaches up into one of the empty cubby holes in the bookcase headboard. "Crap. I forgot Mr. Floppy is in my dorm room. I used to never go anywhere without him."

I kiss his hair and cinch him up even closer to my body. "I'll be Mr. Floppy tonight."

"I can't believe you just said that. Do you know how incredibly bad that sounds?" Jeremy's entire frame quakes with silent laughter.

"Yeah, well, if you tell anyone I said it, I'll deny it. And then I'll whip your ass." As soon as the words are out of my mouth, I feel ashamed. I guess joking about ass whippings doesn't seem quite as funny when your boyfriend has just confessed he's been beaten by his father all of his life.

Jeremy doesn't even seem to notice the slip. He hugs me and kisses me on the lips. "I'll never tell. Your secret is safe with me, Mr. Floppy."

I kiss him back, and soon we're engaged in a full-on kiss fest. We don't move past the kissing, though. Making out like a couple of virgins is more than enough tonight in this dank house, sloshing around on the cold bed where he spent his teenage years.

We trade kisses for what seems like hours, licking and touching tongues, sucking each other's lips. The intensity rises and falls like a tide, lulling us both to the fuzzy edge of sleep. Every now and then, Jeremy stops moving and falls heavily against me, his lips slack and lifeless. *Asleep.* I nudge him, startling him awake, and his kisses become frantic. Sometimes he has to nudge me, and I spring back into fevered action, praying I haven't been unconscious for too long, or snored or drooled on him. It's a surreal, raw kind of experience. We're both exhausted, but neither one of us can give it up.

I'm not aware of the exact moment the kissing finally stops for good, but when I wake sometime in the middle of the night, sprawled out and shivering on his frozen pond of a bed, Jeremy isn't with me. Voices are coming from somewhere else in the house.

"No fucking respect." The man's voice is slurred, so it doesn't take much of an IQ to figure out it's Jeremy's dad. "I told you not to bring anybody in here."

"And I told you we came to see Mama. She wanted to meet him. We'll be out of here in the morning."

"What's it coming to when a man can't even say what's what in his own goddamn house?" Mr. Miller's voice gets louder, only a couple of volume ticks from belligerent.

I roll awkwardly out of the waterbed and slip my jeans on, zipping them as I enter the hallway. Half asleep, I scrub against the wall, loosening even more of the peeling wallpaper.

As I emerge from the darkness, Jeremy and his dad are standing near the sofa, and his mom is passed out on the sofa right where we left her when we went to bed.

Jeremy is in boxer briefs, his dad in a rumpled plaid shirt and khakis that are so worn and stretched he looks like he has camel knees. Both men look at me at the same time, and I'm struck dumb by how much the son looks like the father.

"Beck." Jeremy comes anxiously toward me but not close enough to touch. "I didn't mean to wake you."

His father smirks, letting his gaze slide slowly down my body and back up.

I don't know who he thinks he's dealing with, but being an experienced athlete, I know a psych-out when I see it. I can also smell fear from a mile away. The bastard is intimidated.

Never have I been more grateful for my body and size than I

am at this moment. I take full advantage, tightening my core and meeting his gaze straight on. After years of systematic abuse, he may be able to intimidate his son, but he's nothing to me.

"It's okay, baby." I move in behind Jeremy and snake an arm possessively around his waist. "I heard yelling, and I wanted to make sure you were alright."

I'm pushing some serious boundaries right now, blatantly declaring our relationship to his father, touching him intimately in front of the man. There's no telling how either of them will react, but dammit I'm not backing down.

As of tonight, I've officially claimed Jeremy. He's mine to protect now.

From the look of shock on Jeremy's father's face, I'd bet any amount of money he had no idea his son was even gay. Much less that he was sleeping with a half-naked man tonight in his childhood bedroom.

"You have got to be shitting me," his father says with a condescending chuckle that makes me want to flatten his pathetic ass. "I can't believe it. As many people told me you were a goddamn queer, and I stuck up for you... This is how you repay me? By bringing this—" He gestures at me, unable to meet my eyes or finish his sentence.

As raging mad as I am, I manage to keep my emotions in check. As always. I learned a long time ago that once you lose control in a situation, it's almost impossible to get it back.

"It doesn't have anything to do with you, Daddy." Jeremy stiffens even more, and I rub the small of his back ever so gently with the back of my hand. "Beck is my boyfriend. We're in a relationship, and I wanted him to meet Mama before I go. You won't have to see me— us— ever again."

"What are you thinking, Jeremy? I thought you were going to college for an education. Not—" His father's face reddens with anger, and he finally looks directly at my face. "What the hell have you done to my son? You think you can just waltz up and take what belongs to another man? Tear his family apart? Pervert his only son?"

He suddenly lurches forward, reaching out for Jeremy and trying to pull him out of my grasp.

My head spins, and all I can see is Jeremy as a young boy being hit by his father, wondering why the person he should be able to trust to protect him is the one who's hurting him. The image of that poor little boy curled up terrified in bed with nothing but a stuffed dog for comfort is all it takes to change my gears. My heart squeezes until I think it's going to break, and I shift from reserved defensiveness down into pure aggression.

I shove Jeremy out of the way before anyone can blink, twisting my hand into his dad's shirt collar and backing him across the room. When his back hits the cheap paneled wall, the whole room shakes. Pictures fall to the floor and a lamp topples, but Jeremy's mother remains unconscious on the sofa.

"Listen carefully," I tell his dad through clenched teeth. "You may be able to intimidate a woman and young boys, but with me you've broken off more than you can handle. I'm not a violent person, but when I think about the way you've treated your family, it makes me want to hurt you in a really bad way. So if you don't want to have to depend on your unconscious wife to call 911 to save your sorry ass, you'd better calm down."

I glance at Jeremy, who doesn't look like he has any plans to stop me from manhandling his dad. "Do you need anything out of here before we leave?" I ask him.

"Nope," he says. "Just our clothes. I'll go get them. Don't let go."

"Alright." I turn my attention back to his dad. "Well, Mr. Miller, you're going to get what you want. We're leaving, but I wish you could somehow realize what you've given up here tonight."

Jeremy returns in a heartbeat with our clothes, and I let go of his dad long enough to get dressed. He doesn't try to move. Just stands there watching us. Jeremy bends over his mom on the sofa and kisses her cheek. "Bye, Mama," he whispers.

Then he looks up at me, the glisten of tears in his blue eyes, and yells, "Go! Your keys are in your pocket."

I don't have time to think, only react to the urgency in Jeremy's voice. Like a referee's whistle has just been blown, I run toward the door, leaping over the weak spot in the threshold and landing on the deck. Jeremy is right behind me as I swing off the steps and open my truck door. By the time I crank up, Jeremy is seated on the passenger side.

"Go!" he yells again, and I tear backwards out of the yard, not knowing why I'm in such a hurry.

I shift the truck into drive and press the gas, fishtailing down the worn asphalt roadway toward the front of the trailer park. Just as I pass the third house from Jeremy's a loud sound cracks through the night, and glass shatters down onto my back and shoulders.

"Fuck! Is he shooting at us?"

"Go!" Jeremy screams for the third time, and I don't give him

235

the chance to do it again. I'm out of that trailer park before another bullet can find us, my heart hammering in my chest.

Cold air blows in through the now-nonexistent back glass. I crank the heater to try to offset it, silently thanking Mother Nature for the unseasonably warm weather she's been bestowing on us this year. When I reach a convenience store far away from Jeremy's trailer park, I park in an inconspicuous spot near the back of the building and go in to find trash bags and duct tape.

Jeremy can't stop apologizing, and I feel really bad for him. "It's not your fault, Jeremy," I assure him. "Let's just get this cleaned up and get out of town, okay?"

After we get the hole covered and sealed, Jeremy directs me to a car wash with a vacuum cleaner, where we take turns vacuuming out the glass.

Back out on the highway, I begin to relax. Then, against all logic, I get the giggles. Jeremy stares at me for a minute before joining in.

"Jesus, Jeremy," I say through the laughter. "Why didn't you tell me your old man had a gun and wasn't afraid to use it? I might have gone easier on him. Maybe not pawed all over you in front of him or slammed the man up against the wall."

"Would it have made any difference?"

"Not in what I said. But I might have called it in over the telephone instead of telling him in person." I'm joking, but there is definitely a grain of truth in it.

"He wasn't trying to hurt us. He just wanted to scare you."

"Did you have any idea he might pull a gun?"

"Kinda. But I didn't want to give him the idea if he hadn't

already thought of it, so I just kept my mouth shut. Besides that, I never would've expected him to pull the trigger. You really pissed him off, I guess."

"Well, what do you expect? I'm perverting his only son!"

Jeremy's laughter subsides, and he turns serious. "I'm really sorry, Beck. This whole trip has been nothing but a nightmare for you. First you had to come out to your friends at the mountain house, then you got in an argument with my ex, and now you've been shot at. That's too much drama. You don't need that shit in your life, and it's all because of me."

"In a way, you're right. It is a lot of drama, and it is because of you, but you're looking at it in the wrong way."

His eyes widen, a glimmer of hope in them now. He's waiting for me to take some of the weight off his shoulders, and I want to do that more than anything. I can't stand to see his eyes so sad. I think for a moment, trying to come up with the best way to explain.

"First of all," I begin, "my friends were going to have to find out about me sooner or later. And if you remember, the mountain house was my idea. I promised you we'd be together, and then I let things go too far with Anna before I said something. So you were actually on the receiving end there. As for your ex..." I chuckle quietly. "I enjoyed that. I think when you're in a relationship with someone— anyone— you're going to have stuff like that come up. I mean, you've already had to deal with knowing about me and Dan."

He nods, the ghost of a smile playing at his lips.

"Now your father and his gun were a little excessive, I'll admit. But that wasn't your fault. He's a loose cannon, and you're cutting ties with him. Hell, what if he'd shot at you when I wasn't there? I'm just glad I could use my amazingly awesome stunt driving skills to save your life."

That at least coaxes a chuckle out of him. "How can you keep so positive all the time? It blows my mind."

"Oh, I get wound up plenty. But I just try to step back and see things for what they are, that's all. I think we've been through the worst of it on this road trip. Everything's not going to be smooth sailing, you know. We still have to come out to my family, and I assure you that is not going to be pretty. Hopefully there won't be any guns involved, but there may be some screaming, and possibly even some disowning."

"Really? You think your family would disown you?"

"It's always a possibility. Do you think you can handle that for me? Because I think I've just shown how much I'm willing to handle for you."

"I can handle it. You're my boyfriend, Beck. That means more to me than you'll ever know."

"I think I have some idea. Don't forget I've never had a boyfriend, either. I'm ready to take on just about anything for that— except maybe losing my scholarship. Not quite ready for that yet if it can be avoided." I reach over and pull his head down into my lap. "Now get over here and act like a proper boyfriend; take a nap in my lap while I drive."

# 18

"So tonight's pretty special, huh?" Gretchen runs to the kitchen, grabs a couple of wine glasses and sets them on the table next to the place settings that are already there.

"Yeah." I don't say more, because lately I've gotten skittish around Gretchen. She's been so negative that I've had to close myself off to her. I'd just rather keep things to myself if I'm going to get a lecture or be made to feel stupid.

"What's the occasion?"

"Nothing," I say, straightening the napkins beside the plates.

"Beck, I'm sorry. I know it's too little too late, but I understand how you feel now." She bites her lip and twists her long braid around her index finger. "If I was in love and someone tried to tell me I couldn't be... Well, that's just crazy. I mean first of all, it wouldn't work."

"I'm moving out." My voice is barely above a whisper. "This

239

group arrangement isn't really working for me anymore. It's time I started building a real life for myself."

"I don't blame you. I've meddled in your business, pushed my opinions on you when I should have just been happy for you."

"You told me what you thought was best for me, and I appreciate it."

"But I was wrong," she says.

"Yeah, you were wrong. Hell, I was wrong, too. But now I can see what I was missing." I smile, feeling a little more relaxed now. "I don't know how far Jeremy and I can go together. He's pretty immature in some ways, but only because he's young. And let's not forget how rigid I can be. You know I have a tendency to get tunnel vision."

"Those sound like things that can be worked out."

"Yeah, I think so. But the point is, even if Jeremy and I were to break up tomorrow, I still need to make a change for myself. There's more to life than winning medals, being popular, and having someone else pay for my school. I'm starting to think that the easiest road is not always the best one to take, but I wish like hell it was."

"So are you going to tell the coach?"

"Yep. Jeremy doesn't know it yet, though. That's kinda what this dinner is about." I run my hands through my hair and cast a skeptical eye toward the table. "I want it to be special, but not too cheesy. I asked Jeremy to go steady with me on Labor Day, and I guess this is the official boyfriend dinner." I can't help but laugh out loud at myself. "I've lost it, haven't I?"

"No," she says, patting me on the arm. "You're just in love, hon."

"Um… I wouldn't go that far." But the heat I feel creeping into my face says otherwise.

She smiles knowingly. "Can I at least help you? What are you cooking?"

"Mario's Italian takeout."

"Oh. Well, that's easy."

"My kind of cooking. Just dump it into the plate, and it's ready. It'll be a late dinner, though. Jeremy had a note in his locker today that said to be in the wrestling office at nine tonight. Assistant Coach Bradley called a meeting with some of the new guys. Sucks for my plans, but I'm dealing with it the best I can. Picking up the food at eight-thirty. We can reheat if we have to."

Gretchen frowns. "Why such a late meeting? That coach should be horsewhipped."

"He had some function to go to and couldn't get back till then. I don't know why he couldn't have just postponed it until tomorrow, because he's cutting into my time. But it'll be okay. Jeremy's gonna sleep over."

*And I'm going to bottom for the first time ever.*

I place a big red envelope in the middle of the table, propped against the flower bowl. There's a card for Jeremy inside, and also a condom. They didn't have any *I'm ready to let you fuck me* cards at the drugstore, so I'm hoping he'll understand the symbolism.

241

# 19

*(JEREMY)*

The gym is empty at this time of evening. I've never seen it this way, and it's got me pretty creeped out. In the absence of any noise, I can almost imagine the ghosts of past athletes playing here all around me. Invisible and inaudible, but here just the same. Or maybe they come out after all of the doors are locked and the lights turned off.

The sound of my sneaker squeaking against the polished wood floor makes me jump.

*I wish Beck was here.*

We need to hurry up and get this stupid meeting over with so I can meet him at his apartment for dinner. It's going to be strange eating in together like a real couple. I didn't even do that with my own family. Just grabbed something out of the fridge when I was hungry, or picked up some fast food in town.

I just hope this meeting isn't bad. If I get kicked off the team, I'm not going to be in the best mood to eat dinner, and I definitely don't want to bum Beck out. He had to deal with enough negativity over the holidays to last a good long while.

I practically run through the locker room to get to the wing of offices on the other side. Talk about eerie, that place is even worse than the gym. It's almost completely dark, and the locker room smell seems somehow worse when there's nobody here to cause it.

The door swings shut behind me as I emerge into the office wing. I've only been here once before, but I remember the way, taking a right and then a left before reaching my destination. All of the offices are dark except the one Coach Roberts and Assistant Coach Bradley share.

I knock hesitantly on the closed door, unable to tell if there's anyone inside with the blinds closed.

"Come in," calls a voice from inside the office.

When I open the door, relief washes over me at finally laying eyes on another human being. My muscles unclench, and I smile at the assistant coach, who is sitting at the desk doing something on his laptop.

The overhead fluorescents are off, but a lamp glows from an end table near the window. I take the chair next to it, picking up a Muscle Guy magazine from the table and flipping through it.

In this low light, the coach's hair looks darker than its usual caramel blonde, the hollows under his eyes more pronounced. He looks young, not much past thirty. Funny I've never really paid him that much attention. He's always just kind of faded into the background.

When he doesn't even glance up at me, I decide I'll have to be the one to break the awkward silence. "Um… You wanted to see me, Coach?"

"Yes," he says, still not looking at me. "How are you?"

I flip the magazine pages, not really seeing them. "Fine, Coach. Where's everyone else?"

He shrugs, tenting his fingers in front of his chin and finally resting his watery blue gaze on me. "Jeremy, I invited you here because I have a personal matter to discuss with you, and I didn't want to say that in the note. For your privacy."

"Yes, sir." I clear my throat, thinking this is seeming more and more like I'm about to be cut from the wrestling program. That would make me the first to be let go.

*Talk about embarrassing…*

"How badly do you want to stay on the team, son? Are you serious about having a college wrestling career?"

My heart rate picks up. "Yes, sir. Very serious. I know I'm came from a crappy wrestling program, but I'm working hard and getting better every day. And I'll work even harder on my attitude. Please just give me another chance."

"Well, I'm glad to see you do value your place here. But how about your friend Beck? How badly do you think he wants to stay on the team? Doesn't he have a full wrestling scholarship?"

"Uh… Yes, sir." I'm shaking now, mostly on the inside, but I can feel it making its way to the surface as confusion sets in.

Why would he be asking me about Beck's scholarship? As far as he knows, Beck is only my Monday mentor.

"What would you say if I told you that Beck's scholarship is in jeopardy? That any minute it could be taken away from him... Would you try to help your friend? Or would you just let it happen?"

*Fuck. What the hell does he know? And how?*

"Sir, if Caleb has been saying things, you ought to know he's sort of mad at me and Beck. I wouldn't put it past him to make something up."

The coach perks up slightly. "That's interesting. Why is Caleb mad at the two of you, and what do you think he might have told me?"

"Nothing. I was just saying..." I squirm in my seat, wishing I'd kept my big mouth shut about Caleb.

I'm starting to feel like a character in an interrogation room on one of those TV crime dramas, and it's that potentially self-incriminating moment when I'm supposed to say, *I need to speak to my lawyer.* Only I don't have a lawyer, and the man sitting across from me is not a cop. He's an unimposing wrestling coach with a pleasant face, and now he's piercing me with his eyes, trying to draw something out of me about Beck.

*But why?*

It occurs to me that he's probably bluffing. If he had any real evidence on Beck, he wouldn't have to drag me down here in the middle of the night to answer his cryptic questions. If I play my cards right, I can probably just fake ignorance and this will all blow over.

"You know," he says, watching his finger as he drags it along the edge of the desk. "Sometimes the people who care about us can hurt us more than our worst enemy ever could."

I drop the magazine onto the table and move to the edge of

my seat, trying not to think about my dad after a statement like that. My temper is starting to stand up and take notice of the situation, and I'm about thirty seconds away from storming out of here. Or worse.

*Fuck my dad, and fuck coach Bradley. I don't have to take this.*

"I don't understand what you're getting at, Coach Bradley, but it's late. If you're not planning on making a point anytime soon, I have a date to get to."

"A date, huh?" He muses silently for a moment. "I'm sorry, Jeremy. I don't mean to beat around the bush, but I have something uncomfortable to talk to you about, and it's hard to come up with the right words to say."

The coach stares at me through slotted eyes for a moment before tapping the space bar on his laptop and spinning it around so that it's facing me.

What I see on the computer screen makes my blood run cold.

A slightly grainy video is playing on the screen. Beck has me up against the wall, handling me in that rough, angry way that makes my stomach quiver. But watching the scene playing out on video, seeing it in third person and knowing we've been discovered, fills me with a profound sense of shame unlike any I've ever felt before.

I abused my power over Beck that day, goading him into doing something stupid just to boost my own ego, and now it's coming back to bite us both in the ass.

"Turn it off," I choke out, reeling from shame and fear, breathing so fast I'm nearly hyperventilating. "Please. I've seen enough."

Coach Bradley doesn't turn it off, though. He just continues talking in that same calm voice.

"I have to hand it to you, Jeremy. You're a very persuasive boy. Bagging such a high profile athlete is impressive enough, but to convince him to risk everything he's worked for just to get a cheap thrill in the locker room..." He shakes his head in disbelief, but there's a cruel smile curling the corners of his lips.

*Is he enjoying this?*

"How could you record us in the locker rooms? Isn't that illegal? What, were you recording naked guys to get off on?"

"Of course not. How rude to accuse me of something like that." He shrugs. "For your information, Coach Roberts gave the okay. We've had some stealing going on, stuff disappearing from people's bags and lockers. We had to do something to get to the bottom of it. Most of the time, sports teams try to police their own to keep the authorities out of it, for the good of the team and the members. Jeremy, I'm not a mean person. I haven't shown this to anyone. Not yet."

"Please turn it off." I'm no longer looking at the screen, but the sound of Beck fucking me senseless against the locker room wall is enough to turn my stomach.

Finally, I lean forward and hit the space bar myself, and the video freezes.

"You're not going to tell anyone about Beck, are you?" I'm about a breath away from dropping to my knees and begging. "I don't care if anybody knows about me, but Beck shouldn't be punished for something I caused."

The coach muses for a moment, running his fingertips in small circles over the stubble on his jaw. "I don't know. Beck may not have been crazy about putting on a porn show in the locker room, but that doesn't change the fact that he's queer, now does it? I feel like maybe it's my duty to report something like this. The team members deserve to know who they're showering with and getting undressed in front of."

"It's not like that!" I jump up from my chair and lean across his desk, trying to burn him with a glare. "Just because we're gay doesn't make us perverts. We just like each other, that's all." I drop back into my seat, on the verge of tears now. "He's not going to be messing with anyone else, Coach. That wasn't just some random hookup in the locker room. He's my boyfriend."

That last word does bring the tears, though I'm able to get them under control before more than a few slide down my cheeks.

"Hey, don't cry, Jeremy. I'm on your side." Coach Bradley grabs a tissue from the box on the desk and hands it to me. "In fact, just between you and me, I don't mind a little guy on guy action. I've been with boys before. No big deal." He frowns and rests his forehead in his hand for a moment, contemplating. "This is really hard for me. Do you understand that? I have a job to do, and I don't know if it would be ethical of me to keep Beck's secret. He's on scholarship, and the school frowns on stuff like this. Have you seen on the news lately what's been happening to teachers and school officials who have turned a blind eye to sexual misconduct? I'd probably lose my job if they found out I knew and didn't tell."

I'm staring silently at him now, my brain swirling, trying to make sense of what he's saying. His whole argument is starting to sound strange to me, and it's making me more nervous by the minute. Why didn't he just come forward with the video in the first place instead of asking to meet with me? And at this time of night?

I look around the shadowy room, suddenly and keenly aware of the fact that Coach Bradley and I are the only two people in the entire building.

"I like you a lot, Jeremy, and I don't want Beck to lose his scholarship any more than you do." He turns the laptop back around and starts the video up again, watching a little too intently. "You're both young, sexy guys who have everything going for you. If I was a student here, it could just as easily have been you and me on this video." He drops his hand to his leg, almost touching his dick, and sighs. "I didn't ask to see this video. But now that I have, I just don't know if keeping it a secret is worth risking my job over." He cocks his head to the side and smiles. "Looks like Beck has found something that's worth risking everything. Maybe you could give me something to make my risk worth it, too."

My stomach churns, and the tang of bile burns my throat. I blink three times before I can will my mouth to open to try to speak, but nothing comes out.

"Jeremy, I know you feel terrible about causing this mess for your boyfriend, but you do have the power to make it right."

I know what he's doing— what he's asking for without technically asking. It's more than clear from the way he's watching the video and the way he's looking at me. His carefully crafted proposition puts the full responsibility of action on me, making me the instigator and leaving himself an out— the possibility of claiming that I've misunderstood his intent.

But I haven't misunderstood. I'm certain of it.

The creeping burn is back, making its way slowly across my

shoulders and all the way down my spine, up my neck and onto my scalp. My whole body is tingling with an anger that seems to have a mind of its own. I'm just about to let it loose, but the thought of Beck losing his scholarship because of this stops me. He'd blame me, no doubt, and the worst part is he'd be justified.

*And after everything that happened this past weekend...*

I lean over, resting my elbows on my knees and choking out a sob that's as wretched as they come. "I finally get a boyfriend, and then I go and fuck it all up. If I hadn't pushed him... Gretchen was so right about me. I'm a selfish prick, and I don't deserve him."

"Aw, Jeremy," Coach Bradley says quietly. "Don't be so sad. Come here." He pats his lap. "Come put your head right here, boy. It's gonna be alright. You and I can work through this thing together, help each other out. Beck doesn't even have to know how close he came to losing everything. You can be the perfect little boyfriend and make it all go away."

I move like an unoiled tin man, hitching my way over to his chair and dropping to my knees. It feels like I'm lowering my head to a chopping block rather than a warm lap, but his hand is gentle as he runs his fingers through my hair, shushing me softly.

"Jeremy, please don't let it be weird between us. I care about you, but I can't risk my job for nothing. It wouldn't be fair. And besides, there's nothing wrong with a little harmless fun between friends, right?"

A whimper escapes my lips as he takes my head firmly between his hands and rubs the side of my face against his erection. It's obvious from the way his bulge tents the fabric of his lose shorts that he's not wearing any underwear. In one fluid movement, he lowers the elastic band of his shorts and releases his cock, groaning as it bounces warmly against my cheek, smearing a streak of pre-cum onto my skin. Humiliation washes over me as he guides my head around and pushes insistently into my mouth. In that excruciating moment, I make the decision to do whatever he wants, whatever will save my boyfriend from the awful thing I've done to him.

*This is nothing. It will all be over soon, and Beck will never know.*

# 20

*(BECK)*

WAITING for Jeremy has me tied up in knots. He's excessively late, and he hasn't even called. I've never worried about a guy like this before, and I don't like it one little bit. In fact, it's got me rethinking my decision to date at all. I've had twenty plus possible scenarios running through my head, and none of them are good.

"Chill out, Beck," Gretchen says, pausing the horror movie that's playing on the living room TV. "You're wearing a hole in the carpet with all of the pacing you're doing. Why don't you just call him?"

"I have. Multiple times," I admit with an embarrassed grin. "It just keeps going to voicemail."

"Well, I'm sure there's an explanation. If I were you, I'd just sit down and enjoy the movie. Nothing like gratuitous sex and violence to get your mind off of your troubles. He'll get in touch when he's ready."

Truck pops up from Gretchen's lap, where he's been enjoying a head massage. "Are you saying if I was supposed to meet you for a romantic dinner and didn't show up, you'd just ignore it? Beck's got candles and wine and shit in the dining room, and Jeremy hasn't even bothered to call and say he's late. Even if he forgot his phone or something, he could use the phone in the coach's office. I've done it myself."

"Jeremy doesn't know how much trouble Beck's gone to," Gretchen counters. "It's supposed to be a surprise."

Truck just shakes his head. "I've got a bad feeling that something's not right. He could be lying bloody by the road somewhere, and you think Beck ought to just sit down and watch a movie? That's pretty cold, babe."

Before Truck has even finished his sentence, I'm already grabbing my hoodie from the coat rack in the foyer and heading out the door to go to Jeremy's dorm room. I don't have time to consider options anymore, because it's after eleven, and the dorms go on lock-down at midnight.

"Where's Jeremy?" I demand as soon as Seth opens their door. He's barefoot in a t-shirt and sweats, and his sketch pad and pencils are scattered out on his bed.

His brows draw together in confusion. "I assumed he was with you. He said something about a wrestling meeting."

"Yeah, he was supposed to meet with the coach at nine, but he should have been done with that a long time ago. I offered to go with him, but he said no. The coaches have been a little down on him for being reckless and not following the rules— you know how he is. I think he was afraid he was going to get kicked off the team."

Seth nods. "He's so proud, he'd rather die than let you see something like that if he could help it."

My head spins when I start considering all of the possibilities. "Oh, crap. What if he did get kicked off? He might do something stupid, especially with that temper. Do you have any idea where he might go if he was upset?"

"Uh, maybe Dan's?" He winces as soon as the words are out of his mouth, because he knows exactly what I'm thinking.

*Please don't let it be that. But please let him be safe.*

We both take off up the stairs without a word, each of us trying to be the first to reach Dan's room, and Seth yelps as I step on his bare toes when he tries to overtake me in the hallway. He's running like he's afraid someone's about to get hurt. When Dan answers the door, Seth squeezes between us and asks in a quiet voice if Jeremy has been there.

"I haven't seen him," Dan says, throwing his door wide, purposely letting us see inside. He's wearing nothing but a pair of boxers, and judging from his foggy-eyed appearance, he's just been asleep. His roommate glances up from his desk and fixes us with a look of undisguised annoyance, so Dan steps out into the relative privacy of the hallway, pulling the door to behind him.

"Really, guys, I haven't talked to him at all," Dan assures us after I've filled him in on the situation. "I think there was something wrong with the tacos in the cafeteria today, because I've felt a little sick all afternoon. I told you I didn't feel well, Seth. I went to bed before nine, and you know I never do that."

"It's true," Seth says to me.

Dan is unable to come up with any places he thinks Jeremy might have gone after his meeting, and we're all drawing a blank about what to do next. By the time we get back to the room, Seth and I are both spouting off ridiculous ideas, and the only thing that seems to make sense is that he might go to Hoppers. Which worries me for several reasons I'd rather not think about.

"We'll stay here until almost midnight just in case he shows up," I tell Seth. "Then we'll slip out just as they're locking the doors and head to the club. Grab a change of clothes and your things. You can spend the night at my place."

Seth looks horrified at the idea of sleeping at my apartment, but he agrees nonetheless. "Okay, Beck. Whatever you think."

I glance at my phone, checking to see if I've somehow missed a call or text, and noting that it's only twenty minutes until lock-down. Seth starts running his mouth in the annoying way that he does, and I let my mind wander, barely registering the hypnotic sounds of dorm life that I'd all but forgotten since freshman year— water running in the pipes, slamming doors, rubber soles on linoleum, and the occasional muffled voice or mystery squeak. It's amazing how noisy people can be when they think they're being quiet.

After about five minutes, the bathroom door opens, and Jeremy walks out with a towel wrapped around his hips. Droplets of water cling to his upper body, his wet hair curling at the ends. Even as frazzled as my nerves are, the sight of his svelte, almost-naked body causes a stir in my pants.

"Uh, hey..." he mumbles, staring at me with wide, startled

"What the hell, Jeremy?" Seth jumps up and rushes him, momentarily blocking my view of his face. "We were worried about you. Where have you been? Did you just get here? You must have slipped in while we were at Dan's room. Why do you want to scare the shit out of us like that?"

"Beck..." He ignores Seth's jabbering, pushing past him to get to me, his eyes locking in on mine like we're the only two people in the room. "I was gonna call you tomorrow. It was late, so I figured you were in bed."

*Amazing. How can he be so nonchalant?*

"It's okay, Junior." I hold up my hand to silence him, a confusing wave of relief and humiliation numbing my body and mind. "I'm just glad you're not bleeding by the side of the road somewhere. Now if everything's okay, I'll just go on back to my side of town."

*And put away the stupid fucking candles and wine before anyone else sees.*

"Wait! Don't go." Jeremy says, going from aloof to frantic within seconds. "Take off your clothes and come to bed with me."

"Oh, brother." Seth falls onto his bed face first, groaning into the pillow. "Do you guys have to torture me with your gushy man love when I have no one? Should I put my earbuds in to block out the noises?"

"I don't mean it like that," Jeremy says. "I just want Beck to sleep with me tonight." He beseeches me silently with his eyes.

His behavior is more than suspect. The fact that he stood me up and didn't call me is ravaging my pride even as I stand looking at him, but it's almost impossible for me to resist that sweet face. He's needy in a way I've only seen him once before, at his parent's trailer in Blackwood. And this is worse.

Maybe he did get let go from the team. It's difficult not to ask for an explanation, but I've learned enough about Jeremy to know that asking will get me nowhere. He's got secrets trapped in that pretty head of his, and I just have to trust that he'll share them when he gets ready. Otherwise, I'll always be on the outside to some extent, and that's somewhere I really don't want to be.

As I strip down to my underwear, I catch Seth looking at me, face slack and eyes wide. "I'll get the light." He swallows hard. "And my earbuds."

After Seth has turned off the light, throwing the room into almost complete darkness, Jeremy slides into bed beside me and pulls the covers over our bodies. His skin is cool and shower soft, scented with a mixture of coconut body wash and toothpaste. He wraps his arms around my waist and runs his fingertips down my spine, but as soon as he reaches my underwear, he grunts.

"I said take off your clothes," he whispers where only I can hear. Then he's dragging my boxers down my legs, using both his hands and feet, kicking them down between the covers at the bottom of the bed where I'll have to search for them later.

There's no doubt that he's completely naked already. I can feel every inch of his smooth skin against mine, including the erection that moves against my thigh as he slides slowly down my body. The feel of him takes my breath away. He's all arms and legs and softness rubbing over me and against me, working his way down in the darkness, closing his lips over my nipple and sucking with a fervor that's got my hips moving of their own volition. He takes it into his mouth, teasing it with his tongue until I have the deepest urge to cry out. I clench my jaws together and listen out for Seth in the next bed, hoping he can't hear the rustling of our bodies or the gentle sucking noises. Then Jeremy scrapes his teeth down the sides of my already sensitive nipple, and I do cry out. I can't help it.

Seth flops loudly in his bed, and the volume of the tinny music coming from his headphones increases. Jeremy reaches up and seals his hand over my mouth, keeping me quiet as he swaps sides and gives the other nipple the same treatment. While I'm just concentrating on breathing and being silent, he runs his hand down my belly and wraps his fingers around my cock, stroking me while running his teeth repeatedly along the sides of my nipple, driving me to the fine edge of pleasure and pain.

*Damn good thing he's got my mouth covered.*

Just when I think I can't take another second of the blissful torture, he stops what he's doing and shimmies up my body. I reach down to grab onto his cock, but he slaps my hand away. When I reach for it again, he captures my wrist in his hand and pulls it above my head, using his other hand to bring my other arm up to join it. With one hand, he immobilizes both wrists together and moves over me, kissing me feverishly. I don't understand the way I feel when he holds me down like this, but it makes my stomach clench and my passion go into overdrive.

It's not like I can't move. I just don't want to.

I kiss him back, darting my tongue deep into his mouth, taking everything I can from him— everything he'll allow me to have. Being quiet is nearly impossible when we're gasping against

258

each other like this, starving for each other, unable to get our fill.

He pulls back slightly. "Do you love me at all, Beck?" he whispers, his breath touching my lips in the darkness.

Dizzy with passion, I moan out what is meant to be an affirmation, lifting my head to steal another kiss from him.

"Tell me," he says.

I lift my head even higher, my greedy mouth seeking his, not trusting words, but needing to show him how I feel. Wanting to kiss him until there's absolutely no doubt in his mind how much he means to me.

He pulls back even farther, just out of my reach. I can't see him in the dark, but there's a palpable chill spreading out between us. "Goddammit, Beck..." His voice is hostile. "You tell me right fucking now if you do or you don't. One way or the other, I need to know."

Before he can even flinch, I've flipped him smoothly under me and pinned his arms in the same way he'd done mine, tangling the covers around us. With our positions reversed, he's at my mercy, and I'm not playing. He struggles, but there's no way he's getting free of me until I allow it. He may be quick, but his strength is no match for mine.

"You want to know how I feel about you?" I grate out through clenched teeth, straining against his futile struggles to take back control. "You want me to confess my love for you? I don't think you have any idea what you're asking for. It's not a game. You come charging into town like some badass, challenging wrestlers twice your size like you're David against Goliath, acting like you're gonna dominate me... subdue me... Well, congratulations. You did it. I fucking tapped out, Jeremy. I'm in love with you. So now what?"

"I love you, too," he whispers. "So much."

"Bullshit." I tighten my grip on his wrists. "Don't say those words, because I don't think you know what they mean. Tonight when you stood me up, I was going out of my mind worrying that you were cheating on me, or hurt, or even dead. You know why? Because I thought if you were alive and well, and you felt the same about me as I do about you, there's no way you wouldn't at least call."

"Please don't be mad, Beck. It was nothing. I just needed to walk around and clear my head, that's all." He sobs in the darkness, twisting the knife that's already lodged in my heart. "After I left the meeting with the coach, I wasn't feeling right."

"Did you get kicked off the team?"

"No."

"Have you been with someone else?"

"…No." He hesitates for only a second before answering, but that slight hesitation is all it takes to sow a seed of doubt in my mind.

"Fuck you, Jeremy." I push roughly off of him and roll over in the bed, turning my back to him. I pull the twisted covers around me and shut my eyes tightly, willing the tears away. No way I'm gonna cry.

"Beck." He touches my back, but now his fingers just feel cold, and I jerk away.

"If I could leave right now, I would," I tell him, my voice flat and devoid of any emotion. "But I'm stuck here, so just let me sleep. We'll talk about this later."

He turns away without a word, and we both lie deathly still

for a long, long time. I can't think of anything but the fact that Jeremy may have been with someone else. Images of our abandoned dinner play across my mind, and I hope someone at least put the food away. God, if there ever was a night that went horribly wrong, this is it. Thankfully, just when I think it never will, the oblivion of sleep eventually rescues my tortured mind.

The next thing I see is cruel sunlight through the blinds. I dig my underwear out of the covers at the foot of the bed, get dressed quietly, and get the hell out of there before anyone can make me change my mind.

# 21

*(JEREMY)*

THURSDAY feels like dying. Beck is already gone when I wake, and it takes me three calls to realize he's purposely not answering. I don't call a fourth time, because that would seem desperate. I know Beck thinks I've cheated on him, and I kinda have— but not in the way he thinks.

*Not because I wanted to.*

Is it still considered cheating if it's against your will? And what if you do it *for* the person you're cheating *on*? These are things I would have asked Mrs. Davis, my high school counselor. This is the first time I've really thought about needing her and not being able to see her. I remember reading in the school pamphlet that the university health center offers free counseling, but when I try to set up an appointment, I'm told that no one can see me until next

Wednesday. Too fucking late. Guess I'll have to wait, though. What else can I do? I set an appointment.

Seth is worried about me. "Please go out with me and Dan tonight," he begs on Thursday. "I know you well enough to know you're not in a good place right now, and I don't think you should be alone."

"I'll be okay. They should have another few pages of *GLiF* published. That will cheer me up."

"You really like that one, huh?"

"Yeah. It stands for *Gay Life Forever*. Kinda cheesy, but I feel like I can relate to it, you know? A group of college guys just trying to make the best of things... I just wish they could get the new pages out quicker."

"I know all about it, dude. I'm the one who turned you onto it in the first place." Seth looks back over his shoulder as he leaves the room. "You sure you won't join us?"

"Positive. Y'all have fun, though. I'll be fine."

After he and Dan have left, I try to read some manga, but my heart's not in it. I'm not even interested in looking at the latest installment of *GLiF*. Same with porn. I navigate to one of my favorite sites and type *bareback public* into the search box. There's usually something in those results to fire me up, but not tonight.

*How depressed do you have to get before porn isn't even interesting?*

Friday night is more of the same, but by Saturday afternoon I've decided that maybe a little outing to Hoppers with Seth and Dan is the only thing I can do to keep from going insane. Beck has still not returned my calls from Thursday, and except for periodically checking for calls and texts, I haven't dared to touch my phone for fear I might break down and call him again. It seems he's cut me off completely, and I can't blame him. He absolutely should cut me off before I mess his life up any more than I already have.

"Hello... Earth calling Jeremy..." Seth looks worried. "I've asked you three times if you're ready to go. Are you gonna be okay?"

"Yeah, of course." I try to make my voice light, but I can tell by his expression he's not falling for it. "But I'll take my car just in case I want to leave early."

We grab our wallets and keys and head out the door.

"I'll ride with you, then," Seth says. "Dan's meeting us there, so I can catch a ride home with him if I need to." He turns and wiggles the doorknob to make sure it's locked. "If you're not feeling better by the time we get there, Farrell has something that can cheer you up."

"Seth, I have a confession to make. You know when I said I'd tried smoking pot but that I didn't want to fail any wrestling piss tests?"

"Yeah..." He stops in the middle of the hall to give me his full attention.

"Well, I lied. I just didn't want to sound lame. The truth is I've never tried any drugs except the poppers Dan gave me. I go to parties and stuff, but I hardly ever drink."

Seth wrinkles his brow. "Jeremy, why would you lie about something like that?"

"I guess I just wanted to fit in for a change. The truth is my dad is an alcoholic and my mom is a drug addict, so I don't really have the stomach for any of that stuff, you know? I'll usually have a couple of drinks, but that's it."

Seth reaches over right there in the dorm hall and wraps his arms around my shoulders, giving me a long, lazy hug. "You don't have to try to fit in with me, roomie. We're friends." He rubs the back of my head. Three dorm residents I don't know by name pass by us, but he doesn't stop hugging, and I don't pull away.

When we finally split apart, I'm nearly in tears. He knows it, too. He looks directly into my eyes and smiles. "We're friends," he says again. "You can be honest with me. About anything. I know you have a lot of heavy shit on your mind, and I'm not going to be nosy about it. But I do want you to know that when you're ready to share, I'm ready to listen, okay?"

I nod, swiping the back of my hand across my eyes to catch a couple of tears before they can roll.

By the time we get to Hoppers, I'm feeling slightly better. My entire world is crumbling, and my emotions are teetering on a cliff, but at least I have a friend.

Dan is already out on the dance floor gyrating seductively with some pretty-boy Italian. For a moment, I find myself wondering why it couldn't have been Dan I fell for; he's so good looking, charming, and fun. I sure as hell wouldn't be going through the horror story I am right now with Beck and Coach Bradley if I'd picked Dan, but dammit, my heart didn't give me much of a choice. It's Beck or no one, and right now it's looking more and more like no one.

"Dan can really dance, huh?" I ask Seth, trying not to dwell on thoughts of Beck.

"Oh, yeah," he agrees. "He's one of the best dancers I've ever seen in here, but I try not to dance with him anymore if I can help it. Not only does he put me to shame, but he gets me way more worked up than I ever want to be around him— if you know what I mean."

I laugh for the first time in days. "You're preaching to the choir, brother. Been there, done that."

"Let me go tell him we're here." Seth makes his way slowly through the crowd toward the dance floor, leaving me standing awkwardly near the bar. I shove my hands into my pockets and do my best to look more comfortable than I feel. The usual bravado that kicks in when I'm nervous isn't anywhere to be found.

*I think maybe I'm broken.*

"Hey, stranger," says a voice from behind me. I whirl around, irrationally hoping it's Beck though the voice sounds nothing like his.

Chris, the boy who asked me to tutor him in wrestling, is leaned casually against the bar. His blond hair is slicked back, and he's dressed in a stylish outfit that makes him look much older than he is. In this light, his sprinkling of freckles is invisible.

"Wow." It's the only word that will come out of my mouth at first.

"Yeah, same here," he says with a smile. "I tried to call you a couple of times. Left a voicemail."

"Uh, sorry man. I know I told you I'd work with you, but I've been really busy."

*And my boyfriend thought you were trying to hit on me. Guess he might not have been too far off.*

He shrugs, still smiling. "No problem. You wanna get a drink and sit down? Get to know each other better…"

"Well, I'm sort of seeing someone."

*At least I hope I'm still seeing someone.*

"Who, him?" He gestures toward the dance floor, where Seth has apparently been talked into joining Dan and his dance partner. The three of them are looking pretty cozy, and I'm jealous at how happy they all look. None of them are sulking around like me.

"Okay, Chris. I'll get a drink with you." We approach the bar, and the bartender serves us without question. I order a White Russian again, because Sex on the Beach seems to incite too much drama.

As we pass the dance floor, I raise my glass to Seth, letting him know he doesn't have to babysit me anymore. After we get settled into a table, Chris takes a drink of his beer and slides a little closer to me. "So…," he says with a huge grin on his face. "How cool is it running into each other here?"

"Pretty cool. Is this your first time at Hoppers?"

"Hell, no." He laughs as he peels the label from his bottle and folds it in half. "I've been here lots of times. Can't seem to stay away. When it's a choice between streaming movies in my dorm room or coming out here and partying, I always end up down here. My roommate and I don't really have much in common, anyway. We kind of clash." He gets a faraway look in his eyes, as if he's playing scenes of his roommate strife in his head, and then he snaps back with a deep breath. "I don't drink all that much when I come out, though. Gotta watch my figure." He rubs the six-pack I know he's got under his shirt.

"This is only my second time here. I came with my roommate Seth and our friend Dan… two of the fabulous dancers you were admiring earlier."

"Yeah, I wasn't really admiring them. I was just trying to figure out if you were with anybody. I like a little more muscle on a guy, you know?" He nudges me with his elbow and gives me a very deliberate once-over. "Oh, but you're seeing someone, aren't you?" He cocks an eyebrow like he's not sure if he believes me.

"I guess I still have a boyfriend." I look down at my glass, twirling it around on the table top. "We had an argument, and I haven't seen him in a couple of days, so I'm sort of in limbo right now."

"Ouch." Chris gives me a sympathetic look. "Sorry to hear that. I wish I had a guy to even argue with. My ex and I decided to break up when we got accepted to different schools. Guess it wasn't that serious to begin with, huh?"

"I can't believe you haven't found someone at SSU yet. You're a good-looking guy. These dudes in here ought to be hitting on you left and right."

"A lot of them do." He laughs humorlessly. "I'm just picky, that's all."

"Me, too," I admit. "Seems like there's only one guy in the world I'll ever want, and he's not even speaking to me right now."

"Sounds like you're in love, man." When I don't reply, he continues. "My ex and I were close, but it was kinda more like friends than soulmates. We were so cool with breaking up, it was freaky. We were both like, *See ya!*" He folds his beer label as tightly as he possibly can before unfurling in again.

"That poor label," I chuckle. "You're really giving it hell."

"Fuck. What is he doing here?" Chris drops the label altogether and puts his hands in his lap. "You think maybe we're in trouble? What if he sees us?"

"Who?"

"Beck," he says, pointing discreetly toward the entrance. "No way he's gay. He's too much of an uptight goody-goody." Then he winces. "Oops. Forgot he's your mentor. Don't tell him I said that, okay?"

I nod, my mouth hanging loose. I can't do anything except stare at Beck as Raoul stamps his hand and he pushes his way into the club. He's never looked as gorgeous to me as he does at this moment, wearing a white dress shirt, dark dress pants, and an expression that would shrivel the most confident of men. I wonder if this is how he looks when he faces down an opponent on the wrestling mat. If it is, I can see why he's nearly unstoppable. That look alone could bring me to my knees.

"Should we hide?" Chris is nearly frantic at my side, but I'm too frozen to acknowledge him. "Oh, we're so screwed," he whines, shifting in his seat like he's not sure if he should sit up or hide under the table.

Beck scans the room, searching for someone.

*Could it be me?*

My heart skips a beat when his eyes finally land on me and stay there. I raise my hand tentatively in a half-assed wave, but when his expression goes even darker, my hand falls to my lap.

"Oh, shit, he sees us," Chris says, his voice going high at the end like a girl's. "Crap. He's headed this way."

"*Fuck fuck fuck.*" I'm like a ventriloquist with Tourette's, hissing the words through stiff lips. I know Chris can see the fear in my eyes, though he thinks it's because I don't want to be outed. I

269

almost wish I was a possum, because with the way Beck is glaring at us, I feel like playing dead and hoping he passes right on by. "Chill," I bark at Chris just before Beck reaches our booth.

"What's up, guys?" Beck's words are friendly, his tone anything but.

"N-nothing much," Chris stammers.

"Hey," I manage, unable to make eye contact but also unable to keep from staring at his body. My eyes lock onto the little vee where the top two buttons of his shirt are undone, the collar of a white t-shirt peeking out, and a warmth spreads over my body at the mere sight of him.

Beck slides in beside me without asking, and Chris and I scoot around the booth to accommodate him. His presence is so overpowering I can't breathe properly, especially when anger is radiating so strongly from him.

"I'm not crashing a private party, am I?" he asks. "Is this a date or something?"

Chris leans around me. "Uh, this is our first time here, sir. Good music and cool lights, but I'm just starting to notice there are an awful lot of guys here and not many chicks. Y'all want to head over to the Collegiate?"

"I don't know," Beck says. "Jeremy, do you want to go to the Collegiate and pick up some chicks?"

I shake my head and swallow around the huge lump that's suddenly there.

"Is that what you want to do, Chris?" Beck continues. "Go find chicks? 'Cause this is a gay bar, and most of the guys here are gay." Beck is baiting him, and I can't do anything but sit quietly. I don't know how to make it known that Chris and I aren't together without outing Beck in the process, and I'd rather die a thousand horrible deaths than do that again.

Chris stammers some more. "Um… I, uh—"

"Are you guys gay?" Beck looks him straight in the eye, silently daring him to lie about it.

Suddenly, Chris's expression changes. A visible calm washes over him, and he draws his shoulders up and locks gazes with Beck. "Yeah, Beck. I'm gay. But I don't think Jeremy is. He's just hanging out with his roommate. Right, Jeremy?"

Beck laughs out loud. "So sweet. You're trying to protect Jeremy? How fucking poetic." He growls and runs his hand over his scalp, looking up at the ceiling like he's trying to call his temper under control.

"Beck—" I begin, but he cuts me off.

"Are you two sleeping together? Tell me the goddamn truth, Jeremy. If you have any fucking decency at all." Pain flashes across his face before his voice softens. "Please don't lie to me."

So much for not outing Beck. He's insisting that I do it.

Chris looks confused, but I can see the cogs turning behind his eyes. If I had any money, I'd bet he's very close to putting it all together. He looks back and forth from me to Beck, then away as if he's trying to remember anything that might support his suspicions.

"No. We are not sleeping together, Beck. I promise. I just ran into him here, and the only reason I'm here in the first place is because I was going crazy in my room wondering where you were and why you haven't called." Tears start falling down my cheeks as the uncertainty and despair of the last few days catches up to me, and I swipe angrily at them. "Why haven't you called?"

*Fucking tears. I hate tears.*

Before my heart has time to beat again, Beck snatches me against his body, twining his arms around my neck and burying his face in my neck. He kisses me over and over, his lips moving like fire across my throat. It makes me cry even harder.

Since the incident with Coach Bradley I haven't allowed myself to cry, or even feel anything about it. I've focused only on Beck, channeling all of my emotions into missing him. It hasn't even occurred to me to feel the shock of what happened to me in the wrestling office. Now it all just rushes in, flooding my senses, but only because Beck is drawing it to the surface without even knowing he's doing it— allowing me to feel the pain so that I can get rid of it. He's my hero, and he doesn't even realize it.

He lifts his head from my throat and slants his soft lips over mine, kissing me with a hunger that makes my heart stutter. After he gets through owning my mouth completely, he kisses the tears from my cheeks.

"Don't cry, sweetie," he says, his voice breaking. He leans his forehead against mine. "I don't care what you did the other night— well, I do, but… as long as everything can be okay between us again. God, I've been going out of my mind trying to find you. Been calling since Thursday night when we got to the hotel, but your freaking phone is cut off, and I don't know Seth or Dan's numbers. You have no idea how close I was to catching a bus home. Then on the way back into town I spot your car in the club parking lot, but when I rush over here to see you, I find you here with this creeping sonofabitch."

We both glance at Chris, who looks like he could use a shot of something harder than beer. He gathers his wits enough to scoot far away from me to the other end of the seat. "Don't look at me, Beck," he says. "I didn't touch him."

"Hotel?" I ask Beck. I'm still crying a tiny bit, but heartache is giving way to curiosity. "Catch a bus back from where?"

"The coaches took me and Truck to Atlanta. The school paid a lot of money for us to go to this clinic Friday and today. We had a formal banquet this afternoon, so that's why I'm dressed this way. I meant to tell you about it Wednesday night at dinner, but things went a little haywire."

I look up into his face, embarrassed by my tears but so in love I can't stop myself from kissing him. He returns the favor, pulling me onto his lap and arranging my legs on either side of his hips so that I'm riding him on the seat. Just like that, we're engaged in a full-fledged make out session. I grind against his dick with mine and moan into his mouth, letting him know in no uncertain terms how much I want him.

"I'm sorry." I squeak. "I didn't want to stand you up, believe me. I had all these stupid romantic fantasies of us sitting around watching TV and eating pizza in our pajamas like a real couple."

"Well, what I had set up was a little more formal than that, Junior. Try Italian food, candles and wine."

That almost makes me cry again. "Shit. I missed that?"

Beck shrugs and smiles sweetly. "I'll give you a do-over."

"So we're still boyfriends?" I ask.

"Yeah, baby." He grabs my ass with both hands and hips up into me. "Definitely still boyfriends. I don't give up that easily."

"Oh, shit!" Chris yells. "Guys, I hate to break up your Hallmark moment, but I think we really are in trouble now. What the hell is this, a coming out party for the whole wrestling team?" At our puzzled looks, he nods toward the entrance, where Coach Bradley waits in line. He's dressed the same as Beck, except his shirt is pale blue. He pulls a striped tie from around his collar and stuffs it into his pocket.

"What the fuck—" Beck throws me roughly off his lap when he sees the coach, then looks frantically around the room as if he's trying to figure something out in a hurry. Probably planning an escape he doesn't have the time to pull off.

Chris and Beck are squirming in their seats on either side of me. I'm the only one who doesn't react. Of course I'm not scared of being found in a gay bar by Coach Bradley. The man knows in vivid digital detail just exactly how gay Beck and I both are, and I know first-hand just how twisted he is. A cool calm spreads over my body as he spots our little group and approaches.

He waves in that friendly, unassuming way he has. "Hi, Beck."

"Uh, hi coach," Beck says with a nervous smile. "What are you doing here?" I feel sorry for him, thinking he's got to play anything off, and knowing this situation has the potential to get extremely ugly.

"Well, you seemed really distracted at the clinic, so I was worried about you. I wanted to talk, but you took off like a bat out of hell when we got back to the school, so I followed you. What is this place?" He looks around as if he's clueless he's in a gay bar, but I have all ideas he knows exactly where he is.

"Just a local watering hole," Beck says with a shrug. "We make the rounds on Saturday nights. We were just debating whether or not we should go over to the Collegiate to pick up some chicks."

Amazingly, that's not a lie. I feel a hysterical giggle fluttering in my guts, and I fight to snuff it out.

*Don't lose it now, Jeremy.*

"Mind if I join you?" the coach asks. Again with the disarmingly genuine manner that makes me want to puke.

"Sure," Chris says a little too eagerly. "Have a seat, sir."

"Um, first things first." The coach hands Beck a couple of twenties. "Could you buy us all a round of drinks? I'll have a rum and Coke." After Beck gets our drink orders, he slides out and is well on his way to the bar when the coach turns to me. "Jeremy, would you please show me to the restroom? I don't do well in crowds."

*Fuck me.*

"Sure, Coach." I slide out and lead the way through the sweaty bodies, glancing over my shoulder at Beck as he muscles his way up to the bar and calls for the bartender.

I try to leave the coach at the restroom door, but he grabs my hand and pulls me in with him. "Wait for me, will you?" My chest constricts with fear as he opens his pants, but he only positions himself in front of one of the urinals and talks to me while he's taking a piss. "You know, I hate to tell you this, Jeremy, but your boyfriend is losing his edge. He's slipping, and it's all because of this drama with you. He doesn't know I can see it, but it was all over his face at the event this weekend. He's terrified someone is going to find out he's gay."

I wish I could tell him that Beck's not afraid of anything, but

275

the truth is he's probably right.

"I watched him very closely," the coach continues. "He was hesitant about touching his competitors, and it cost him quite a few matches. He was detached from everyone for the whole trip, like his mind was somewhere else. Coach Roberts is very worried about him, and so am I."

"Why are you telling me all of this?"

"I think you know." He shakes and puts himself away before turning to face me, looking deceptively respectable in his suit. "Beck is our star, Jeremy. He's a favorite for nationals, and I think he can go all the way... *if* he can stay focused. That will be the first number one title for SSU. Do I need to explain how important that is— for all of us?"

I shake my head, registering my own horrified expression in the mirror on the wall.

"I think the best thing for everyone involved," the coach continues, checking his hair in the mirror, "would be for you to back off. Not forever, but at least until after nationals. Give Beck a chance to shine. I'm not trying to hurt your feelings, boy, but the fact is you're poison to a guy like him. He was chugging along just fine, about to make a real name for himself and for this school, and then you showed up with all your trailer trash drama." He laughs humorlessly and shakes his head. "I mean, I don't know how the hell you did it, but you've managed to get our entire wrestling program by the balls. I just want you to stop and think about what you're doing. Don't fuck this up for everyone." He finishes primping his hair, then pushes past me without a glance and heads back out into the bar.

*Don't do well with crowds, my ass. Such a liar.*

But he's right, isn't he? Beck was doing great before I came along, and now everything is upside-down. He's losing matches, being filmed having gay sex in the locker room, stressing out about our relationship. Hell, he admitted he almost left the wrestling clinic just because my phone is out of service. That definitely doesn't sound like the Beck I met on the first day of school.

When we return to the table, Beck is already back. "They'll bring our drinks to the table in a minute," he says.

It hurts to look at him now. He gave me his heart, asking only that I respect his wish to keep our love a secret, and what have I done? I've nearly destroyed him. I should have ended it the night I met with Coach Bradley— the night the unspeakable happened.

In fact, I'd planned on doing just that, but when Beck showed up in my room I lost my nerve. Now it's time for me to remedy the situation I've gotten both of us into.

Coach Bradley slides in next to Beck before I can get to the table. I start to go around to the other side where Chris is, but the coach pats the seat next to him. I hover for a moment, unsure what to do next, and then the cobwebs clear out of my head and it's suddenly clear.

"I think I'm gonna go dance," I announce to everyone. "I came here with Seth and Dan, and I've been ignoring them the whole time."

I take off before anyone can protest, quickly rounding the corner and jumping onto the dance floor. Seth and Dan are gone, probably to the back room where Farrell no doubt has something for them. The hot little Italian guy who'd been dancing with them is still out there shaking his butt, and I wiggle right up to him.

"Where did my friends go?" I yell over the music.

He points toward the back room. Then he moves close to me, changing his style of dance now that he's no longer solo. I'm ashamed to admit it even to myself, but I find myself doing a lot of dirty stuff on the dance floor just because it's easier than learning dance moves. Sex moves I already know.

So Mr. Italy and I are getting down pretty well when Beck grabs my arm and snatches me off the dance floor, pulling me into a dark hallway that runs along behind it. A red exit sign glows from the other end.

"What, no dirty dancing this time?" I ask.

"If you were hoping for a replay of you, me and Dan, you're gonna be disappointed." He glares at me, but I can't quite get a bead on his mood. "You don't have to do this, Jeremy."

"Do what?"

"Show out in public, try to break up with me..."

I shake my head. "I'm not—"

He kisses me. "You're not what?"

"Not—"

He kisses me again, pushing my back against the wall. "Not what?"

"Um—"

"Spit it out, baby." He kisses me again, lingering longer this time, swirling his tongue around mine until my brain is mush. "What are you trying to say?"

"Stop!" I flatten my palms against the hard contours of his chest and push half-heartedly against him. "I can't think with you doing that stuff to me."

"Well, that's too bad, because I'm not stopping." My thoughts of protesting are long gone within seconds, as he claims my mouth again, covering my body with his and enveloping me in a warm embrace that feels safer than anything in the world. If only I could just stay wrapped up in him like this forever while everything else just faded away into oblivion. "I've got something to tell you," he says. "But it's a secret. Can you keep a secret?"

I nod against him, not wanting to break the mood by speaking.

"I know where you were Wednesday night."

My heart stops beating, and I lean back to look into Beck's eyes.

"When I was in Atlanta, I ran into a couple of Coach Bradley's old students, and they told me an interesting story." He searches my face before continuing. "This one guy named Greg said the coach planted video cameras in their locker rooms to catch the wrestlers doing things they shouldn't. Seems he caught a close friend of Greg's making out with a football player. His friend was really shaken up about the whole thing. He didn't want to talk about it, but when Greg pressed him, he admitted that he was gay and that the coach was a raging homophobe. Coach Bradley had threatened to go public with the video unless the guy quit the team."

I swallow hard, so dizzy I think I might fall down if Beck wasn't holding me up. "Did he quit?"

"He did worse than that. He left school."

"If they knew what the coach did, why didn't he…"

"Get in trouble?" Beck finishes for me. "I asked the same

question. After his friend dropped out of school, Greg went forward with the information that the coach had cameras in the locker rooms. They found them, but the coach claimed he'd put them in to find out who was stealing stuff out of people's gym bags and lockers. The school wanted to avoid a big scandal, so they just asked Coach Bradley to leave quietly and swept it all under the rug. But I have a feeling the assistant coach is up to his old tricks again, huh Jeremy?"

"Is that all?" I ask.

"All what?"

"Is that all of the story? All that happened? All Greg's friend said?"

"Yeah. But it was enough for me to put two and two together." He threads his fingers into the back of my hair and rubs gently. "The way you were acting after you met with him, being so upset, wanting me to tell you I loved you... I kept playing it over and over in my head, but it wasn't until Greg told me his story that I figured it out. The coach got us on video, didn't he? Fucking in the locker room... He threatened to expose us if you didn't break up with me. Did he try to make you quit the team?"

I start to tremble in Beck's arms. "He... um..." The trembling is getting worse by the second.

Beck bends to look at me, a concerned look on his face. "Don't worry, sweetie. I've got it all handled. As we speak, Truck and Caleb are taking Coach Bradley's laptop to our apartment. When I went to get the drinks, I texted them, and they lifted it out of his car right here in the Hoppers parking lot. We've got a plan. That bastard is going to regret ever messing with me and my boy. I wish like hell he'd tried that shit on me. I would've told him to shove that video right up his ass."

"Really?" I croak.

"Yeah." He rests his lips against my hair, and I can feel him smile. "If you'd shown up for dinner that night, I would have told you that I was going to come out to Coach Roberts. I had it all planned. But I'm learning more and more that you can't always stick to a plan, no matter how well thought out it is."

"You were going to come out?"

"That's right. But you know what?" He kisses the top of my head and squeezes me close. "I already did it."

I snatch out of his grip and step back. "You what?"

"I told Coach Roberts on the way to Atlanta." His hesitant smile turns into a frown. "Isn't that what you wanted?"

"No!" I slam my hands into the sides on my head as the noise of my own thoughts overtakes me. "I mean yes. Oh, God. What have you done? What the fuck have *I* done?"

*I never had to do it...*

"It's okay," Beck soothes, taking a cautious step in my direction. "Coach Roberts said it would be fine. You were right, as usual; he already knew. He could see the attraction between us as far back as that day in Hotrod's and was so happy I'd finally found someone. But then he noticed I was avoiding you because I was scared to get involved. That's why he was quizzing me about you over dinner. He said the whole reason he started the Monday Mentors was because he was tired of watching us moon over each other from across the gym. Who'd have thought Coach Roberts would end up playing Cupid?" He stops for a moment, musing, laughing quietly. "So you see, everything is alright."

"No, fuck, it's not alright." Horrified, I stumble backward until I bump into the opposite wall, unable to get any farther away from him. Only days ago, this news would have been the source of my greatest joy, but now it's the source of the worst sorrow imaginable. "Beck, they got it wrong. The coach, the boy... that's not what happened."

Beck holds his hand out to me, concern wrinkling his brow. "What's wrong, Jeremy? Talk to me. How do you know that's not what happened?"

"Because it happened to me. Christ, don't you see? Oh my God, I'm sorry. I'm so, so sorry."

I run as fast as I can toward the exit, depressing the bar handle and throwing the door wide open. Outside it's drizzling cold rain, but I'm so distraught I can barely feel it. I never lock my car, so it's easy to hop in and get it started.

As I back out, I can see Beck in the rear view mirror. He lunges out of the way and comes up to my window, banging on the glass.

"Jeremy, talk to me," he yells, squinting from the rain falling into his eyes.

He's so beautiful, and so perfect. He deserves better than a fuck-up like me, tainted beyond repair because of my own stupidity and fear.

In that moment, I know exactly how that other guy felt— the one Coach Bradley blackmailed before. We're the same, he and I. Damaged goods. He left school to escape the humiliation, and right now that's all I can think of doing. Just getting as far away as possible and trying to forget.

For the first time, I think I understand my mother's need to lose herself in drugs. It's better than being conscious while your life falls to pieces around you.

# 22

*(BECK)*

STANDING in the rain watching Jeremy squeal out of the parking lot and almost get T-boned by a passing car, I can't do anything but wonder what went wrong. I thought telling him I knew about the coach would bring him relief, but instead he freaked out and ran away.

What did he mean when he said that wasn't what happened? And why would he apologize to me?

In my mind, we were in it together. He didn't force me to do anything in the locker room. I was the instigator. And if I hadn't been such a coward about coming out in the first place, the coach never would have had anything to leverage.

*What did Coach Bradley want?*

That's a question I haven't really asked before, and now it's

284

got me thinking. Jeremy hasn't quit the team, and he hasn't left school. No one has approached me or threatened me.

*That's not what happened.*

I roll the words over in my head, twisting them around and trying to make them mean something significant, but I can't. Not without Jeremy.

*Or Coach Bradley's computer.*

I snatch my phone out of my pocket while climbing into my truck. "You got it unlocked?"

"Vlad just got here with his password recovery CD, and he's working on it. Says it should only take a couple of minutes."

"Well hurry up and get everything copied over. Farrell says that stuff they put in the coach's drink should keep him out of commission for several hours. He won't know what hit him. He was already swooning when I left him at the table, and Chris and Farrell are keeping an eye on him for me."

"You on your way home?"

"Yeah. I'm driving through Spangler Hall right now." I scan the parking lot for Jeremy's car. "You seen Jeremy?"

"No," Truck says. "I thought he was with you."

"He was, but he got upset and left. I'm worried about him."

"Do you need to go find him? We can handle this operation here. As soon as we get the files copied, Caleb will return it to Coach Bradley's car right where he found it. Did Farrell turn off the surveillance cameras?"

"He said he did. Now if the cops come around, there will be no video evidence of what went down tonight. I can't believe how quickly this has all gone down, and how we've had to wing it all.

From the second the coach walked into Hoppers, it's been like a whirlwind."

Truck laughs. "This is so cool. I feel like fucking MacGyver." He clears his throat. "I mean, not like *fucking* MacGyver, but just... you know. I feel like MacGyver."

Despite my dark mood, I have to chuckle. "I wish I could share in your enjoyment, buddy, but there's something really wrong with Jeremy. I don't know where else to look for him, and his phone isn't working. But I have a feeling I'm going to find a clue to what's going on when I get a look at that asshole's laptop. I think it's the key."

"You think there's more to see than all of us cruising around in our skivvies and you and Jeremy going at it?"

"Unfortunately, yes. And I've got a really bad feeling about it."

I slip my phone into my pocket as I pull into the parking lot of my building. When there's no sign of Jeremy's car, I head up to the apartment. I feel awful not searching for him, but without an idea of where he might go, there's really nothing else I can do until I figure out what's got him so upset.

My imagination keeps offering up possibilities, but I won't listen to it. I don't want to even consider the horrific things it's suggesting.

"Anything yet?" I ask, entering the living room and peeling off my wet dress shirt.

"Easy peasy," Vlad says with a cocky grin. "Cracked it in less than four minutes, and the files are transferring as we speak. The videos were in a locked and hidden file, but the password was the same. Apparently we're dealing with an idiot. Anyway, I'll re-hide them when we're done, and the guy will never know we've been in his computer. He'll think he's gotten away with... everything."

He looks at Truck and Caleb and clears his throat, the smile dropping from his face. The other two look equally uncomfortable, and nobody seems to want to look directly at me all of a sudden.

"Come with me," Truck says, grabbing me by the arm and pulling me into my bedroom.

"What is it?" The look on his face tells me I may not want to know.

"Um, you know how you said not to watch the videos? That you wanted to see them first?"

I glare at him without speaking until he continues.

"Well, don't worry. We didn't actually watch anything. That's your business, and we respect that. But there are some videos with interesting names and screenshots, and we couldn't help but see them. There's a lot of disturbing shit on that computer, Beck. It's so bad I *almost* feel embarrassed for the guy. There's raw footage of the locker rooms of both schools, and those videos just have dates for names. There's a video called Beck and Jeremy, and from the screenshot it looks like it's probably the one you were talking about. But there's also..." He looks nervously away.

"Also what?" I touch him on the arm, encouraging him to finish.

"Shit, Beck. I don't want to be the one to tell you this. It's gonna break your heart, man."

I clamp my teeth together and brace myself, my body going completely still. "Tell me."

287

Truck takes a deep breath. "There are other videos that look like Coach Bradley recorded himself doing stuff with guys. One of them is called Jeremy."

"Is there a screenshot?" My voice sounds calm, flat, and like someone else's.

Truck nods slowly. "It doesn't look good."

"Fuck." My mind seizes up as all of the fears I've just been battling become reality.

"I don't get it, Beck. I thought Coach Bradley was supposed to be some kind of homo-hater, blackmailing gay guys and forcing them out of the wrestling program. But that's not what this is at all, is it?"

"No, it's not." I sit down heavily on my bed, bewildered by this mind-numbing turn of events. "He lied."

"Who lied?"

"That kid from the other school. The one who got blackmailed. That's what Jeremy meant when he said that wasn't what happened. This crazy bastard is just getting his rocks off, and in at least two cases, he's using these boys' fear to get his way." Now a picture of what must have happened to Jeremy that night is beginning to crystalize in my mind.

"Are you thinking what I'm thinking?" Truck asks.

"I don't know. Are you thinking that Coach Bradley captured me and Jeremy on video and saw an opportunity to use me against him?"

Truck nods silently.

"Dammit, this is all my fault! If I hadn't lost my cool that day... The worst part is that I kept whining to Jeremy that I didn't want to come out because I was afraid of losing my scholarship. He wanted to be open about our relationship from day one; I was the one who wanted to keep it a secret. Even after I'd decided it wasn't that important to me anymore, I still didn't tell him. I hesitated." Falling onto my back on the bed, I drop an arm across my face to cover my eyes. "Jesus Christ. While I was over here fussing with candles and wine, waiting for him to show up for dinner so that I could tell him I'd decided to come out, he was at the gym. I guarantee you the coach showed him that video, scared the shit out of him, and told him he was going to turn us in."

"And Jeremy did whatever he wanted. To protect you."

"Aaahhh, goddammit!" I jump up off the bed and start to head out the door, but instead I punch the shit out of the wall, putting a huge hole in the sheetrock. Then I return to the bed, falling face-first onto the mattress. "Why is this happening? This is so fucked up. That night, he asked me if I loved him. He'd just sacrificed his body and his pride to keep me safe, and all he wanted was to know that I cared. You know what I said to him? I said he didn't even know what the word meant."

"Don't beat yourself up, Beck. You didn't know what had happened."

"I could have trusted him. He trusted me." I rub my tears into the covers, hiding my weakness in the only way I can. "How ironic is it that it was me all along? That I'm the one who didn't know what the word meant."

289

# 23

*"I love you," Jeremy says, jumping onto me and wrapping his legs around me. Taking me down to the mat and ravishing me. He's naked except for a yellow jockstrap, and he laughs at the goofy way I'm looking at him. I can't get enough.*

It's just a tiny piece of a dream, and so simple. But it means everything.

By mid-morning I'm exhausted from not sleeping during the night, so I keep falling in and out of sleep and having these vivid dreams. That goes on until the afternoon. Through it all, I am always aware on some level that Jeremy is missing. I wish I could take away the pain I know he's feeling, but there's no way I can do that when I don't know where he is. My own inability to help him makes me want to stay in bed.

After the guys took Coach Bradley's computer back to his car last night, I called Farrell. True to his word, and with the help of

Seth, Dan and Chris, he'd kept a close eye on things at Hoppers and made sure everything went smoothly. As far as the coach knows, he had too much to drink and blacked out, though he expressed confusion at only remembering getting two drinks. Chris reported that before the coach passed out, the guy was coming onto him so hard he had to physically fight him off.

His car and laptop were just as he left them, and when he was able, he drove himself home in the dim light of dawn after thanking Farrell for not booting him out or calling the cops.

It's the calm before the storm now. Something big is about to happen, though none of us has a clear plan about how things should unfold.

Thanks to Farrell, I have both Seth's and Dan's phone numbers, and each of us know to contact the other two if we hear from Jeremy. The waiting is torture, because I know he doesn't think he can trust me. He's ashamed and scared, and he doesn't think I'll understand what has happened to him. I wish I could set his mind at ease and let him know that I don't blame him for anything.

"Is there something I can do for you, hon?" Gretchen asks when I finally venture out of my room just after three in the afternoon to get some water. "Anything at all?"

"Afraid not, Gretch." I take several huge gulps of water, only just now realizing that I'm starting to get dehydrated. "Not unless you can locate my boyfriend for me and make sure that pervy asshole Coach Bradley gets what's coming to him."

"Oh, I have a feeling you're going to do both of those things. Wish I could speed it up for you, though."

I down half the bottle of water and set it on the counter.

"You're a psych major. Any ideas about where he might go?"

"Well, normally I'd say someone who's been traumatized would probably go home. But from what you tell me about his family life, I don't know. Didn't he say he was never going back there again?"

"Yeah, he did, but I don't know. I'm not sure where else he has to go. His friend Eric from high school might know, but I have no idea how to get in touch with him. I don't even know the guy's last name."

"Can you get in touch with his mom?"

"Not unless I drive down there. Believe me, she would have been the first person I called."

"You said his Dad's an abuser, right?"

"A real piece of shit." I squeeze my fists so hard my nails bite into the palms of my hands. "Looks like he takes out the misery of his own existence on his wife and son. She's a druggie, and Jeremy's just lost."

Gretchen shakes her head and comes over to run her nails softly up and down my arm. "You and Jeremy have a lot in common."

"My family only ignores the hell out of me. I don't know what I might have done if my dad had beaten me like Jeremy's dad has him. I can't even imagine. And he so does not deserve that. He's such a sweet person, and really a lot more optimistic than you'd imagine for someone who grew up like that. He has every reason to be an emotional wreck, but he's not. He's so... strong."

"Is he?" Gretchen asks.

"Yeah. Wish I had been stronger for him."

"You can be strong for him now," she says. "Thanks to his dad, Jeremy's been a victim all his life. The victim mindset is a very real thing, and it can give a predator a distinct advantage. Victimizers are drawn to people who have been abused. They emit a siren's song to those bastards that they can't resist. It probably wasn't too hard for the Ass Coach to spot Jeremy and then get his claws in."

*"Ass Coach?"*

"Sorry." Gretchen laughs. "Abbreviation for Assistant Coach. It suits him, doesn't it?"

"He may be an ass, but let's not use that nickname for him, okay? It puts images in my head that I'd rather not see."

"Okay, baby. Point taken. So what are you planning on doing to take this guy down?"

"The plan is still fuzzy. But I assure you I'm going to take him down if I have to physically do it."

Gretchen's mouth drops open. "Beck, don't do anything stupid. You don't need to end up in jail or something. Try to keep your temper in check."

I laugh, but there's not a bit of humor in it. "Easy to say, not so easy to do, darlin'. That fucker messed with what's *mine*. Do you understand that?"

"Yes. Unfortunately, I do."

Gretchen bites her lip and looks uncertainly up at me. "Have you seen the video? Of him and Jeremy, I mean."

Just hearing her say the words tears me up inside.

"Nope. I don't think I'll be watching it, either. Someone might have to die."

"I guess I can't blame you. I don't think I could watch Truck

293

having sex with someone else."

I grab her by the ponytail and pull her closer, looking into her eyes. "I guarantee you as much as you think it would bother you, it would mess with Truck's head way worse if someone took advantage of you."

"Why do you think that?"

"Because you're his, and he's supposed to protect you. Just like I'm supposed to protect Jeremy. I just hope Truck would do better at his job, because I failed mine."

My phone buzzes in my pocket, and I nearly break my fingers trying to dig it out in a hurry. I don't recognize the number, but I answer it anyway.

"Is this Beck?" a shaky female voice warbles on the other end of the line.

"Yes, it is."

"Oh, thank goodness! This is Gina Miller, Jeremy's mom." She sighs heavily. "I thought I'd never find you."

"What is it?" My face heats with fear. "Is Jeremy okay?"

"He's stable."

*Stable? Why does that sound like a medical term?*

"He hasn't come to yet, but they've got his heart rate and his blood pressure down."

"What are you talking about, Mrs. Miller? What's happened?" My own heart feels like it's stopped beating, and I can tell I'm in very real danger of passing out.

"He overdosed, Beck." She's crying now, unable to control her voice. "I'm such a terrible mom. He's my only baby."

Somehow I find the presence of mind to rush to my room

and grab my truck keys off the night stand. As an afterthought, I change into a sweatshirt and jeans when I realize I'm still wearing my dress pants and undershirt from the wrestling clinic banquet. I have to put Jeremy's mom on speaker phone.

"What the hell did he overdose on, Mrs. Miller?"

"Meth. Crystal meth."

I stop dead in my tracks. "He doesn't do crystal meth."

"I know, Beck. I'm sorry. I had some at the house, and he found it." She chokes. "I think I'm probably going to end up going to jail, but I don't care about that. I just want my baby to get better."

"I'm on my way right now," I tell her as soon as I'm out the door. I don't even bother telling anyone else where I'm going. There will be time for that later. Right now I've got one singular purpose, and nothing is going to distract me from it. "Is he at the Blackwood Hospital?"

"Yes, Beck. Hurry."

"I'll be there in an hour and a half. Take care of him, please. Make those doctors fix him."

Mrs. Miller whimpers as she hangs up. *Not a good sign.*


The drive drags and whizzes by at the same time. In a town as tiny as Blackwood, it's not hard to find things. I remembered that the hospital was near the Huddle House, which was on Highway 280 going out of town on the east side. There are only about fifteen cars in the entire parking lot. That worries me a little, making me wonder if this hospital is large enough or good enough to care for Jeremy properly.

295

*If not, I'll drive him out of here myself if I have to.*

"Beck!" Jeremy's mother practically attacks me when I come through the double doors of the ER. "He's in here, honey."

I walk through the main area of the ER, which has a nurse's station on the left and three private patient rooms on the right. At the end of the short walk is the main room, where there are two beds with crash cart setups. The two beds are separated only by curtains, which are open at the moment, and even from this distance I can see that Jeremy is lying still on one of them.

It appears he's the only patient they've got tonight except for an elderly woman who is leaning out through the doorway of a side room door listening to us, watching closely with cloudy blue eyes as if Mrs. Miller dragging me through the ER is the most interesting thing she's ever seen.

Suddenly, I'm afraid. The sight of my boyfriend lying pale and unconscious on the hospital bed, hooked up to a heart monitor and an IV, makes my heart jump into my throat. I've been in such a hurry all the way here, now I pull back like a puppy on a leash as Jeremy's mom tries to pull me forward.

*What if he dies?*

When I dig my heels in and pull back even harder, Mrs. Miller looks over her shoulder at me, her eyes pleading. "Beck, he needs you. Come on."

I let go, allowing her to pull me along as tears fall from my eyes. By the time I reach his bedside, my eyes are so blurry with tears I can barely see his face. But I know it by heart.

All of those expressions of his that I've come to recognize and adore play like a home movie across my memory. The sweet puppy-

296

dog look that tells me he looks up to me for some damn reason, that fiery-eyed look that means he's about to break rank and dominate me in the bedroom, that unyielding mask that drops into place when someone's picking on him and he's done taking it... and especially that look of love, when he cuddles against my chest and the corners of his mouth quirk up like he knows he's got me.

"Tell him you're here," Mrs. Miller urges.

"You think he can hear me?" When she doesn't answer, I lean down and wrap an arm across his sheet-covered chest, nuzzling in close to his ear. "Jeremy, I'm here. I... I'm sorry I let you down, baby." I push down the sheet and discover he's naked except for a pair of jeans, and they've got him strapped down to the bed. "What the hell?"

"It was for his own good, Beck," his mother says. "He was pretty wild. They had to get him sedated or he might hurt himself or someone else."

"I can't stand to see him this way. Can I undo him? He looks calm enough."

"Uh, I don't think we should do that without the doctor here. He'll be back in a few minutes."

A pretty nurse with light brown hair appears to be charting something while talking on the phone at the nurse's station. She pushes an errant curl behind her ear, chewing on the end of a ballpoint pen. No one is paying attention to us, but as much as I want to get him out of these restraints, I put it aside for a moment and concentrate on trying to get through to Jeremy.

I thread my fingers through his hair, and it feels sweaty like he's just been training hard for hours. "Jeremy, if you can hear me...

I know everything that happened between you and Coach Bradley. It's not your fault, okay? It's his and mine. Not yours. You were just trying to protect me, and that means—" my voice breaks, and I have to take a few deep breaths before I can continue. "That means everything to me. I love you, Jeremy. Please wake up and tell me you love me, too."

I glance back at his mother just as fresh tears wash her cheeks, and she turns and faces the corner, her frail shoulders trembling.

"Truck and the guys are pulling for you. They said—"

A door on the other side of the room swings open, and a doctor enters the room. He's extremely good-looking, more like a TV doctor than a real one, with dark hair and piercing green eyes. But the most striking thing about him is that he looks so in control, like he can handle anything that comes along.

"How's our boy?" He asks with a slight smile that instantly puts me at ease. "Has he been staying calm?"

Jeremy's mom and I both nod.

"Dr. Ben Hardy," he says, taking my hand in firm shake. "You're Jeremy's boyfriend?"

His directness takes me by surprise, and I flounder for a moment before finding my words. "Yes, sir. Call me Beck. Is he going to be okay?"

"He's not out of the woods yet," Dr. Hardy says, turning away to listen to Jeremy's breathing with his stethoscope. "We had to give him a sedative to calm him down, and some nitro. The scariest thing in a meth overdose is the possibility of a cardiac arrest."

"Oh my God," I moan, and for a split second the room goes black in front of me. Dr. Hardy steps around to support my elbow with his hand. "I'm okay. Hearing the words *cardiac arrest* in relation to Jeremy just threw me for a loop." I struggle to retain control, because I'm no good to Jeremy if I lose it. "How much of a chance is that?"

"At this point, it's pretty slim," the doctor assures me. "We've headed it off with meds, started him on fluids to avoid dehydration, which could lead to cardiac arrest and liver failure if left untreated. We've got his body temp down. Honestly, everything is looking pretty good. I don't think he took enough to do any real damage." He frowns. "This just doesn't seem like Jeremy. How long has he been doing meth?"

"He hasn't!" Without thinking, I glare in his mother's direction. "He doesn't do drugs at all. This was... he was upset."

"Upset?" The doctor leans against the crash cart, waiting for an explanation.

"Um, there's been some bad stuff going down at school. Not his fault, but he kind of got mixed up in something. Let's just say he had a good reason to be upset, but now that reason is being *dealt with*."

Dr. Hardy raises his eyebrows but doesn't press me any further. "Beck, I know you're losing your mind right now with worry, but I'm about ninety-five percent certain he's going to pull through with no problem. I'm familiar with his history and feel very confident in my assessment. He's been my patient and friend for several years now. As you know, he's in excellent physical health, and he's got a will like a rodeo bull. Trust me when I say nothing keeps this kid down for long." He cuts his eyes over at Jeremy's mother crying in the corner before lowering his voice. "If you care about him, keep him close and look out for him. He's tough, but he's also vulnerable, and if anyone deserves some good in his life it's him."

Without waiting for a response from me, Dr. Hardy calls to the nurse, and she hurries in.

"I've gotten everything arranged, doctor. He's to be transported to Southeastern Memorial, right down from SSU."

"Thanks, Julie." The doctor turns to me. "We don't have an ICU here, so instead of transferring him to County where we send most of our patients, his mother asked that he be sent to the hospital near the school. He wouldn't be near any of you at County."

"Perfect," I say. "It's his home now, and that's where he needs to be."

*Close to me.*

Dr. Hardy addresses the nurse again. "Julie, please come release him from these restraints. Get him cleaned up and changed into a hospital gown and these fresh underwear his mom had brought over, too. He threw up all over his pants."

"Yes, sir," Julie says and moves to do as she's been told.

I grab the clean underwear off the bed rail. "If you can just undo his restraints and pull the curtain, I'll do the rest. If you don't mind."

The nurse smiles. "No, of course not." She releases him from the straps and pulls the curtain.

It takes a lot not to cry as I manipulate his limp body to get him dressed. I could have let the nurse dress him, but it just bothers me when he's vulnerable and can't speak for himself. I just get all mushy and protective, and I don't want anyone else near him.

"I'm glad you're here, Beck." Jeremy's mother has composed

herself by the time I pull back the curtain and stuff Jeremy's crusty jeans into a plastic hospital bag hanging from the bed. "Jeremy and I talked a lot last night. He really cares about you, and I know that there's no one in the world he trusts more than you. I didn't know how to get in touch with you, though. Jeremy had his phone with him, but it doesn't have any minutes, and the phone store's not open on Sunday. I didn't recognize any of the names in there except Eric's. He hasn't told me about any of his new friends, and I don't even know what his roommate's name is. Some mother I am. All I know is you, and it didn't look like he even had you in there at first, but…" She blushes fifteen shades of red. "I started reading text messages, and I figured out which one you must be."

"He didn't have me programmed in?"

"From hearing him talk, I'm assuming he was worried about anybody seeing his phone and figuring out it was you. That's why I didn't just start calling around to his other friends asking for you. Didn't want to cause any trouble. He said you were kinda secretive about things."

"Oh. Funny that he would think of that when I didn't. I just had him programmed in under his real name."

She smiles, showing her gapped teeth. "He had you in there as *Batman*. I guess because Bruce Wayne has a secret identity?"

As tense as things are, I can't help but laugh. "Uh, yeah. I'm sure that's exactly why."

By the time the ambulance arrives to transport Jeremy, I've calmed down a lot. Dr. Hardy has checked in regularly and reassured me in a way that someone with less authority never would have been able to pull off.

"Time to go." A tall EMT wheels a stretcher up beside the bed. He's got an untamed sensuality about him, with unruly black hair and a face that could grace the cover of a magazine.

*What is this? Playgirl General Hospital?*

"Can I ride in the back of the ambulance with my son?" Mrs. Miller asks. "My husband is going to meet us there."

"Sure, no problem," says a female EMT who has come up beside the hunky one.

"Are you kidding me?" I ask Jeremy's mom. "He fucking shot at me!"

The female EMT smirks. "Welcome to Blackwood. That's par for the course around these parts."

"Well I'm from out of town, so please excuse me if I don't just accept getting gunned down by my boyfriend's father as *par for the course.*"

"He's sorry, Beck." Mrs. Miller's voice is so soft I can barely hear her. "He's real sorry about what he did. Said he wished he could apologize, but that Jeremy probably wouldn't ever come back around anyway."

"I don't know how stupid I'd have to be to stand still long enough to see if he's gonna apologize or fill me full of lead."

She shakes her head. "He won't. When he sobered up and realized what he'd done, he gave me his gun and told me to get rid of it. So I did. He was so afraid he'd hurt one of you. William's a real hard man, I'll admit that, but he's no killer. And he loves in his own way."

I roll my eyes at her. "Whatever. Let's just get Jeremy to the other hospital."

Pretending to feel anything for William Miller besides disgust is not something I can do at the moment. Maybe I can trust that he's not going to shoot at me again, and maybe I can stand in the same hospital room with him, but nothing is going to change how I feel about the way he's treated Jeremy.

"Are you coming along now?" the male EMT asks.

"Yeah, I'll just follow you."

"Officially, I have to advise you that you're not allowed to follow us. Trying to keep up with an ambulance en route to a hospital or emergency is considered a safety hazard." He smiles. "Unofficially... stay behind us, man. We'll try our best not to lose you."

Jeremy is still unconscious. It makes me nervous watching them load him onto the ambulance, and when they close the door and all I can see is his mom's head through the back glass, I start to feel a full-blown panic attack coming on.

*What if something happens to him on the way and I'm not with him?*

"He's going to be fine," Dr. Hardy says as he passes me. He's in good hands, I promise. Corey is going to be riding in the back with him."

I nod and trot over to my truck, cranking it up and pulling in behind the ambulance to wait. Dr. Hardy and Corey are talking at the back corner of the ambulance, and I roll my window down to hear them, hoping to get a little inside information about Jeremy's condition.

"Take good care of this kid," Dr. Hardy says. "And please be safe coming home. There's supposed to be a storm coming."

"You know I'll be careful. We'll pull over if things get bad. The first responders can handle anything that comes up while we're gone, and you can always call one of the other crews in for a few hours."

"I'll handle things here. You just worry about getting back here in one piece. That road between here and Cedar Glen can get completely washed out when the creek rises."

Corey chuckles and puts a hand on Dr. Hardy's shoulder. "Why are you so anxious? More than usual, I mean."

"I don't know." The doctor sighs. "Actually, I do. This boy has a stubborn, naïve way about him that reminds me so much of you it's scary. And he's had a rough time of it, too. I hate to see him defeated like this."

Corey takes a step closer. "Is that all?"

"No," Dr. Hardy admits. "It makes me think about what I'd do if anything ever happened to you."

*Well, well... what do we have here?* I'm starting to get an idea that the relationship between Jeremy's doctor and Corey the EMT is more than just strictly professional.

"The boy is going to be fine," Corey says. "You're the doctor, and that's what you said, right?"

Dr. Hardy nods, fiddling nervously with his stethoscope.

"And I'm going to be fine, too. I'm not going anywhere. Not when I have you to come home to."

Corey bends and kisses Dr. Hardy tenderly on the lips, lingering just long enough to make every muscle in the doctor's body visibly slacken, but not long enough to be inappropriate. Just the sight of it makes my own stomach quiver.

"You two quit smooching and come on," the female EMT yells through the driver's side window.

They part slowly, and Dr. Hardy winks in my direction before waving goodbye to his man. I look away, feeling like an unwelcome intruder on their private moment.

After Corey swings his long body lithely into the back of the ambulance and we head out, my mind is spinning. In addition to worrying about Jeremy and plotting revenge on Coach Bradley, now I'm contemplating the inspiring glimpse Dr. Hardy and Corey have just given me into their relationship. I'm so in awe of them my stomach quivers anew every time I think about it.

For the first time, real hope begins to take root inside me. After seeing how two confident, successful men can be so secure in themselves and each other that they don't give a damn what anyone else thinks, I know there's a future for me and Jeremy.

*If he survives this nightmare, I'm going to devote myself to making sure of it.*

# 24

As soon as they get Jeremy settled into the ICU, he begins to come around intermittently. He's very confused at first, but by Monday noon, he's more coherent and they've moved him to a room. I try to get a moment with him to tell him how I feel, but it just never seems to be the right time. It was easy to pour my heart out to him while he was unconscious and dying, but now that he's got his eyes open and looking at me, I've suddenly gone shy.

Seth stops by for a while between classes to cry over Jeremy and drop off Mr. Floppy at my request, and Truck and Gretchen bring flowers, and Caleb and Stephie tag along with them. I pull both wrestlers into the hall before they leave.

"I called the police first thing this morning," I tell them.

"What's the plan?" Truck asks.

"Not sure. I'm kinda winging it."

"Don't worry." Caleb holds up a fist for me to bump. "We've

got your back, man."

"Hey, it's not just Beck and Jeremy," Truck corrects. "That asshole has been recording us all. No telling how many times he's cleaned his rifle while watching your ugly ass, Caleb."

"Ew." Caleb shudders. "He could've at least asked."

Truck and I both raise our eyebrows at that.

After they leave, Jeremy's mother goes to the cafeteria for some lunch. Mr. Miller is supposed to meet her there. Hopefully he'll behave for his son's sake.

I lower the bed rail and sit down beside Jeremy. I haven't left the room except to grab a soda and stretch my legs.

"Jeremy," I say quietly, torn between wanting to wake him and wanting to let him sleep. He doesn't answer, so I tie Mr. Floppy's long front legs around his neck.

"Is he sleeping?" Grace, the red-haired nursing student who's been in and out all morning, bustles in with a pan and a rag and fills the pan with warm water from the sink in the corner. She brings a little trail of brightness with her every time she comes in the room, with her sunny disposition and scrub top covered in lemon yellow suns.

"Yeah, he's been out for a while now." I move back to my chair to give her room to work. "How long do you think it will be before he can carry on a conversation?"

"Hmmm... Shouldn't be too long now. The sedatives just have to wear off." She puts the pan of water on the side table, squirts in a little body wash, and begins to run the warm rag over Jeremy's skin. When she gets to his neck, she giggles and unties Mr. Floppy. "Awww, that's so sweet," she says, placing the dog gently at the bottom of the bed and patting his head. "You know, his vitals are looking good, and they're saying he can probably go home tomorrow."

I had no idea how tense I was until I feel my shoulders relax at the good news. I slump down in the seat and lean my head onto the cushioned chair back, closing my eyes as exhaustion starts to set in.

"You're Beck, right? The wrestler from SSU?"

"Yeah." I don't bother moving or opening my eyes. Right now I'm far too tired to be polite.

"I recognize you from school. You and Jeremy must be close. Is he a wrestler, too?" Her voice seems to float to me from far away.

"Mmmm hmmm…" I mumble, almost dozing.

"He's really cute. Haven't seen a girlfriend come in to visit."

That gets my attention enough to open my eyes, and I lift my head weakly to look at her. I'm still not fully alert, so when I laugh it sounds like I'm drunk. "That's because he has a boyfriend, darlin'."

She gasps and puts a hand to her mouth. "Really? I had no idea." Her voice drops to a whisper. "Who is it?"

"You're looking at him." I smile and lean my head back onto the chair, a strange giddiness coursing through my body. Who knew being open could feel this damn good?

"Oh." Grace swallows hard, looking like she's considering crawling under the bed.

"Yeah, we've been dating since school started," I continue, infatuated with the sound of my own honesty.

"Well, he's really cute," she says again. "Are you in love?" She mouths the last bit, tapping her fingers over her heart for emphasis.

"Definitely in love. He's my baby." Bolstered by my newfound courage, I get up and climb into bed with Jeremy. "Could you please put this rail up behind me so I don't fall out?" I ask her. "I've got a rough afternoon ahead of me, so I'm just gonna take a little nap right here." I set my cell phone alarm before yawning and collapsing onto the pillow.

Grace snaps the rail into place and pats me on the arm. "You sleep tight, okay?"

My alarm has barely started beeping before I'm out of the bed and standing, wondering how I made it over the rail in my sleep. Some part of me has been ready for this moment, even while I was unconscious.

Jeremy's parents are sitting in the chairs watching TV, and Jeremy is still asleep. Mrs. Miller smiles, looking chipper enough that it makes me suspect her husband has brought something to reverse the obvious withdrawal symptoms she was beginning to exhibit. "Hope you had a nice sleep, Beck. You were worn out."

I run my hands over my head and drag in a huge yawn. "Wow. Yeah, I was running on fumes." I move to the sink and splash my face with cold water. I can't afford to be groggy right now.

"Hey, Beck," Mr. Miller says in his lazy drawl. "Sorry about your back glass."

*My fucking back glass? How thoughtful.*

I flail my hand in his direction, unsure of what to say. I don't want to let the man off the hook, but I don't want to start anything with him, either.

"I have to get to the school," I tell them, jamming my cell phone and truck keys into my pocket. "It's extremely important. If Jeremy wakes up while I'm gone, tell him I'll be back as soon as I can."

They both nod.

My hands are shaking as I pull into the school parking lot and squeeze my truck into a narrow space. I'm pretty good at keeping my cool under pressure, but this is some pretty extreme pressure. There's a hell of a lot riding on my ability to pull this off, and it's going to take a hefty dose of luck.

It looks like a typical Monday wrestling practice when I enter the gym. No indication that anything is amiss. As soon as I come through the doors, Coach Roberts approaches me. "You're late, Beck. Is everything okay?"

"It will be soon, Coach." I push past him, walking directly toward Coach Bradley, who stops working with one of the freshman students when he notices me.

"Hi, Beck," he says. "How's it—"

I push up into his space, bumping my chest right up against his and growling into his ear. "If you want to hit me, motherfucker, you'd better do it now, because it's the last chance I'm going to give you."

There's raw fear in his eyes when I pull back. In that instant, he knows that I know.

"Beck, come to the office and we'll talk in private."

I laugh humorlessly. "There's no privacy around here. You've seen to that."

His eyes go wide, and I know what he's thinking. His laptop

310

is in the office, and it's got all the evidence on it. He steps in the direction of the office, but I snatch his collar as he passes, drawing him up short.

He turns around and rushes me in desperation. His fist connects with my jaw, and pain radiates up the side of my face.

*There you go. That's all I needed.*

I release all of the pent-up anger, channeling it into the coach's flesh. One lunge is all it takes to get him down onto the mat beneath me, where I pummel him with a fury unlike anything I've ever felt in my life.

"Jeremy's in the hospital, you sonofabitch."

"Not my fault." He fights back hard, and I realize that I've underestimated the strength of a man who's desperate, not to mention a wrestler. Before I know it, he rolls me half over and lands a few painful punches to my ribs. From the sharp sting of it, I'm pretty sure he's just cracked some of them.

Finally, I muster enough strength to get him rolled back under me. Now that I'm on top again, I'm not about to let this go any way but my way. I attack the coach with the limited amount of street-fighting skill I have, aware that if I let up even a little bit, he could take over.

I'm vaguely aware of Coach Roberts and JoJo moving in to break up the fight, but suddenly Truck, Caleb, Vlad and Chris are surrounding us with their arms crossed like a team of mean-ass bodyguards. Caleb shakes his head slowly. "Let them go," he says.

"What the hell's going on here?" Coach Roberts asks, alarmed. "I can't condone a ghetto beat-down, boys."

"This ain't no ghetto beat-down," Truck says. "This is

somebody getting what's coming to them. Besides, the coach hit Beck first."

The entire wrestling team is huddled around us in a circle, astonishment and confusion etched on every face.

"Police are here, Beck," Chris says loudly, making sure he's heard over our grunts.

Out of the corner of my eye, I see an officer approach Coach Roberts with a paper in his hand. Once I've heard the word *warrant*, I'm satisfied.

The cop doesn't glance twice at our showdown on the mat. He probably assumes we're just practicing, which is good, because I'm not quite finished making my point. As the officers make their way toward the locker room and the offices, Coach Bradley makes a concentrated effort to escape me.

"Let me go," he growls.

"Not until you admit it, you scumbag."

"Admit what?" He gasps and covers his face, protecting it from my blows.

"Jeremy." I grate out between punches to the man's midsection.

He lets down his guard on his face long enough to slam his fist into my side while he uses his knee to pop me in the kidney and topple me onto him.

*Fuck.*

He's on me, battering my right ear until the sound of the crowd has faded into a sharp ringing. When he's got me shaken up, he tries to get up and make a dash for the office where his precious laptop is. What he doesn't realize is that it's too late. The police know everything, they know exactly what they're looking for, and they have a warrant to get it.

*All over but the crying, asshole.*

I grab his ankle as he runs away, getting him back down onto the floor.

"Harmless fun..." he pants. "Both adults... he made the choice."

I get his arms pinned firmly beneath my knees and sit hard on his diaphragm, knocking the wind out of him. He grunts and closes his eyes.

"He's *mine*," I yell. "You used me to blackmail him, and you forced him to give up something that wasn't his to give anymore. It's mine." I wrap my fingers around his throat, and his eyes stretch wide. "Since I can't get back what you stole, I'll have to settle for taking it out of your worthless hide."

I feel his arms try to break free as I let go of his throat and crash my fists into his face repeatedly. With strength fueled by helpless anger, I rock into his face over and over until I feel a crunch of bone and the arms beneath my legs are limp and no longer struggling.

Then Truck and Caleb are pulling me off of him, gentling me with their words and calm voices. "Time to stop," Truck says. "He's beaten. The police will take care of the rest."

"He's done for," Caleb adds. "I don't think he'll be hurting anyone else."

The two of them escort me to a supply room off the side of the gym where we won't be disturbed, and they check me over.

"Gonna have to drain this ear, buddy," Truck says.

313

I groan. "Just take me to the hospital. I have to go back there anyway."

Coach Roberts pokes his head in. "Were you boys aware that we had cameras all over the freaking locker room?"

We all nod, and the movement makes my head hurt.

"Yeah, Coach," Caleb says. "There's been a lot of stuff going on around here lately that you don't know about, but once the police haul that Bradley bastard off, things will be back to normal."

"I'll go talk to the police, then." The coach tips my face up to assess the damage. "Get him to the hospital. Where's Jeremy? Do I need to call him?"

"He's in the hospital, too," I say around a swollen lip.

The coach frowns. "You fellows need to keep me more in the loop. I feel like an outsider on my own damn team." He's still grumbling as he walks back over to join a couple of police officers and Coach Bradley, who is being lifted onto a stretcher. I did the damage myself, so I know he's going to be okay.

As angry as I was, I was ultimately able to keep control of myself and avoid committing a felony. I want to take first place at Nationals. I want a successful future in Sports Medicine. And I want to be with Jeremy, not talk to him from the other side of the glass on visitation days. Those are my goals, and I'm not about to let anything stand in my way of achieving them.

# 25

*(JEREMY)*

"Perfect!" Beck says, brushing his hands like he's really done something big.

"I'm glad at least one of us knows how to hang a picture straight. I never did get that painting just right in the dorm room."

"Well, you just sit around and look pretty and leave all the hard stuff to me."

I smile, looking around the half-decorated living room. The beams on the ceiling, thick crown molding, and hardwood floors give it an expensive look that thrills me. After living in a trailer all my life, renting a fifteen-hundred-square-foot bungalow is like winning the house lottery.

Beck has insisted on staying true to the history of the house with a modernized forties-style decor, and I'm letting him run the show. He's done tons of research on the internet and is trying to involve me in the decorating process, but I'm not as good at it as he is. All I've ever known is paneling, floral wallpaper, and shag carpet.

"Your roommate— well, ex-roommate— is a really good artist," Beck says, admiring the abstract painting he's just hung.

A knock at the door makes me jump. "Who the hell…"

Beck just smiles and opens the door. Gretchen and Truck stagger in, carrying a huge rolled up carpet, bumping into the door frame and yelling at each other. Finally, they drop it into the middle of the floor, and Gretchen collapses onto the couch.

"Glad you finally got your sofa delivered," she says, breathing heavily. "I need it now."

"Nice color." Truck takes a seat beside Gretchen, running a hand along the upholstered arm. "I like green."

"Silver sage," I correct, and Beck laughs at me.

"My little decorator." He grabs onto one of my belt loops and pulls me close. "By the time we're finished with this house, you'll be ready to open an interior design shop downtown."

"Fuck that."

While Truck rolls out the fluffy white rug he and Gretchen have brought, centering it in front of the sofa, Seth backs in through the open door carrying one end of a huge sheet-covered canvas. Dan is on the other end with the canvas in one hand and a bottle of white wine in the other.

"Leave it to Dan to bring the alcohol," I tease.

He shrugs. "Hey, it's not too late to return it."

I snatch the chilled bottle from him and take it into the kitchen. "Do we have any wine glasses?" I yell.

"Top shelf to the left of the fridge," Beck yells back.

"Oh no, there are only four. Guess you and I will have to share, Beck."

Gretchen giggles and grabs her boyfriend's huge hand. "Truck and I can share, too."

"I'm not sharing with Dan," Seth yells.

Dan punches him in the arm and laughs. "I can drink out of the bottle if I have to."

I return to the living room with the glasses and the wine and set them out on the table.

"Thanks, guys," Beck says. "You didn't have to do all of this."

"Sure we did," Gretchen says. "We want to get invited over sometimes. Just consider it a bribe."

Seth shrugs. "I've got a lot of paintings lying around that I need to get rid of."

"Yeah, right." I punch him in the arm, careful not to make him spill his freshly-poured wine onto the new rug. At least it's white wine. If it was red, Beck would probably make us stand in the yard to drink it.

"Let's see it," Beck says, and Seth and Dan get up to remove the cover.

The other four of us gasp when the full painting is revealed. Seth and Dan both have smug smiles on their faces.

"I can't believe it." My mouth is hanging open from shock. "That's me and Beck."

The painting is gorgeous— manga style, predominantly black and white with splashes of color here and there. Beck and I are shown from the waist up, both dressed in t-shirts, his white and mine black.

Beck stands tall, holding me in a one-armed embrace, his impressive muscles drool-worthy even rendered in oils. My head rests against his powerful chest, my pale blue eyes focused straight ahead and communicating a love that practically jumps off the canvas and squeezes your heart. Beck's eyes are downcast, his pained expression heartbreaking, looking at me like he'd do anything at all to protect me.

Tears spring to my eyes, and I jump up and hug Seth so hard he has to squeal to get me to let go.

"Dang, brother," he says. "No need for the waterworks. This is just some old thing I had gathering dust in storage."

"You're a liar," I accuse through tears. "It's the most beautiful thing I've ever seen, and you painted it just for us. But that's not all I know."

Seth quirks an eyebrow and grins. "Oh? What else, kohai?"

"You're the author of *GLiF*. It's your artwork I'm waiting for with bated breath every Wednesday on my favorite online manga." I turn to the rest of the group. "This guy's a freaking celebrity. He's got a following like you wouldn't believe."

"Shut up, man," he says, blushing. "No one is supposed to know that."

Everyone tries to speak at once, all promising not to tell. Except Dan. "I've already told half the school," he says.

Seth rolls his eyes at his friend. He knows Dan would never sell him out.

Beck carries the painting over to the fireplace and props it up on the mantle. "Couldn't fit any better," he says. "It's amazing, Seth. Thank you." He looks at the others. "Thanks for all of the gifts, guys.

This is a very special day for me and Jeremy. We're getting out and pretending to be adults now, and your support means so much."

"Speak for yourself, old man," I tell him. "I'm still pretending to be a kid, and we are so getting a game system for Christmas."

Beck frowns. "I think we need a bigger TV first."

"Uh-oh, trouble in paradise." Gretchen laughs.

"Hey, speaking of TV, did y'all see the latest on Coach Bradley on the evening news last night?" Truck scoots to the edge of the sofa, his eyes wide. He doesn't wait for anyone to respond. "They were prosecuting him for the illegal videotaping, then you guys introduced the malicious intent thing, and then there's the pornography thing. But then they announced today that the guy he was blackmailing at the other school was only seventeen years old. He had a late birthday or something. So they've got him on several counts of child porn and having sex with a minor."

Truck leans back in his seat and cracks his knuckles with a self-satisfied grin, as if he's singlehandedly caused the turn of events. Seth and Dan are stunned.

"They're going to bury him," Dan breathes.

"Good." Beck reaches unconsciously for his ear, then grabs the wine bottle and pours what's left into our glass.

The unfortunate truth is that we don't need Truck to update us on the case. It lives with us, climbs into bed with us at night, tries to dominate our world. But it's all worth it to see a bad man get what's coming to him, and to keep him from making other athletes' lives a living hell.

Beck gathers the glasses and wine bottle from the coffee table after our guests are gone, setting the glasses in the sink and the bottle on the counter. "I think we'll save this bottle, what do you think? A memento of our first housewarming."

"I think that's a great idea."

His ass is so perfect in his jeans; it calls to me as he washes the glasses and sets them in the dish drainer. I come up behind him and put my hands on it, feeling the hardness and the roundness of the muscles through the worn denim. My hands follow the contours, running over the swell, down and down until I hook my fingers under and find the sweet spot just behind his balls. I press upward in firm, massaging strokes, and he sucks in a noisy breath.

"Jeremy, I..." He hesitates for a moment while I continue to rub him. Just when I think I've succeeded in making him forget what he was about to say, he turns to face me. "I need to take a shower, okay?"

He gives me a quick peck on the lips and pushes past me, disappearing into the bedroom and the master bath beyond.

*Why is he acting so weird?*

It occurs to me, not for the first time, that maybe all of the Coach Bradley stuff is starting to get to him. I've been paranoid all along that at some point he would decide he couldn't deal with what I did. I wouldn't blame him. He's so possessive of me, I can't imagine it's an easy thing for him to accept.

Sometimes I sense a sort of hesitation on his part when we're in bed together, like he's got something on his mind that he can't talk about. But I've figured out a trick that works like magic when he gets like that. All I have to do is get all submissive and sweet, trailing my fingertips over his skin and kissing him softly, and before I know it he's slamming into me, his troubles forgotten.

This evening, he seems even more distraught, especially after Truck brought up that piece of shit coach. It's not Truck's fault. He thought good news would be welcome, but both Beck and I prefer complete silence on the subject unless we're having to deal with the police or lawyers. We've already said pretty much everything there is to say about how it's affected our relationship. Now it's just down to healing and forgetting.

The counselor I've been seeing at the school health center assures me that a month is not long enough to have completely recovered from what basically amounts to a sex crime followed by a suicide attempt. Beck seems to have been dealing pretty well, but now I'm beginning to wonder. Maybe he's having a delayed reaction.

After I hear the shower come on, I shuck down to my boxer briefs and kick back on the sofa to watch a little TV and end up streaming a poorly produced action movie. Sometimes I actually enjoy low budget movies more than watching a slick Hollywood production, if for no other reason than to pick apart the worst ones.

My mind's not able to focus on the movie tonight, though, and I reach over and re-read the card we got in the mail today. It's from Dr. Hardy down in Blackwood. He says he finally talked my mom into going into rehab and that she checked herself in a week after my episode. I'm glad she's doing it. It may not take, but at least she's finally making an effort. As for my dad, I couldn't care less what he does. I tolerate him the best I can when I have to, and that will just have to do.

Dr. Hardy and Corey also invited us to their annual New

Year's party, which we both agreed we wouldn't miss for the world. I take the card and lean it on the mantle in front of Seth's painting, thinking how lucky Beck and I are to have such good friends. I got off to a rocky start, but it looks like college life is going to turn out great after all.

*As long as we can weather the storm just a little while longer.*

Finally, when the movie is halfway over, Beck comes out of the bathroom. I can hear him shuffling around in the bedroom before he strolls out into the dim living room wearing nothing but a towel, looking firm and tan in the flickering light coming from the TV. His muscles still make my stomach flip every single time I see them. Especially when he's like this, all clean and damp, running a hand over his buzz cut.

"There's not a sexier guy in the state," I tell him as he approaches.

"Only the one I'm looking at." His response makes my heart soar, and I squirm to the edge of the sofa so that he can slip in and lie down behind me in our favorite movie-watching position.

"This movie isn't too bad. Want me to start it over or find a new one?"

"I don't want to watch a movie, sweetie." He comes closer until he's standing directly in front of me, so close I could tear the towel off with my teeth. "I want to give you a gift."

He brings a small box from behind his back, wrapped in solid black paper and encircled by a white bow.

"A housewarming gift? But I didn't get you anything." I'm embarrassed now, thinking I've missed some important piece of new house etiquette. "Crap." I poke out my bottom lip, dreading opening

322

it, hoping it's not too expensive.

He laughs. "Just quit pouting and open it, okay?"

I pull the ribbon loose, and my hand shakes as I work the edges of the paper free. Inside the box is a pair of expensive spandex boxer briefs like I've admired so often on Beck. I pull them out and set the box on the coffee table, holding them up to admire the pattern of vintage stills of Batman from the old TV show. "Wow. These are really nice. I could never afford—"

"Put them on," he interrupts. "Right now."

"Yes, sir." I stand immediately and drop the ones I'm wearing, kicking them toward the fireplace, and pull the new ones up over my thighs. They fit like a glove, so smooth and supportive. I start to get semi-hard just from the feel of them cupping me so closely.

"Mmmm..." I run my hands over the slick fabric and look up to thank Beck again, but as soon as I look at him he unwinds the towel from around his waist and lets it fall to the floor.

My jaw drops when I see that he's wearing a pair of underwear similar to mine, but with images of Robin on them. His words from that first night in my dorm room replay in my head.

*I'm Batman, you're Robin. I do all the fucking in this duo. Got it?*

I stare at him in open-mouthed silence, glancing first at him, then his underwear, then back at him. Worry that I could be giving meaning to a mere coincidence makes me hesitate, but only for a moment. As soon as my rock hard dick has convinced my brain that I've read the signals right, it's all over for Beck and his ass-virginity.

"You don't have to tell me twice." I step up and grab him

roughly by the back of the neck, pulling his mouth down onto mine and leading him in a primal kiss. Our tongues duel furiously as we grope each other's bodies with abandon. The contours of his muscles, his biceps, his pecs, his ass. I explore it all as if I can't make up my mind just where I want to touch him. "Christ, you are so hot." I run my hand down inside the back of his boxers and grab onto his ass, sucking his tongue into my mouth at the same time. "I can't believe I get to fuck this."

Beck leans in and kisses me again. "I love you, Jeremy. I really do." He rubs my erection through my underwear. "I never wanted anyone to do this before. To make me—"

"Mine," I whisper.

"Yeah." He closes his eyes and leans his head back as I suck one of his sensitive nipples into my mouth. I feel goosebumps pop up all across his skin when I take my mouth off long enough for the cool air to hit it, moving to the other side to give its twin some attention.

"Get down on the rug." I put my palms on his muscular shoulders and push him down to the floor. Then I move the coffee table out of the way, and Beck stretches out on the rug, waiting nervously for me like he's offering himself up for sacrifice. I'd laugh if he wasn't so adorably earnest.

"Don't forget the lube," he says. "In the bottom of the gift box."

"Awww, you got me lube?" I chuckle as I remove the bottle from beneath a tuft of tissue paper. "If I'd seen that, there wouldn't have been any question what you wanted."

"You didn't know?"

"Not at first. But it didn't take me long to figure it out. Trust me, that's the first place my mind went. I've been dying to do this since the first time I laid eyes on you. Now take off those underwear. I want to see you."

When I've got him lying flat on his back with his knees bent and legs spread, admiring him, he asks, "Is this going to hurt?"

"Oh, you're not too concerned with pain when it comes to tearing me up, but now that you're going to be on the receiving end, it's a different story, huh?"

"Hey, I try not to hurt you."

"I know, I'm just teasing. Just trust me, okay? I do know what I'm doing. Have you not ever experimented with toys or objects?"

"Yeah, of course." He offers a shy smile. "But small stuff. Nothing like what you're about to shove in there."

I push his knees back, exposing his asshole to my hungry gaze. "I'm about to ruin you, then. You're gonna love me even more when I'm done."

His nervousness certainly hasn't affected his erection. His dick is so hard and tempting, for a split second I consider climbing on top of him and having him do me instead. But this is his special night, and there's nothing in the world that could stop me from getting inside him now that he's asked me to. I'm obsessed with it.

I bend and kiss both of his exposed cheeks. Deep, slow, hot kisses with tongue and suction that have him quaking beneath me, gradually moving toward the center until my mouth is hovering over his hole, letting my warm breath fan across his flesh. I look up and smile to myself when I see that he's got his eyes squeezed shut, and he appears to be holding his breath.

*And this is where he loses control.*

I lower my mouth to his asshole, kissing it in the same slow way I've been kissing the rest of him. His body tenses and comes off the rug for a few seconds before he relaxes back down and begins to squirm. I dart my tongue out, letting him feel it circling the crinkled edges before going in for the kill. He's lost as soon as I start really manipulating him with my tongue— fucking him slowly with it, wiggling it in, wetting him, warming him, loosening him, driving him crazy.

"God, Jeremy, Jesus Christ that feels so good. I might come." He reaches for his dick as if he can't help himself, but I push his hand away and take it into my mouth.

"Oh, shit. Don't do that." He's panting now, on the verge of losing it. I back off a little, but it's difficult when I'm bringing him such pleasure.

I grab the lube and drizzle it on his warm, softened hole, rubbing it in with my fingers, pushing partially inside to prepare him. I've got a steel rod between my legs, and it's not content to wait any longer. One finger, two fingers, and I'm going in.

Using my fingers to assist, I work my cock in, nearly blowing as soon as the head passes the opening. Beck moans loudly. I'm not sure if it's from pain or pleasure, but I'm guessing a little of both. I've done my very best to prepare him, but the rest is just a matter of doing it.

"You're so tight and hot," I tell him as I move ever so slightly inside him. "I can't do much here. Not this time. I've been waiting too long, and— Christ almighty that's good."

Beck is just moaning. I've never heard him nearly as vocal as he is tonight, but it seems he's also lost all ability to form words. He's writhing gently beneath me, his bottom lip sucked into his mouth and his eyes at half-mast. He looks so sexy and aroused, and I realize neither one of us is going to be able to do a whole lot of fancy moves. It's going to be over soon. But that's okay, because it feels so damn good.

"Hang on, Beck," I tell him. "Put your hands behind your head. I'm about to make you come."

He does as I ask with an eagerness that really turns me on. What I'm about to attempt is going to make me come, I already know that. I just hope like hell he comes along with me.

I alter my angle slightly so that the head of my cock is massaging his prostate, and he arches and moans to signal that I've hit my mark. He's aware of what I'm doing because he's done it to me, so he moves in just the right way to help me along. He opens up to me, encouraging me with his movements and his sounds, letting me know he's loving everything I'm doing to him. There's a moment when we both let go of rational thought and give ourselves completely over to the sensations. Then we're rocking in such perfect unison, both gasping, crying out, bucking against each other with wild abandon.

It takes less than thirty seconds for Beck to start shooting like a fire hose onto his own belly, chest and face. The sight sends me careening over the edge into blissful orgasm, and I push feverishly into him again and again until every drop of semen has been spilled. Then I collapse beside him.

Both of us are silent for a long time. I can't come up with any words to express how I feel about what just happened between us,

327

and I have all ideas Beck feels the same. We've done something meaningful.

Eventually, I break the silence. "Well, that was the most awesome sex ever. I told you you'd love me topping you, but damn. You really got into it, you bad boy." I slap him playfully on the ass. "That was fucking hot!"

Even in the low light, I can see that he's blushing.

"That reminds me," he says, "I never did prove to you what a good bad boy I am. Remember?" He draws his eyebrows together, looking like he's going to burst something he's thinking so hard. "Ooh, I know… how about mud bogging? I can redneck with the best of 'em. Wouldn't you love to see your man all sexy and dirty, maneuvering that powerful black beast of a truck through a treacherous mud pit?"

He flexes his delicious muscles for emphasis, and I find myself appreciating his perfection anew.

"And watch you destroy your pretty truck or get hurt? No way. How about knocking over a convenience store? That would be bad boy enough for me, especially if you grab me a Yoo-Hoo and a couple of Cow Tales while you're in there. I'll sit in the getaway car and cheer you on."

He shoots me a withering look and pinches the tender inside of my naked thigh, making me yelp. But instead of moving away, I crawl over and twist my body up with his in the closest, most intimate way I can manage.

"You don't have to prove anything to me, Beck. Are you feeling vulnerable after giving it up to me?"

He chuckles so quietly I feel it rather than hear it. "Yeah. I guess so."

"Well, let me put your mind at ease." I reach down and trace circles in his happy trail while I talk, grinning when his breathing ramps up noticeably. "You are so sexy and dirty to me already that I don't think any amount of mud could help. Watching you wrestle is like an aphrodisiac to me. The way you move, so manly and powerful, I literally have trouble catching my breath. And knowing you can whip pretty much anybody in the country is— well, that makes you like the ultimate bad boy. But…" I pause for a second to steady my voice, because just thinking about my feelings for the man in my arms is enough to choke me up. "The way you take care of me, worry about me, calm me down when I'm upset… No one has ever done that for me before. You came out for me, stood up for me, put my dad in his place, watched over me in the hospital, and beat the shit out of Coach Bradley to defend my honor. I hate to disappoint you, Beck, but you're even more of a good man than a bad boy. And that's what makes me love you so much."

I press up to kiss him in that cute little chin cleft.

"Damn, Jeremy. I don't think I've ever heard you say that much at one time." Though he's being flippant, I can clearly see the tears welling in his eyes. It's incredibly sweet, but I'm not about to point it out. He might try to bench press me just to prove he's not sappy.

*Hey, now that I think about it, that might be kind of fun.*

# THE END

# Books By Maris Black:

*Owning Corey*
*Pinned*

# About the Author

Maris Black lives in the Southern United States. In college, she majored in English and discovered the joys of creative writing and literary interpretation. After honing her skills discovering hidden meanings authors probably never intended, she collected her English degree and got a job at a newspaper. But she soon figured out that small town reporting wasn't going to pay the bills, so she went to work in the medical field. Logical progression, right? But no matter what she did, the self-proclaimed compulsive plotter couldn't stop writing fiction.

"The M/M genre feels sort of like coming home," she says. " I can't quite explain it. I've always had openly gay and bisexual friends and relatives, the rights and acceptance of whom are very important to me, so it feels great to celebrate that. But there's also something so pure and honest about the love between two men that appeals to me and inspires me to write."

**Visit Her Website:** http://marisblack.com
**Connect on Facebook:** Facebook.com/marisblackbooks

35299296R00190

Made in the USA
Charleston, SC
05 November 2014